Christmas at Gingerbread Inn

Christmas at Gingerbread Inn

A SUGARPLUM FALLS ROMANCE

JENNIFER GRIFFITH

Christmas at Gingerbread Inn

© 2023 Jennifer Griffith All rights reserved. No part of this book may be reproduced or transmitted in any form or by any means, electronic or mechanical, including photocopying, recording, or by any information storage retrieval system without the written permission of the author.

ISBN: **9798366687539**

This is a work of fiction. Names, characters, places, and events are creations of the author's imagination or are used fictitiously. Any resemblance to actual persons, living or dead, events, or locations, is purely coincidental.

Cover art credit: Blue Water Books, 2023

For Aunt Shauna and Her Girls—Who Exemplify Hospitality

"Mankind was my business. The common welfare was my business; charity, mercy, forbearance, and benevolence, were, all, my business. The dealings of my trade were but a drop of water in the comprehensive ocean of my business!" –Jacob **Marley,** in *A Christmas Carol* by **Charles Dickens**

Chapter 1

Cliff

Cliff Rockingham's feet pounded on the frozen ground of the jogging trail near the roaring waterfall while his brain roared even louder.

What am I going to do?

His soul *needed* Christmas giving—in a *real* way. Toy drives and groceries and gift certificates for those in need in Sugarplum Falls hadn't cut it last year, or the year before, or the year before.

No, it's got to be deeply meaningful this year. Not just changing a holiday morning. Changing a *life*.

But what? And for whom?

Cliff rounded the corner of the jogging trail where the waterfall came into view—his favorite sight, Falls Overlook. The view of Lake Sugar, stretching to the western horizon, with the waterfall spilling off the lake's southern edge, was famously inspiring.

Cliff needed inspiring, since even being on his roof hadn't helped him think. Maybe the view would inspire him to—

His train of thought screeched to a halt.

Someone was already standing at the Falls Overlook. And—wait a second! What was she doing? That was dangerous.

"Hey!" He picked up speed. "Hold up!" He ran faster, his thighs catching fire.

Don't jump!

A young woman leaned precariously over the railing protecting Falls Overlookers from the churning waters below. Her blonde hair lifted in the breeze while her arm arched backward, as if giving herself momentum to dive.

"Stop!" he cried, breaking into a dead run.

"I've got you!" Cliff reached her side and yanked her backward, toppling both of them—but not before a blue cylinder flew from her hand, soaring toward the frigidly cold lake below.

Oof! They smacked onto the ground, but the woman was safe! Cliff clutched her to his chest, his breath coming in heaves.

"Are you okay?" Cliff pushed himself to his feet and pleaded with her. "Whatever is going on in your life, it's not as bad as it seems right now. Things always get better."

He reached to help her stand, taking in her appearance. She looked *very* familiar, but he couldn't place her. Soft, feminine features, natural and without makeup. With her straight blonde hair that glinted in the winter sunlight, she could've been an actress.

She accepted his help and stood, dusting herself off.

She definitely wasn't from Sugarplum Falls. He would've noticed. The stunner had to be a tourist. Sugarplum Falls couldn't keep a secret as pretty as she was.

"Look, I get it. I've seen some dark days, too. They pass."

"I was"—she squeezed her hands into fists—"just looking at the lake." The tourist's honey-brown eyes stared back at him in pure annoyance.

Hey, what was with that reaction? He'd saved her life!

Most other people might have said that her lake-leaning was none of his business, but Cliff lived by Jacob Marley of Dickensian literature's maxim, *Mankind was my business!*

"Well, the lake is prettier when it freezes solid." *But that would hurt even more if you plunged into it, so don't.*

"I bet it is." She glanced over the railing, her fair hair catching a breeze, lifting and falling—her frown deepening and revealing more complex feelings churning inside her than sightseeing. "I'm sure you meant well."

Uh, of course he'd meant well! "I'm just glad you're safe."

"Safe's a relative term." She gave him a little, sad smile, while rubbing her shoulder. "Well, bye." She stepped around him and headed toward the parking lot.

Cliff, being a dingbat, tagged along after her. "Where are you staying?"

"At the Gingerbread Inn."

"Really? Gingerbread Inn?" Not *that* place! *Why not Sweetwater Hotel?* Argh!

"You've heard of Gingerbread Inn?"

Yup. He'd heard of it. He'd wanted to pull his hair out because of it.

"Newly remodeled place on Orchard?" The kitschy, boutique lodges in Sugarplum Falls were killing him—and his business, Sweetwater Hotel—especially Gingerbread Inn. "Sure. This is a small town."

Maybe I should offer her a free night's stay at Sweetwater Hotel. Show her what she's missing. Except that would sound like a pickup line. Maybe even a creepy one.

"You look like you just choked on a candy cane." She paused beside a red jeep. "Is there something wrong with Gingerbread Inn?"

Her phone chimed a holiday ring-tone—the song "I Heard the Bells on Christmas Day"—cutting off his reply about Gingerbread Inn and the bed and breakfasts popping up around town—with their low ceilings, their cramped rooms, and their dark, fairytale cottage vibes—being signs of the End Times for Sweetwater Hotel, the premier lodging in Sugarplum Falls.

"A little dreary for a ring tone," he commented instead.

"It's my alarm." She pulled it out and shut off the tune of the Wordsworth poem's song. "Gotta go. It's almost check-in time at the inn."

She climbed into the jeep and started the engine.

Wait. Was she really leaving? But—but, he hadn't gotten her name, even.

She rolled down the window halfway. "Have a good day." She gave him a partial smile. "Sorry for getting upset when you tackled me. I know you were just being a knight in shining armor."

Mercy! The radiant sunshine of even that small smile could've melted the iceberg that sank the *Titanic.*

The jeep began to back up, but Cliff put his hand on the door's frame, as if he could keep her from driving off by sheer force of will. "What's your name?"

"It's Sam-Jessamyn."

"Sorry?" *It's I'm Jessamyn?* Is that what she'd said? "I'm Cliff Rockingham." He offered his full name. "It was nice meeting you, Jessamyn …" Hint, hint. *Give me your last name?*

But why? So that he could … what? Internet stalk her?

I do not stalk. Not women who look like movie stars. Not blondes with honey-brown eyes. And especially not tourists. Tourists are temporary. I'm permanent.

"Bye, Cliff Rockingham." The window swished upward. He stepped back so the jeep wouldn't run over his foot. The jeep disappeared down Orchard Street.

A countdown clock began ticking down the hours and minutes until he could see her again, until he could try to be her knight in shining armor again.

No! He yanked the battery out of that dumb countdown clock. He didn't crush on tourists. Tourists, by their very definition, didn't stay.

And Cliff had had far more than his share of impermanent relationships.

Chapter 2

Jessamyn

In the parking lot of Gingerbread Inn, Jessamyn gripped the jeep's steering wheel.

Sam-Jessamyn?

No, no, no!

That guy! He'd looked at her as if he recognized her. And then she'd almost introduced herself as Sammie before she caught herself. Why was she such a self-sabotaging idiot the second she saw a pair of crystal-blue eyes and an earnest face, or when a guy thought of himself as her knight errant.

Idiot! She smacked the steering wheel, and the horn sounded.

Oops. She turtled her neck in, but no one came out of Gingerbread Inn to investigate.

She pressed a fingertip to her forehead and shut her eyes.

All this time, I thought I was so well hidden! The different hair color and style, the makeup change, the clothes she now wore—no vestige of her former outward appearance remained. Whether anyone in Sugarplum Falls knew it or not, she was Sammie.

Sammie, the famous and glamorous starlet, now gone from the public eye. For good.

Unless she herself whipped back the curtain, by introducing herself to kind-eyed men as Sammie Westwood instead of Jessamyn Fleet.

Sometimes she was her own worst enemy.

For instance, when I agreed on live television to marry Douglas.

She'd fallen into his net and hadn't even tried to untangle herself until it was too late. But there'd been so much glitz, so much energy and excitement. The neon lights and shooting stars had temporarily blinded her—and her entire family. Well, other than Grandma Ginger.

Well, no more. And never again.

She turned up the radio on the local station, which had already begun playing holiday songs. Year-round Christmas music could be a thing in a town named Sugarplum Falls.

Muffled by the raised window and the too-loud blast of "Silver Bells," she hollered, "I'm Jessamyn Fleet! Nice to meet you!" And then, she said, "My name is *Jessamyn Fleet.*" She popped the *t* sound at the end of the word. "Fleet, Jessamyn," she said in a James Bond voice, following with, "Shaken, not stirred."

And shaken she was. The possibility of being recognized made her shake. Literally. As if she were outside on a freezing street corner listening to the silver bells of Christmastime in the city.

Stirred, too, if she dared admit it.

Cliff Rockingchair's chivalry had stirred her insides. No, she hadn't been about to jump, and he'd probably bruised her shoulder in the rescue attempt, but something about him undeniably affected Jessamyn.

She squeezed her abdominals to stop the aftershocks. Those had to be from post-fear adrenaline let-down, right? Not the reaction to that man's ocean-blue eyes, or to his kindness and reassurances, or to the fact that a man had—albeit mistakenly—tried to *protect* her instead of *exploit* her.

For once.

All she'd meant to do was send out that forlorn wish into the world, er, the lake. It was silly. Who put a message in a bottle in real life? At least no one would ever see it.

Then again, if no one saw it, no one would ever grant her Christmas wish-list.

Not even Cliff Rockinghorse, Knight in Shining Spandex.

Cliff with the crystal blue eyes and jet-black hair. Like Clark Kent! Oh, good grief. Not only was he a knight, he was a superhero now? Please. What was wrong with her today? All this sentimentality and confusion. Maybe she'd hit her head when Cliff body-slammed her to the ground during his so-called rescue.

Wake up, Jess! She could *not* make connections in Sugarplum Falls with anyone but the scant housekeeping staff and the guests at Gingerbread Inn. To do so would be just as dimwitted as almost telling that wannabe knight her real name.

Just because Cliff Rocktheboat was initially chivalrous and knee-gellingly handsome didn't mean he was *actually* noble. Life had taught her looks and first impressions could be wildly deceiving.

No more getting taken.

Not for her.

Not for *Jessamyn Fleet*.

It was past check-in time already. She gave the wheel one last grip and then shut off the engine. The radio went dead.

Jessamyn Fleet headed inside Gingerbread Inn.

Where she'd be safe.

Chapter 3

Cliff

Back on the jogging trail, Cliff kept hearing Jessamyn's words, *knight in shining armor.* Were they a compliment or a cut? Had that been his motivation when he tackled her? No, mankind was his business, as Jacob Marley said.

Her face floated before his eyes. One more glance at her, just one, and he'd be fine. Maybe she'd be at one of the local holiday events, or he could run into her at Sugarbabies Bakery or at Mario's.

"Hey, Cliff." Andrew Kingston took up half the trail while walking Beast, his little brown and black Chihuahua. "Who was that woman I saw you talking to in the parking lot? Is she new in town?" Beast yapped from the end of his leash.

"Tourist." Cliff slowed and walked alongside Andrew and the dog. They came to the trail's slope beside the waterfall and headed downward along the tree-lined path.

"Too bad for you." Andrew shrugged. "She did look interested."

"Haw," Cliff scoffed. "Hardly. She didn't even give me a look-back when she drove off."

"Harsh. Women usually give you at least one look-back." Andrew chortled. "But, as we all know, no tourists for you."

"Yep. How's Beast?" Cliff bent over and gave Beast's pointy ears a ruffling. "How are you, Beast? Is Andrew treating you well? I heard there's going to be special doggie toboggan run at Kingston Orchard this winter."

Beast yapped again. It was his best skill.

"Where's she staying?" Andrew asked, not taking Cliff's change-the-subject hint. Some people were like bulldogs, even if they owned Chihuahuas. "Sweetwater Hotel?"

"Nope. Somewhere else." Cliff suppressed a Beast-growl. He couldn't even say the words *Gingerbread Inn.* "New topic. How's the legal business? Any new court cases?"

"Some, but I'm branching out, too. Taking some P.I. work." Beast started barking at a cardinal.

"Seriously?" No way. Cliff measured his tone away from shocked and concerned. "Private investigation? In Sugarplum Falls?" The place had a crime rate hovering near subzero. "Forgive me for asking, but why?"

Andrew dropped a treat for Beast, and Beast quit yipping at the bird for two seconds to chomp it. "It started with Poppy's devotion to a Korean TV show featuring a private detective. I watched it, too, and thought, *I could do that.*"

Everyone who ever went to Andrew's wife Poppy's beverage shop knew of her Korean television obsession. And of Andrew's obsession for Poppy.

"Just because a person *can* do something really well, that doesn't necessarily mean they should." Cliff tread carefully. "Remember when we were into poker as teens for a while and realized your cousin could've turned professional?"

They were all glad when Owen had dropped poker and took on the running of the family orchard instead of a career in Vegas.

"I totally remember that!" Andrew lit up like the town Christmas tree in front of the recreation center. "So, you're saying you think I could be a pro at investigating? Thanks, man. I appreciate the compliment."

Not what Cliff had intended. But he wasn't one to stomp dreams, even misguided ones.

Andrew crouched down to pat the barking Beast into a calmer state. "If you hear of anyone who needs private investigation, let me know."

"Will do." Cliff poised himself to return to his run.

Andrew's brows pushed together. "Uh, you doing all right?"

"Yeah, why?" That was weird.

"Nothing. Well, I just heard around town that you turned over the *Presents for People* holiday gift drive to Mayor Lang and the Sugarplum Falls Chamber of Commerce. Isn't that your pet project every Christmas?"

9

"It was."

"Past tense because …?"

Cliff hadn't told anyone about his change of direction this year. "It was time to let it go."

"Why? It was going great." Andrew rambled off some of the well-publicized stats of the number of gifts *Presents for People* had collected the Christmas before. "You made a huge difference, Cliff."

"Like you, I'm branching out." It had been worthwhile, he knew, but—"I want to accomplish something *significant*." Why had he mentioned that aloud?

"*Presents for People* is significant." Andrew dropped barking Beast another treat. "Don't minimize the good you've achieved in the past."

"And it can still achieve good. Mayor Lang and the Chamber of Commerce will continue it." He might have said this with a little too much finality because Andrew put his palms up.

"Hey, if you choose to change up your charitable giving, who am I to argue?"

"You're the town's most capable lawyer. You argue for a living."

"True." Beast strained at the leash, but Andrew held firm. "By significant, you mean …?" There Andrew went again, a bulldog when it came to a conversation topic.

Cliff capitulated and told him the truth. "I probably should've said *individualized*. Depth over breadth. It might sound stupid. Or full of hubris—assuming I could make an actual difference in someone's life. But hey, thanks for not calling me out for *flaking out on the needy*." A few grumblings of that sort had met his ears.

"Thank *you* for not telling me I'm an idiot for starting a P.I. business in Sugarplum Falls. We all gotta follow our dreams. Listen, I don't know what you're planning, but if you need a private investigator to help you *find* a project, I now know a guy."

"I have your number." Cliff slapped Andrew's back, Beast barked goodbye, and Cliff resumed his jog.

Cliff headed for the last stretch of his run: the slope alongside the falls. At the base of the falls, he'd turn off and head back to Sweetwater Hotel. His feet pounded down the steep trail, and the waterfall rushed nearby, roaring and spraying—for now. It would freeze soon. It had to! Or else a lack of *winter wonderland* vibes would endanger the high tourist season of Sugarplum Falls.

Including the number of rooms filled at Sweetwater Hotel.

Truly, the lack of cold weather was an even bigger threat to his hotel than Gingerbread Inn—or any of the other perplexing troubles that now plagued Sweetwater Hotel.

Why? His business used to seem invincible!

No, first he'd focus on his Christmas goodness plan.

How could he create something lasting? Lasting things were so rare. Which was why he couldn't pursue tourists—and why he couldn't stand these fly-by-night boutique hotels that would probably only last a year before closing.

Andrew was right. Cliff had set himself a tough challenge, including the timeframe. The weeks between now and Christmas were few and shrinking fast.

For another, even discovering a significant need was another huge hurdle. Around these parts, if anybody really hit rock-bottom, they rarely spoke about it.

Plus, there was the looming question of whether Cliff *could* help, once he determined who to help and what was required. Cliff was a pretty capable, competent guy, but some needs were beyond the scope of his resources.

And yet, his heart whispered that he absolutely must accomplish something that *mattered.* To *someone.*

Whatever it ends up being, I will *do this for Christmas.*

Chapter 4

Jessamyn

"Welcome to Gingerbread Inn." Zinnia gave Jessamyn one of her broadest smiles, her white teeth shining in contrast to her dark skin. "Can I interest you in a complimentary caftan in lieu of a fluffy robe after your bath?"

"Zinnia!" Jessamyn joined her one-and-only full-time employee behind the desk, glad to be out of the jeep and back at work. "You haven't actually offered guests caftans, have you?" A lot of them would probably accept. Zinnia's signature wardrobe item—which she wore that day and every day, just in varying prints—did look incomparably comfortable. But they weren't in the budget. Zinnia hadn't purchased any, had she? Jessamyn's heart clutched.

"No, but trust me, if they'd just try one out, they'd be hooked for life."

"It does look comfy. Maybe I'll order some next year—if we can afford them." During the remodel, she'd ordered everything else. She was on a first-name basis with the drivers of every delivery service in town.

"Christmas colors, maybe? Or patterns!" Zinnia tugged at the bell sleeve of her flowing dress. "Something in microfiber but in an angel print, or—get this!—with gingerbread men."

"Gingerbread men! Imagine!" Jessamyn fake-swooned. Just talking to Zinnia made her forget the distress of a few minutes ago. "I'll see what types of fabric I can find online later on." If Jessamyn sewed them herself, they could pinch a few pennies. "Have any of tonight's guests checked in?"

"We only have three check-ins scheduled. The other rooms were booked for multiple nights."

Together, they quickly reviewed the guest list, as well as the breakfast menu, which Jessamyn needed to start tonight, since overnight oats needed to go into the crock pot with extra fruits and spices to fill the air with goodness and warmth.

Ah, it was nice to be in Gingerbread Inn. *I hope this makes you as happy as it makes me, Grandma Ginger.*

A soft glow filled Jessamyn.

Coming to Sugarplum Falls and opening Gingerbread Inn had been the right call. Her gut knew it a hundred percent.

As long as no one discovered Sammie was here, she could live on in happiness indefinitely.

I won't check Douglas's website today. I'll grant myself just one afternoon of peace.

Chapter 5

Cliff

Cliff hadn't jogged far before yet another sight interrupted his run. At the bottom of the hill, fifty feet beyond the falls, trouble brewed—again.

An elderly woman waded into the shallows of the icy water, clinging to a tree branch. What in the world was going on with people? Why did everyone seem to want to take a polar-bear plunge?

Cliff put on another burst of speed, again yelling as he went.

"Mrs. Vanderhoff?" Cliff splashed into the shallows. Grief, that water was cold. "Wait up! What could be so important that you'd risk thirty-three-degree water?"

"Litterbugs are ruining this earth, don't you know!" Valerie Vanderhoff, the local Litter Warrior, leaned farther forward, wielding her pincher-fingers cane. She could've toppled head-first into the river, but that didn't seem to bother her. "I've got it, I've got it."

Cliff took a handful of her coat's fabric and gently pulled her backward toward the safety of dry ground. "Let me, Mrs. V. I'll get whatever it is."

When he turned back around, he saw the offending debris—a blue cylinder. Hey, not just any blue cylinder, *the* blue cylinder Jessamyn had hurled into the lake. It had already made its way over the falls. Now, it bobbed in the shallows near a stand of quaking aspens along the shore.

What's more, it appeared to have a sheet of paper rolled up inside. *A message in a bottle?*

Cliff balked, pulling his hand back instead of grabbing the offending trash. "It's probably better to leave it, Mrs. V." It rolled in the ripples from the falls.

"Are you off your gourd?" Mrs. Vanderhoff whacked his back with her litter-grabbing stick. "Don't you care a whit for the good Earth God gave us? I'm ashamed of you, Cliff Rockingham. Your mother would be, too, if she were alive to see you." Valerie pushed him aside and soon was up to the middle of her galoshes—and getting deeper by the second.

"No!" Cliff cried. If she went in, she'd chill and likely catch pneumonia. "I'm getting it."

He passed her and splashed out into the icy slush. With lunge after lunge, he grabbed for the bottle, but without luck. The rotten thing floated just out of his reach every time.

"See what I mean? It's a sneaky one." Valerie splashed back to shore. "Get it. Don't let it get away and choke a turtle!"

"You might be thinking of drinking straws."

"They'd choke on a bottle given the chance. Save the turtles, son! They're all going to choke!"

On the single bottle? Cliff was this far into the depths, he might as well finish off the job, if it took finishing off *himself*. Gah! It was cold! "There are no turtles in Lake Sugar."

"How do you know? There would be if they hadn't all choked on trash, I'm sure."

Soon, Cliff had waded knee-deep into the frigid slush—which would've reached well over short little Mrs. V's galoshes tops. *The things we do ...*

Finally, he caught it by the neck. "Got it!" Phew. Feet sticking in the mud and cold surging deep into his bones, Cliff carried the bottle out of the water, shivering like his veins were made of jackhammers. "Aren't you cold, Mrs. Vanderhoff?"

"No. Any sacrifice is worth it. Day or night. Heat or subzero. I'll warm up with some hot soup and so will you. Now, give it." Mrs. V held out her palm for him to deposit it there. She was already sitting in her famous golf cart, on the side of which she'd added its name, *The Warrior*.

Cliff pulled the bottle back. "Wait a second." No way. Mrs. V should not have possession of this bottle. Well, at least not of the letter it held inside. Valerie Vanderhoff might read it. The note in the bottle was no one's business. Not even Cliff's. Maybe *especially* not Cliff's, since he knew its writer's identity.

"I'll throw it away when I get back to Sweetwater Hotel." Cliff placed the bottle inside his jacket.

"Nope." Mrs. V shook her head, pushing her palm toward him insistently. "It needs to be recycled."

"I think it would"—he scrambled—"make a nice vase for some poinsettias."

"Poinsettias do not work as cut flowers, young man."

The woman thwarted him on every front! Cliff shivered violently. Wet workout clothes and near-freezing air weren't a good mix.

Finally, he did the only thing he could think of. "See you later!" He jogged off before she could protest.

"Cliff Rockingham!" *The Warrior* followed for a hundred yards. "You'd better promise to recycle *immediately*. No waiting! And absolutely no throwing it in the garbage can. Promise me, Cliff! Promise!"

"Thanks for caring about the Earth God gave us, Mrs. V.," he called over his shoulder, running hard to get warmth back in his blood.

Back at Sweetwater Hotel, Cliff dodged his business partner Tarquin, who manned the front desk this time of day, and dove into his personal quarters. His heart pounded, and not just from his run.

In his room, he did not throw the bottle in the recycling bin. Or the trash.

Instead, he set the bottle on his nightstand, and then sat himself down on his bed beside it. He should take a hot shower. He should drink hot soup. He should not stare at that bottle or its contents.

What does that note say?

He shouldn't open it. Of course not. It was private, which was why he'd snatched it away from Valerie Vanderhoff before she could either dispose of it or discover the note inside.

Cliff lifted the bottle and turned it over and over, making the paper tumble inside.

Okay, he shook it a little, too. Inside, the furled paper unrolled slightly, revealing seven words at the top of the handwritten message:

Dear Santa Claus. I need your help.

Chapter 6

Jessamyn

"**S**ign here, Miss Fleet." The UPS guy, Manuel, pushed a sheet of paper in her direction. "Last delivery of the evening."

Jessamyn Fleet, she scrawled, crossing the *t* with a bold stroke.

"Thanks, Miss Fleet." Manny took the paper back without a glance. "I've never delivered a package from"—he squinted his eyes at the envelope in Jessamyn's hand—"from the Moluccas. Who are the Moluccas? Sounds foreign."

"Not a who, a where. It's a chain of volcanic islands near Indonesia."

"Indonesia!"

"Even if the origin sounds exotic, inside it's just cloves that I plan to grind for my spice cake."

"Oh, I like pumpkin spice."

"Me, too." It wasn't exactly pumpkin spice, but close enough not to argue. Cloves were one of Grandma's favorites. Hints of camphor, cinnamon, pepper, and allspice—cloves had it all. Warm. A scent to live by. "If you come by tomorrow morning, you can have a slice of warm spice cake."

"I'll be here—whether or not I have a delivery!" Manny gave a thumbs up and then headed back out to his brown, boxy-shaped delivery truck in the dark, dry-pavement parking lot.

Winter was coming to Sugarplum Falls soon, whether or not snow had fallen yet.

It'd better fall soon, or Gingerbread Inn could be short on guests. Without snow, no skiers or sledders, and a lot fewer ice skaters, she would guess.

The door swung shut behind Manny, and Jessamyn caught her reflection in the glass.

Oh! The straight blonde hair shocked her every time. That tackle at the waterfall had skewed her ponytail, moving it to the side. She hadn't been able to wrangle it back into place, and now there was an unsightly crease. Ew. She winced and whipped around, turning her back on the reflection and walking quickly toward the hotel kitchen with the packet of cloves.

Douglas isn't here. He won't see this messy ponytail. I don't have to have perfect hair anymore. Perfect hair was Douglas's thing, not mine.

At the counter, she measured the dry ingredients. Then she stirred the spice-scented bowl of cake batter as if whipping it would turn memories of Douglas to froth.

Jessamyn pulled out her mortar and pestle and added the cloves from Indonesia. She crushed them until they were nothing but dust. Possibly too crushed. The scent enveloped her, and the tension in her shoulders finally relaxed.

I'm at Gingerbread Inn. No one knows me here. I'm safe. Douglas hasn't found me in all this time. I'm back to my original blonde hair. I'm back to my legal name. He might not even know my legal name.

Or did he? Jessamyn's heart clutched, with that vise-pinch that came every time she thought of Doug and his relentless nature. It had seemed so charming at first, when he'd pursued her. Now, however, it was a different feeling altogether.

She tipped a half teaspoon of the ground cloves into her batter, finished mixing in the dry ingredients and then poured the spice cake batter into the prepared loaf pans. Just breathing all those mingled spices helped erase Douglas's face from her thoughts.

A different face replaced it: Cliff Rocknroll's.

She blinked it away.

"You okay, sugar?" Zinnia, wearing a red velvet caftan this time, took up the full doorway to the Gingerbread Inn's kitchen nook. "You got that look like someone just jump-scared you."

"I'm okay. Just having a bad hair day."

Ovens and waffle-makers and ten flavors of syrup covered the countertop of the hotel's kitchen. Overnight guests would end up sampling all ten flavors tomorrow morning, like every morning.

"Whatcha making this evening?" Zinnia came into the room. "Mmm. That smells heavenly. Cloves, nutmeg, cinnamon, ginger? What else?"

"You nailed them all for this recipe. Impressive."

Zinnia inhaled deeply. "Spices are why people come to Gingerbread Inn."

"Spices make a harsh world feel cozy and safe." Grandma Ginger had used them to change lives, and Jessamyn wanted to change lives, too. Including her own. "Grandma Ginger called them warm spices, and as a kid I thought she made up the term."

"That Grandma Ginger of yours was really something, I bet."

"I wish you could've met her." Jessamyn held out a spoonful of batter. "Wanna taste? This is spice cake, but I'm also going to bake pumpkin gingerbread cookies—to make ice cream sandwiches for the late-night snack for the guests." Which reminded her, Jessamyn had better get going on the homemade vanilla ice cream.

With a flourish of the spoon, Zinnia tasted the mix. "Bless me!" She rolled her eyes heavenward and patted her puffy hair in its unruly bun. "This is everything, girl. Can I get another?"

"Sure." Jessamyn handed her a clean spoon, and Zinnia dipped again. "Glad you like it."

Zinnia made delicious, taste-savoring sounds again. "It's no wonder your breakfasts and late-night snacks bring the repeat guests."

The front desk's bell jingled. "They're playing my song." Zinnia scooted back to the lobby.

Truly, Jessamyn couldn't have been luckier than to have found Zinnia as her hotel manager. The content retiree with the wide, welcoming smile and chill personality was the perfect person to make every guest feel embraced. *I just hope I don't have to let her go if ...*

She wouldn't think about *if*.

Jessamyn *would* get that millstone of a loan repaid.

I never should've borrowed any money, let alone that unholy amount, from that ... shark!

Ouch. And then a physical ouch followed. She rubbed her elbow. It must have been bruised when Cliff Rockstar tackled her. Bless his heart. Bless Jessamyn's elbow.

A commotion arose from the lobby area, and then footsteps and Zinnia's voice rang through the hallway air.

"Once you've had the best night's sleep of your life, you can come downstairs and our property's lovely owner will make you a delicious, soul-filling breakfast." Jessmyn turned. Zinnia and a nice-looking older couple peered into the kitchen nook. "Mr. and Mrs. Houlihan, this is Jessamyn Fleet, owner of Gingerbread Inn."

"It's nice to meet you." Jessamyn set aside her bowl, wiped flour specks from her hands, and went to greet them. "I hope your stay is healing and wonderful in every way."

"It's already starting out great," Mrs. Houlihan said, leaning on a cane. "This hotel is even better than it looks online. The details! And it smells even better in person than I imagined it would when I saw the photos." She inhaled deeply, closing her eyes.

Mr. Houlihan, however, pinned Jessamyn with a stare. "You look incredibly familiar."

A zing darted through Jessamyn's chest. She scrambled for one of her prepared excuses. "I get that a lot."

"No, I'm sure I've seen you somewhere." He rubbed his chin. "Have you ever done any acting?"

Far too much. "Um …" Jessamyn resisted the urge to pull her hair in front of her face.

Zinnia clued in quickly, coming to her rescue. "You may be thinking of her second cousin, Sammie Westwood."

Second cousin! That was a great cover. Jessamyn took up that baton. "Other than our hair color, we're practically look-alikes, but I've only met her a couple times in person. Family reunion when we were twelve. She was too cool to hang out with the likes of me."

Please buy it, please. Jessamyn could barely breathe.

"Sammie Westwood!" He slapped his hands together. "That's it! I wasn't imagining it. She was on that reality show. Man, you're a dead ringer for her.

Other than the hair, of course, like you said."

"Right," she managed, feeling sick. Unfortunately, *dead* was exactly the word Jessamyn was trying to avoid. Maybe she needed to do something more drastic about her appearance than just a change of hair color and dropping her famous makeup. Did Sugarplum Falls have a plastic surgeon? Maybe she could look into a chin implant. Or changing up her nose's shape. Anything to throw everyone off her track.

"Jessamyn gets that all the time." Zinnia waved the air, as if to clear all the tension Jessamyn must be exuding. "Would you like her to say hi to Sammie for you if she sees her at a family wedding someday?"

"Would you?" Mrs. Houlihan clutched her chest. "We're the Houlihans of Honolulu. Easy to remember, right? And would you tell her how much we missed her when she decided to leave the show? It wasn't the same afterward. My friends and I decided we might never forgive Douglas for letting her go."

"Of course. I'd be happy to give her the message. If I see her, that is." She filled her tone with doubt. Bringing them all back to the front desk, Jessamyn showed them the guest book. "Be sure to sign in. And place a star next to your name? Then I'll be sure to check it before I go to any family events."

Mrs. Houlihan signed, and she added a brief personal note to *Sammie* on a fresh page. It was very sweet, expressing Mrs. Houlihan's concern for Sammie's health and for her broken heart.

The next guest might see it—so as soon as Mrs. Houlihan wasn't looking, Jessamyn would remove the page and tuck it into her own journal.

After all, the note was for Jessamyn. Er, Sammie. Er, Jess.

Being three people was exhausting.

Even after the guest book had been replaced and the Houlihans had their room keys, Mrs. Houlihan was not ready to let it drop. "What's Sammie doing these days, anyway? Do you know?"

Jessamyn forced a laugh. "If I kept up with all my second cousins, I wouldn't have time to make gingerbread pancakes for your breakfast tomorrow morning."

Mrs. Houlihan lit up. "You'll be making gingerbread pancakes?"

21

"Yes. Family recipe. With homemade applesauce."

Mrs. Houlihan got a faraway look. "My mama used to make homemade applesauce for me when I was sick. I think it has healing properties."

"I think you're right." Jessamyn couldn't have asked for a kinder compliment. "An applesauce a day keeps the doctor away."

They talked food for a bit, thank heaven, and Mrs. Houlihan promised to send Jessamyn a copy of her holiday apple cake recipe later, after she returned home to Honolulu.

Zinnia helped wrap up the chit-chat by saying, "Now, don't hit the hay too early. As a late-night snack, Jessamyn will have a batch of pumpkin cookie and vanilla ice cream sandwiches ready at nine."

Mr. Houlihan grasped his wife's hand. "This is the best hotel ever."

They disappeared down the hall into their cozy room with a fireplace.

Jessamyn squeezed Zinnia's shoulders hard. "Thanks for saving me with the Sammie thing again."

Eyes narrowing, Zinnia tapped her chin. "Why *do* you get all defensive when people say you look like Sammie? She was beloved on that show! Nobody didn't like Sammie—well, until she broke Douglas's heart, that is." Zinnia's messy bun wagged atop her head, curls zinging out everywhere. "Leaving a great guy like that at the altar, what a shame."

Uh-huh. That's how the producers had played it. Keeping Douglas in *almost* everyone's good graces. Well, not Mrs. Houlihan's or her friends' high esteem, apparently—but everyone else still loved Douglas to distraction.

"I guess I'm disappointed in Sammie like everyone else," Jessamyn said—more truthfully than Zinnia would ever have guessed. "I'll try harder to keep a poker face anytime I'm wishing we weren't so similar."

Maybe Jessamyn should have written *gift certificate for rhinoplasty* in her letter to Santa instead of the things she'd penned there instead.

Thank goodness no one would ever see that desperate, embarrassing letter. Cliff—Rockingham, had he said?—hadn't seen it, thank goodness. She'd been able to chuck the bottle into the lake before he asked about it. If he'd even seen the message in the bottle, he hadn't mentioned it, or her littering ways.

Bless him for that.

She placed the spice cake pan in the oven and sighed at the memory of him. He'd been unbelievably good-looking. How awkward had she been, trying not to stare at him while she attempted to escape before he asked where he'd seen her before? Because, no doubt whatsoever, he'd been about to ask that. The look of confused near-recognition had dawned there in his crystal-blues, bright as the sun at eight thirty a.m. in the wintertime.

Oh, those eyes. And the kind sincerity in his looks. It'd been a long, long time since Jessamyn had even let herself notice any man's good looks. Honestly, she shouldn't now.

Where are you staying? he'd asked, just as if he were a tourist. Tourists were so plentiful in Sugarplum Falls, it was a safe assumption.

Maybe she shouldn't have told him Gingerbread Inn. He wasn't a spy for Douglas, was he?

Stop being so paranoid! Douglas can't find you here.

In truth, she'd likely never see Cliff Rockabilly again. It didn't matter, then, if she were to appreciate his mountain-lake-in-Switzerland eyes and all those piled swirls of jet-black hair.

So dreamy.

Except, like his Superman theme look, that old save-the-girl attitude was written all over him. Wrant-wrant-wrant! Her inner klaxon warned hard. The very *last* thing she needed was to be the object of another crusade. Douglas Queen had been more than enough caped warrior for one lifetime.

Zinnia had scooped up a pile of clean towels and was heading toward the linen closet. "I probably shouldn't have lied to those people about you being related to Sammie. I feel like I sinned."

Sinned! Hardly! "Oh, Zinnia. Don't let that weigh on your conscience. I'm sure Sammie and I *are* related in some way. We couldn't look this much alike otherwise. How about if I get in touch with her and she and I do some genealogy match-up thing. Or a DNA test. Until then, you just sleep with a clear conscience, okay? You don't know it *wasn't* a lie."

Jessamyn did know it hadn't been a lie. Jessamyn's DNA and Sammie's were an identical match.

"Knock-knock!" Esther Lang popped in at the front door. "I brought Mario's!" She held up her hands and shook two large bags with the logo of the Italian restaurant. "Yes, it's for a bribe—before you ask. And there's enough for Zinnia if she wants some."

"You can leave that in the fridge for me, Esther Lang." Zinnia hugged the pile of towels. "I have a few things to take care of, like calling my mama in Darlington. Bye, now." She headed up the stairs to her personal room where she boarded.

"Mario's. Ahhh." Jessamyn took Esther into the Gingerbread Inn's breakfast nook, where she rummaged for plates and cutlery. They sat down at one of the bistro tables and dished up the food. "Give me tortellini and my spine turns to linguine." Jessamyn took a big bite of cheesy, pasta deliciousness and sank back against the chair.

"Are you officially in a weakened condition?" Esther twisted noodles coated with alfredo sauce onto a fork.

"It's official." Jessamyn popped another of the little turtle-shaped pastas into her mouth. It exploded in a cheesy, oregano-laced deliciousness. "I'm as spineless as a boneless chicken ranch."

"Good. My mom sent me over here to trick you into showing up at the Sugarplum Falls Chamber of Commerce meeting on Thursday night."

"Oh, no." She set down her fork. "My spine returned."

"Please?" Esther batted her long lashes. "Pretty please, with grated parmesan on top?" She waved a breadstick at her, and the garlic tantalized the air.

"I do owe you. And not just for the Italian food. You know that." When Jessamyn met Esther in Los Angeles, Esther had told her about Sugarplum Falls. Otherwise, Jessamyn's life might've still been a never-ending round of dodging the press and yearning for freedom. Now, she was living out her dreams, her higher purpose in life, all thanks to Esther.

"Forget about that. We were there for each other, you know."

"And as much as I'd do anything for you, Esther, going to a meeting?" She winced. "I'm not really a joiner." Plus, Jessamyn had to lie low. Esther should recognize that. Seeing guests was one thing, but getting to know the people of Sugarplum Falls? Not wise.

"You keep saying that." Esther poured marinara sauce onto her dish and dredged her breadstick through the tomato-y goodness. "This one time, I'm telling you, you want to be there. Trust me."

"Why?"

"My mom's doling out perks, but it's one of those *you must be present to win* things. I don't know what they are, but I do know Mom doesn't exaggerate when she promises something will be good. One time, she offered to use Chamber of Commerce funds to upgrade a winning business's sign, and another time, she featured a business on our town tourism billboard down in Darlington for six months."

"Really?" Jessamyn's bottom line could use those kinds of perks. *So many visits from the soul patch-sporting debt collector!* "Can you give me any advice for winning?"

Oh, no. The limp spaghetti spine was taking over Jessamyn's will to stay hidden.

"Nope, but I *can* give you some unrelated advice: stay out of her *other* crosshairs."

"What *other* crosshairs?" The mayor took aim at business owners, like who refused to show up at Chamber of Commerce meetings? "She wouldn't orchestrate a bunch of bad reviews online for my hotel or anything, would she?"

"Of course not! She's all about improving businesses in Sugarplum Falls, not wrecking them. Please." Esther looked horrified and set down her fork. "I'm talking about her matchmaking crosshairs. My mother thinks of herself as Emma Woodhouse."

"Like from the Jane Austen novel?"

"Yep, and like Emma, she's absolutely not-self-aware. She forgets that she's totally hit-and-miss with her matchmaking successes." Esther pointed her fork at her chest. "Case in point, she really missed when she turned Fargo and me into Estargo." Esther raised her palm and waved a circle in the air.

"Oh, dear. Tell me Estargo wasn't your mom's idea." Estargo, the snail-like couple-name for Esther and Fargo had made everyone cringe—including poor Esther. "I'm so sorry you had to leave Fargo at the altar." It had happened a few Christmases ago. "But I'm glad I met someone who knew how emotional something like that could be."

That had been the common experience that bonded Jessamyn and Esther when they'd met in Los Angeles—even though Esther still didn't know that Jessamyn was, in fact, Sammie Westwood of *Queen of the Queendom* fame.

"My mom means well." Esther rolled her eyes and took a big bite of breadstick. "And she hasn't been wrong every single time, but she's definitely not batting a thousand. Unfortunately, that doesn't stop her from trying to improve her average every time she meets a single person in town."

"I'll keep out of her crosshairs. No more almost-trips to the altar for me. I'm a businesswoman now." With a slight crush on a blue-eyed tourist who'd tried to save her un-endangered life. Luckily, that would pass. Soon. "So, okay. If—and it's a big if—if I do go to the Chamber of Commerce meeting, I'll lie low and stay off Mayor Lang's matchmaking radar. A new man is the *last* thing I need in my life right now." No matter how piercingly blue that tourist Cliff Rock-solid's eyes had been, or how earnestly kind his face.

Nope. Nope-a-dope-ity-nope.

Esther stabbed at her tortellini. "How about we go back to talking about Jane Austen."

Yes, a much better topic than dating or past relationship failures. "If your mom is an Emma Woodhouse, who does that make you?" Jessamyn took a crispy bite of a garlic breadstick. Delicious. Garlic was a soothing spice, too. She instantly pinpointed which Austen character she was, herself. Or which Sammie had been, anyway: Kitty Bennet. The weak one who went along with whichever personality dominated the room.

"Well, I was going to ask which film version of Mr. Darcy you prefer, but this is good, too." Esther nodded. "I obviously have a history as a Lydia Bennet, with my own Mr. Wickham near-miss."

"Cringe."

"Total cringe. Jessamyn! I was such a blind idiot! When my cousin Chelsea—the smartest person I know—and Fargo broke up, I should've taken that as a glaring warning sign."

"Don't beat yourself up. We don't always trust our family's opinions. Nor should we." Jessamyn shouldn't have listened to Mom and Dad's approval of Douglas, that was for sure. "At least you didn't actually go through with marrying Fargo. You didn't make vows you then had to break."

"True." Esther sighed. "What I want to know, and I'm being serious here, is can a person switch characters? Like, past the age of twenty-five?" Her voice cracked. "Jessamyn, am I *doomed* to stay Lydia Bennet forever?"

"You're not doomed!" Jessamyn could've reached across and grabbed Esther's hand if Esther hadn't been using her fork right then. "You can pick your non-Lydia life from this moment forward."

I want to, too. That's what Jessamyn had, more or less, asked Santa Claus for in her message in a bottle, if not in so many words.

"You really think so?" Esther's fork stopped midway to her mouth. "If so, then I want with all my heart to become a Lizzy Bennet."

"You can. It's all up to you."

"You really think I can shed my Lydia past, then?"

"As a recovering Kitty Bennet, I'm banking on it."

Esther pointed a new breadstick right between Jessamyn's eyes. "Please! Kitty is weak-willed. That's *nothing* like you."

"See? Evidence of someone changing Jane Austen types." *I'm done being Kitty Bennet.*

"Well, since I didn't know you before, I can't say, but there's something I have to point out: Kitty never found love by the end of the story. I can't picture that type of outcome for *you*."

"I'm resigned to whatever happens." Jessamyn gave her best *I don't care* shrug. "I'm happily single."

"Especially by comparison to before when you were together with someone, I take it? Who was he? What was he like?" Esther pointed the tines of her fork at Jessamyn's heart. "Whoever he was, he sure did a number on you if you really mean you're *never* going to fall in love again."

"I'm over it." So over it that she'd gone into hiding. *If only Douglas were over it.* "These days I'm striving to be a true Jane—serene, a reed that's flexible enough to bend in strong winds but who never breaks."

27

"I can see it." Esther studied Jessamyn thoughtfully. "Calm during storms, taking the bad but hoping for the good. Always making the right choice."

"Ha! If only!" Due to her impatience to get the hotel purchased and remodeling started, Jessamyn had committed a huge error. Maybe a fatal one. If she'd been in her right state of mind, she never, *ever* would've put herself into that viper's power. "I'm what they call a work-in-progress. No overnight transformation, unfortunately."

"Well, we're all works in progress, so here's to our Lizzy and Jane futures." Esther held up her Styrofoam cup of diet soda for a toast.

"Cheers." They touched foam cups and sipped from the straws.

They finished their meals, and Esther put on her coat.

Jessamyn followed her out to the lobby to say goodbye. Just as Esther exited, in walked Jessamyn's nightmare.

"You've been tardy with your loan installment." Blue Soul Patch, whose name might be Bertie, cracked his knuckles, the soul patch on his chin bouncing. He'd dyed it blue now? It should've at least been green for the season—to complement the red rims beneath his eyes or the red veins on his bulbous nose. "My boss don't like it when you're tardy. He don't want to put anybody in detention."

Heart racing, Jessamyn panicked. She raced behind the desk, crouched and twisted the combination to the cash box. Who even knew how much was inside it this time?

Blue Soul Patch heaved his asthmatic breathing. "What's taking so long? Didn't you expect me?"

How could she? He showed up at the worst times. What if Mr. Houlihan wandered downstairs and saw Jessamyn paying a loan shark's lackey? That could totally taint her online reputation and ruin everything she'd invested and built.

She popped back up, holding a stack of bills. "Should I count it for you?" *Please say no and just leave. Get that disgusting facial hair out of here.* "Or are you going to trust me."

He grabbed it from her hand. "Just show me the empty cash box, and I'll believe you're making a good-faith effort. Unless you got another cash box somewheres else and you're not dealing fairly with my boss."

"That's all there is." Her throat constricted.

He pocketed the money and then pulled the hood up on his jacket and took off, the door jingling a joyful sound behind him, a crummy contrast.

Jessamyn flopped down on the chair, then pulled her knees to her chest and hugged them hard. Bright side, bright side. There had to be one.

At least I've been able to make every payment he has demanded.

So far.

How much had she forked over in repayments up to now, anyway?

What a Kitty Bennet thing to not have a clue about the repayment amounts! Jane Bennet would have kept a careful record. By now, it felt like the full debt should've been repaid. Would Blue Soul Patch just keep on showing up forever?

If so, whose fault was that? No one's but her own.

She should've included a job transfer to Mars for Blue Soul Patch in her message in a bottle to Santa Claus.

If only.

Chapter 7

Cliff

The Chamber of Commerce meeting droned on in the Sugarplum Falls Recreation Center. Metal folding chairs scraped on the shiny tile floors while the chairs' occupants squirmed.

Couldn't the mayor just make her points and set them free?

As was his usual habit, Cliff strategically positioned himself behind Owen Kingston, orchard owner and cousin to Andrew the budding PI, who had taken to wearing a ten-gallon hat lately. Thanks to the mega-hat, Cliff could attend these meetings to hear the updates and yet never land in Mayor Lang's direct line of sight—always a dangerous location for a single person in Sugarplum Falls.

While someone droned on about upcoming holiday events—which Cliff had attended so many times in his life he had them memorized—Cliff stared at the photograph on his phone and re-read the letter.

Dear Santa. I need your help.

He'd snapped a picture of the letter in the bottle and then stashed the original deep between his mattresses.

I'm not a kid anymore, so I have no right to write to you. I don't need toys, which are your specialty. But I truly do need help, and there's no one in my life I can ask right now.

He should not be reading Jessamyn's letter. Er, re-reading. Memorizing every curve of her handwriting as he went.

Foolishly, I put myself in the power of someone awful, more or less a storybook villain. Now, I'm at his mercy, and even though it's my own fault, I can't help wishing there were a way out. It's not really your line of work, I know. But I am sending this wish out, hoping and praying for a Christmas miracle. If you have one, email me.

Love, JW

JW.

J had to be for Jessamyn. What did W stand for?

In almost a knee-jerk reaction, Cliff had typed in a cursory search on social media for Jessamyn W. Way too many results had popped up—though a lot of them were for *Jessica* not Jessamyn. He hadn't sifted through them.

Sifting through them would be wrong. All he'd wanted to know was whether a Jessamyn W existed.

Answering the letter using the email address scrawled at the bottom of the letter would *also* be wrong.

Super wrong.

Through the din of the chamber meeting, the address JW@giantmail.com sang to him, softly, insistently, a siren's song, ready to smash him on the rocks of *super wrong.*

A response to the letter composed itself in his brain. A lame one, telling her she was beautiful, and that he'd like to get together sometime. Super stupid, as well as being super wrong.

Besides, she was a tourist, and even if she was still in Sugarplum Falls today, she wouldn't be around after her vacation.

What's wrong with me? Why am I so drawn to her? Duh, besides how pretty she was. Cliff saw beautiful women all the time.

Suddenly, like sunshine breaking over the ridge in the morning, Cliff's Christmas project dawned bright and clear.

The dilemma of whether reading the letter had been ethical or not faded to nothing. Obviously, the Universe or Fate or Heaven above had ordained that Cliff get that note! The siren song wasn't for him to *fall* for her, it was that she was the one he needed to help this Christmas. It had to be fate. Remember how immediately prior to finding it Cliff had been asking for guidance about who personally needed help in this life!

Cha-ching! Answer from Above! Hallelujah!

A split second later, those angels' songs fell dead silent, however.

How on Earth was Cliff supposed to help this Jessamyn woman, tourist from who knew where, when he'd never see the woman again? He knew nothing more than her first name and last initial: Jessamyn W.

Dang it. The blasted email address gave Cliff no clues as to her identity. GiantMail was a generic search engine company that gave out free email addresses. JW at GiantMail told him nothing about her job, her education, or her whereabouts. Just like his cursory social media search had been fruitless.

All he knew was her beauty, her despair, and the fact she'd been staying at Gingerbread Inn a couple of nights ago.

La! Angels sang again. Cliff could sneak into the loathsome Gingerbread Inn and peek at the guest book, assuming they kept a written one. Kitschy boutique places like that always did. He'd at least get her last name and her hometown that way.

Easy. Easy peasy. Easier than peasy.

Ethical standards reared their heads again. Lots of them. He silenced them with a stern warning. This creepy sneaking around was for a good cause. The woman had literally sent out a cry for help, and Cliff's gut just *knew* he was her destined rescuer. Otherwise, all these coincidences were too unlikely to deal with.

So what if he was turning into a stalker?

He craned his neck to look around the room. Where was Andrew Kingston? Once Cliff knew Jessamyn W's hometown, he could hand Andrew his first P.I. case.

Except for one thing: Cliff wanted to keep this investigation secret, as well as his methods of helping the woman with her needs. Alms before men, and all that. Christmas giving was best kept quiet—another problem with *Presents for People,* frankly. Far too public.

Most of all, Cliff ought to keep secret the fact he'd plucked her bottle from the freezing water and read its contents.

Cringe much? Cliff had not awakened the other morning intent on turning into a sneaky weirdo who read other people's private, heartfelt missives to Santa Claus.

The clock on the wall of the meeting room crawled slower than spilled molasses. Mayor Lang needed to wrap up this meeting so Cliff could truck over to find that guest book.

Frankly, there were too many of these Thursday night things with nothing new. A peek at the agenda showed five more speakers listed. Five! *Kill me now.*

Well, in the meantime, Cliff could at least get the project's ball rolling. With a few taps on his phone screen, Cliff composed a new, different, non-stalkerish and non-flirtatious answer to the message in the bottle.

An anonymous one.

Dear JW ...

It filled the screen. It took the first three speakers' time for him to compose it, but Cliff waxed witty and insightful and encouraging.

Then he deleted it all and typed a new letter.

Which he deleted.

Finally, he composed something succinct and yet kind.

Perfection! *Send!* He punched the screen and a slow smile spread over his face. Good deed, accomplished! Well, ball officially rolling, anyway.

The microphone screeched.

"Ladies and gentlemen, thank you for your time, and thanks to our previous speakers. Now, it's time for the best news of the night." Mayor Lisa Lang stood much closer to the microphone than anyone speaking earlier in the meeting. "Our last item of business is why you're all here."

"Not all of us." Next to Cliff, a lean, elderly guy—George Milliken of Angels Landing bookstore—sniffed, speaking in a mumble only Cliff could hear. "I'm here for the refreshments, personally. Sugarbabies Bakery caters these meetings, or else I'd never show up. Way too many blowhards."

"Bring on the Nutella-filled cupcakes." Cliff's stomach growled. He'd been so busy stalking tourists online he hadn't grabbed dinner.

"Or the raspberry thumbprint cookies." Lean old George patted his belly. "Spiced-cream-filled croissants, too."

Now Cliff *really* wished this meeting would end.

Mayor Lang's voice boomed through the conference room of the Sugarplum Falls Recreation Center. "Thanks to all of you wonderful businesspeople, Sugarplum Falls has drawn the notice of the state tourism board."

Wait, really? Cliff sat up—and he leaned around Owen's huge hat. "The *state* tourism board?" he said too loudly, drawing Mayor Lang's gaze.

"That's right." She beamed at Cliff and then spread the grin toward all her other long-meeting hostages. "Sugarplum Falls has been chosen officially as the Most Christmassy Town in the state."

Applause erupted, and even George Milliken stopped looking longingly toward the buffet table. "That's incredible." George held up a hand to high-five Cliff. "Who'd have dreamed?"

Cliff was almost too stunned to clap. State tourism ad dollars meant more guests at Sweetwater Hotel. Maybe even enough to offset his lost bookings due to places like the Gingerbread Inn. *Maybe* even enough to make up for the crazy money-gush caused by incidental plumbing repairs that kept cropping up lately.

Wow—everything suddenly looked rosier.

"Stuff to know. One, Sugarplum Falls will be featured on the state's tourism website, which gets more hits per day than we get in a month." After Mayor Lang patted out the enthusiasm, she continued more gravely. "However, although they've agreed to feature individual businesses, they'll feature only *one* business from each industry on their website.""

Beside Cliff, Milliken harrumphed. "Works for me. Angels Landing is the only bookstore in town. My boss will love it."

Cliff harrumphed right back. "Not as great of news for the lodgings industry." Cliff folded his arms over his chest. Sugarplum Falls teemed with hotels, motels, and bed and breakfasts. "There will be some sad hotel owners."

"Maybe, but not you." Milliken elbowed Cliff. "You run Sweetwater Hotel—the biggest, best, most well-known place in town. It's the obvious choice for the state tourism website."

Maybe it once was. But these days? What did tourists want? And why were his numbers falling at Sweetwater Hotel? In fact, thanks to all the expensive repairs, Cliff's numbers had been running in the red for the past three quarters.

"More details will be in your weekly newsletter, so check your inboxes tomorrow, people."

Finally, the speakers were done. Cliff stretched his legs and poised himself to make a fast getaway—to the Gingerbread Inn's lobby.

Unfortunately, Mayor Lang had more to say. "We have one more item of business, even though it's not listed on the agenda."

There was an audible groan.

Mayor Lang ignored it. "Tonight, in attendance is a new business owner in town, one who hasn't come out to our meetings before, and who hasn't officially joined the Chamber of Commerce." No subtlety about the guilt trip there. "Please, everyone welcome Miss Jessamyn Fleet. Jessamyn, stand please?"

Jessamyn! That name twice in three days? What were the chances?

Cliff craned his neck to see what this other Jessamyn could look like. Obviously, she wouldn't be as gorgeous as the message-containing-bottle-littering tourist, Jessamyn W.

From around the edge of the ten-gallon hat came a flash of straight blonde hair, the kind that glinted even in dim lamplight. Jessamyn from the Falls Overlook? It couldn't be!

Then, she turned toward Cliff, as if in slow motion, and she met his gaze with those one-of-a-kind, arresting honey-brown eyes.

Cliff grasped the base of his chair, a weak attempt to steady himself—and not just because she was the most beautiful woman in the room. In the town, for sure. Maybe in the whole state.

She wasn't a tourist. She owned a business in Sugarplum Falls.

Something shifted inside him, like a continental shelf.

"Thank you, Miss Fleet!" Mayor Lang said over the applause as it grew while Jessamyn waved to everyone shyly. "Everyone, please give your support and friendship to the owner of Gingerbread Inn."

Gingerbread Inn! She owned it? She had told him she had to get back for check-in time, but he'd assumed it was because she was a guest. Not the owner!

His continental shelf smashed into another one, like when India hit Asia and created the world's highest mountain range.

Because he'd irretrievably pressed *send* on that privacy-invading email.

And she wasn't a tourist.
And she was standing right there.

Chapter 8

Jessamyn

Worst fears realized!

Jessamyn had tried desperately to exit the Sugarplum Falls Recreation Center quickly and quietly without drawing any more attention. Talk about crosshairs! Being forced to stand in front of everyone was far worse than being love-matched by the mayor.

Unfortunately, practically every other business owner from the whole town seemed to want to follow the mayor's instruction to make friends with her. They completely blocked her exit.

"I hope your hotel gets the spot on the state tourism site," a short woman eating a cookie said.

"Yeah, you did a great job remodeling your hotel this past year," a tall guy in a huge Stetson said.

Cookie woman spoke through a mouthful of crumbs. "It totally screams Christmas. It's the very essence of Sugarplum Falls."

A woman wearing a red- and green-striped scarf smiled. "I love Christmas so much. Mayor Lang will see how perfectly Christmassy Gingerbread Inn is and pick you, I'm sure."

Jessamyn looked longingly at the doorway. "Being featured would be really good for business," she found herself repeating. "I appreciate the encouragement so much, but I'm new. I'm sure the mayor will choose an established hotel."

Like Sweetwater Hotel. Established. *And generic*. Something to appeal to all types of travelers, not just the ones who wanted a holiday experience year-round.

Oh, but—getting featured on the site could be a game-changer for Gingerbread Inn, and for Jessamyn personally. Then that loan shark would quit

37

sending his collections officer to shake her down for money.

Being free of the debt would make her world halfway better. If only Douglas would quit looking for her, it'd be the first freedom she'd experienced in literally years.

Man, how had her life gotten so messed up?

You date one wrong TV superstar, and ...

"You're a shoo-in," Poppy Kingston from The Cider Press said. "You want me to lobby Mayor Lang for you? My cider-drinking tourist customers all give your place the best reviews."

"That's so nice of you." Jessamyn kept her words neutral and her tone of voice as monotone and indistinct as she could. She probably sounded rude or cold. But what choice did she have?

Please, don't let anyone say I look familiar tonight. The fewer times she had to repeat that second cousin fib, the better.

And yet she still couldn't leave!

Jessamyn's phone chimed an email notification. "Excuse me?" She escaped a conversation about fresh-ground spices with the Sugarbabies bakery owner and opened her message.

Dear JW. I received your letter. Please let me be of service. SC

Jessamyn stared at the short note, her face puzzling into a frown. What letter?

Then, alternating hot and cold sensations washed through her veins. The message in the bottle!

She gulped, but her mouth was dry. Someone had read it?

Who? The sender's address read:

SantaClaus@SanNouveau.SN

San Nouveau? Wasn't that an island off the coast, inhabited by ... billionaires?

Finger hovering over the delete button, Jessamyn nearly sent the message to the trash. It had to be a prank, right? Besides, how could her message in a bottle have floated out to the ocean and all the way to San Nouveau in three days? No, less than three days' time. Impossible! Or, was it?

She swiped over to the search engine to ask the wide world of the internet how fast rivers flowed.

"Jessamyn!" Up walked Mayor Lang, interrupting the frantic info-search.

She shoved the phone back in her jacket pocket and prayed for mercy to keep herself out of the *other* crosshairs. *Please, please, please.*

"Jessamyn, Jessamyn." Mayor Lang had a presence, dominating, but loving at the same time. "You're not only lovely, you're also doing a great job adding value and charm to Sugarplum Falls with your instincts about Gingerbread Inn's remodel. I'm glad you came tonight so I could introduce you *and* thank you publicly."

"Thank you so much." Jessamyn darted her gaze toward the door. "It's been a lot of work and a big risk." Bigger than anyone could have guessed.

"It's like you have an instinct for hospitality."

"More learned than instinctive," Jessamyn found herself admitting, as if Mayor Lang's engulfing aura were some kind of truth serum. "My grandmother ran a bed and breakfast down on the coast. She really blessed her guests."

"She taught you how to love strangers into friends."

"Exactly!"

"I wish I'd known her."

"I wish everyone had," Jessamyn said, meaning it truly. "Their lives would've been better for it."

"I believe that."

Huh. Even if she was an Emma Woodhouse matchmaking busybody, Mayor Lang was a whole lot of all right if she could pinpoint Grandma Ginger's magic so instantly.

"Well, Jessamyn Fleet, since you're new to Sugarplum Falls, I have a plan to help your lodgings level up."

"Really?" Jessamyn asked. "Thank you. How?" This couldn't be happening already, could it? Was Poppy Kingston, owner of The Cider Press, already proving to be a prophetess? Mayor Lang couldn't be simply choosing the Gingerbread Inn as the state tourism board's featured location, could she?

Jessamyn bated her breath.

Instead, however, Mayor Lang looked across the room and called out,

"Cliff? Cliff!"

Something in the base of Jessamyn's stomach quaked. *Cliff?*

On the far side of the room, a man turned around, his extra-dark hair shiny, and his crystal-blue eyes piercing.

Jessamyn's heart did something funny and scary and electrifying at the same time.

Hadn't Knight in Shining Spandex been a tourist? He'd asked where she was staying, and …

If he's at the Chamber of Commerce meeting—Jess's tongue dried into sandpaper—*that means he's a business owner. In Sugarplum Falls.*

What kind of business? If it was Mario's restaurant, she might *really* be in danger of being interested in him and his mistaken, knightly ways.

"Cliff?" Mayor Lang summoned him with a beckoning arm held high and waving. "Come on over and meet your newest fellow hotelier."

Fellow hotelier! What in the—

Cliff walked up, stood next to Mayor Lang, but he stared at Jessamyn's shoes.

Jessamyn shrank. This guy had pulled her from what he had assumed was a self-destructive path. Oh, geez! What must he think of her?

"Cliff here," Mayor Lang said, oblivious to the stifling awkwardness brewing, "owns Sweetwater Hotel, just a stone's throw from your place. But don't throw stones, please." She chuckled at her own joke. "We're all neighbors in Sugarplum Falls."

Sweetwater Hotel? Of all places. She shriveled. She must look like such a loser to him!

Cliff lifted his eyes for a split second, darting one uncomfortable, unhappy glance at her.

Oh, great. He did remember her. He must be thinking of Jessamyn as unstable—or as a woman who tossed litter into America's lakes and streams.

"Come on, Cliff. She's beautiful, I know," Mayor Lang said far too loudly. "But pretty girls aren't all threatening. Jessamyn's a darling! And you two are going to be working *together*." The word dripped with meaning, and matchmaking alarm bells clanged.

"Together?" Jessamyn gulped. "But ..."

"Don't say no until you've heard what I'm *proposing.*" Again with the dripping meanings. "Jessamyn, you're going to be working with the biggest hotelier in Sugarplum Falls. I should say, biggest in hotel *and* heart."

"That's great." Her tone did not ring with the appropriate level of enthusiasm. More like with the doom of "I Heard the Bells on Christmas Day" alarm chimes. But neither did the tension in Cliff's intensely uncomfortable-looking stance.

"Yeah," Cliff said, looking anywhere but at Jessamyn. He did take her hand, though, and shook it.

"Cliff! Show some manners!" Mayor Lang whacked him with a tourism pamphlet. "Now. Our Sugarplum Falls official town website needs content. Since the tourism site will redirect to our town's site, I need help. From both of you."

"Mayor Lang—" Cliff began.

"Starting tonight," the mayor said, bulldozing ahead, "the two of you will be working *together* to create articles about each and every one of our town's traditional holiday festivals."

"But isn't all that already on the website?" Jessamyn asked, a wish in her tone.

"*Fresh* content! For search engine optimization we need *updates.*"

Updates. Oh. Jessamyn wished the ground would open up and swallow her. Or, better yet, Mayor Lang.

"Our festivals feature new aspects every year. You know this, Cliff, after living here your whole life."

"Not my whole life." Cliff pulled a tight smile and looked wistfully toward the exit. Wow, someone who wished they could escape as much as Jessamyn did!

"Close enough." Mayor Lang rolled forth. "You can help familiarize Jessamyn with the annual festivities. We'll need pre-event articles for buzz, and then post-event stories with your experiences. It'll be great. The more I talk about it, the more I love this idea."

Cliff's mouth went from tight smile to pinch-faced grimace. "Okay,

Mayor." It came out forced, pained even. "On it. I can have content written up for you by midnight, with details from last year's events."

Was she that repugnant to him that he wouldn't even talk to her about the events?

Wow.

"Cliff!" Mayor Lang boomed. "I said *fresh*. Would you eat last year's gingerbread men?"

Good question. Jessamyn might, depending on how they smelled and where they'd been stored. Cookies with very little fat stayed edible for a long time.

Not the point.

"It's all right, Mayor." Jessamyn offered him a way out of spending time with the lunatic lady from the Falls Overlook. "If Mr. Rockingham isn't interested—"

"If he's not interested, then he takes himself and his hotel out of the running for placement on the state's tourism website."

Cliff's jaw dropped.

"But Sweetwater Hotel is iconic in Sugarplum Falls!" Jessamyn protested on his behalf. "It's the biggest, nicest hotel."

Cliff side-eyed her, as if shocked.

"That's right," Mayor Lang said, lifting a brow that declared she wouldn't budge. "However, sometimes good things come to those who earn them."

"Are you saying ...?" Cliff began but was cut off.

"I'm saying"—she peered over the tops of her glasses at them—"if you two do this project together, I will use my influence with the state tourism board to select one of your hotels for the website."

Ooh, so that's how she was going to play it. Manipulative, this Emma-Woodhouse-wannabe.

"To clarify, do we have to do the content-writing together?" Jessamyn asked. *Please say no, for his sake.* "Wouldn't it be more efficient to divide and conquer? We could get the content to you twice as quickly."

Mayor Lang dug in. "I'm looking for dual perspectives. For *all* events."

What choice did Jessamyn have? Website placement was an opportunity she couldn't squander. Maybe Cliff had the financial solvency to walk away from such a big prize, but not Jessamyn.

"I'm in," she said.

Mayor Lang broke into a triumphant grin. "Cliff will get you a schedule of events. Give him your number. He will pick you up and escort you to all of them." She patted Cliff's shoulder, as if he'd actually agreed to sell his evenings into festival-attending servitude. "When you've finished any write-ups, send them over. Cliff has my contact information."

Speaking of messages, Jessamyn's inbox contained that ominous message from SC in San Nouveau. What did SC stand for?

SC.

Santa Claus?

Her stomach flipped. There could be financial help on the horizon—via the North Pole, hardy har har. More likely a prankster. It flipped back.

Man, she could get seasick from the rise and fall of *hopes* and *dashed hopes*.

Then again, if Gingerbread Inn received the state tourism board's feature placement, Jessamyn just might be able to solve her own woes—without needing outside help from some San Nouveau billionaire, Santa Claus himself, or anyone else.

For once, I would frankly like to be my own white knight.

The mayor smiled in smug triumph and left Jessamyn standing with Cliff Rockingham.

Cliff again refused to look up. Instead, he tapped something onto his phone screen. Stinking phone addicts.

"I'm supposed to give you my number," Jessamyn said. "Unless you'd rather communicate by email?"

"No!" Cliff's head snapped upward, his alarm crackling everywhere. "Text!" He shook himself. "Text," he said again, more calmly this time. "I'll put your number in my phone."

Jessamyn almost repeated her old number, from her Darlington days, but she caught herself and gave her Sugarplum Falls digits. "Hey, you spelled my name right the first time. Almost nobody does that."

"Uh, yeah. Lucky guess. So when can we set up a date to plan our schedule?"

"Date!" Jessamyn set her jaw into stone. "Just to be crystal clear"—as crystal clear as his dreamy blue eyes, bless them and may they please look the other way before she got caught in their net again—"even if we are being required to attend all these events together, we can't consider this dating."

Cliff recoiled, blast him and his honest reactions. "Of course not!" he said much too quickly for Jessamyn's ego. "When I said set up a date, I didn't mean *date* date."

Jessamyn's face flushed so hot she probably turned Rudolph's-nose-level red. "Sorry. It's just that I heard Mrs. Lang is a hopeless matchmaker, and I—"

"Don't worry. We're not letting her arrange anything other than our website placement."

Exhale. And yet, why was she a fraction disappointed? "Good. Let's make some plans." *And not use the term set up a date so that I get all confused and fluster-brained.*

Cliff scrolled his phone screen again. "The first thing up on the calendar is the Orchard Lights Walk grand opening on Monday night. Let's meet this weekend to iron out a schedule. Sync our calendars."

In other words, set up a date.

Jessamyn pulled a tight smile. "I'll get my full-time staff to cover for me while I'm gone." Meaning, her full-time staff of *one*. Zinnia, plus two part-time housekeepers, Breanna and Brynn. As opposed to Superman here's likely staff of hundreds. Gingerbread Inn was shoe-stringing it by comparison. Jessamyn did the accounting, gardening, and the baking. Zinnia managed everything else. "Saturday? The Cider Press?"

"Noon," he said. And then he walked out without giving her another glance.

Not even a glance back!

Pardon her vanity, but usually men gave her at least one glance-back.

And for this guy, it seemed extra weird, since when they'd met at the falls, he'd acted so eager to please her. He'd even stood watching her drive off. She'd caught that fact in her rear-view mirror while she'd given *him* a serious glance-back. Much to her current chagrin.

It was lame to wish—even faintly—that Cliff Rockingham would show interest in her again. Maybe he only liked tourists.

Well, at least he hadn't asked why she looked so familiar.

Bless him for that.

It didn't matter, though! A relationship was impossible as long as Douglas—with his anxiously waving marriage certificate—was still looking for her.

Chapter 9

Cliff

The Cider Press's warm air smelled of apples and oranges and cloves, but Cliff couldn't even sip his hot cider with cherry and cinnamon add-ins.

Jessamyn Fleet was late.

His nerves frayed every time he thought of her. *She's not a tourist.* He kept his eyes on the door. She'd come in soon, right? Unless she was a computer-sleuthing genius and she'd somehow discovered he was passing himself off as SC of San Nouveau.

Not possible, right?

Dang, he shouldn't have read the letter in the bottle.

Worse, he shouldn't have responded to it.

Even worse, he shouldn't have kept on corresponding with JW last night by email, while lying about not knowing her and about his own identity.

JW@giantmail.com: *Wow. Head spinning here. Your response from San Nouveau hit me much sooner than I expected. First, I need to apologize for sounding so desolate. I didn't think anyone would find the note, let alone read it. Anyway, I don't want to be a burden. I'll be fine. You have a great day.*

She'd given him the perfect out. But had Cliff used his head and taken it? Nope. Not at all! Instead, he'd lain on his back on his cold, hard bedroom floor after doing planks, and tapped out a response.

SantaClaus@SanNouveau.SN: *No burden. To be honest, I'm looking for a Christmas project. Besides, if I'm a stranger, how can you be a burden? We'll never meet. If it becomes burdensome, I'll ghost you like you're Ebenezer Scrooge and I've delivered my message. Okay? Now. Who's this storybook villain? How can I help?*

Suddenly, they'd become those people in the movie *Shop Around the*

Corner. Except Santa Claus knew who JW was, and not the reverse.

The Houstons, Cliff's and his sisters' stand-in parents after their mom and dad's accident, had set an example of serving anytime an opportunity arose. They'd be ashamed of him if he were to let this chance pass him by—even under the awkward circumstances. Besides, it was fate that he help her, right?

Cringe.

Now that she *wasn't* a tourist, and now that Mayor Lang had paired them up, it could get very sticky if Cliff didn't watch every step carefully.

JW@giantmail.com: *I owe someone a lot of money. It's putting my business in danger. If I can't keep my business, I'll lose everything that matters to me.*

Instantly, Cliff the Dingbat had fired off a reply.

SantaClaus@SanNouveau.SN: *I'm great at business. What's going on with yours?*

From a safe, unnamed distance, he could offer this beautiful woman in distress his best advice, he'd reasoned in his sleepy brain. Risk-free. Besides, she'd unwittingly struck his most confident chord. Cliff had lots of business experience—in fact, it happened to be in exactly the same business as hers. Why hoard that knowledge-gold like a dragon in an underground lair? That would've been selfish.

She hadn't responded yet. He opened his phone again, but Andrew pulled up a chair.

"Dude." Andrew plopped down at Cliff's bistro table. "My wife knows how to bring in clientele, doesn't she?" He glanced over his shoulder at Poppy Peters-Kingston, who helped customer after customer, while simultaneously keeping tabs on the Korean TV show playing on several screens in the room. "Cool that the mayor is going to feature her on the website, right? Only drink shop in town, but hey."

"Uh, totally. Yeah."

"Ooh, sorry if that's a sore spot." Kingston leaned back and folded his arms over his belly. "I heard that you were given a *special assignment* to earn your placement."

"Yep." Cliff unwrapped his tiny straw and stabbed it through the hole atop the cider cup's lid. "You know the mayor."

"This is one of her more creative coercion schemes, I have to say." Andrew pulled a napkin from the dispenser and folded it into a square. "You have to date the competition to get the coveted prize."

"It's not dating." Cliff pushed his drink back. "We're not dating."

"That's not what Mayor Lang is telling everyone." Andrew smirked, but then leaned in, talking low. "Look, I know better than anybody why you're still the town bachelor."

Not Kiva. Kiva could not be a topic.

"But Cliff, come on. Your failed Christmas wedding to Kiva was ages ago."

Ages? Not when it came to Kiva. All-things-Kiva were present-day, as though they'd occurred last week and not back when he was nineteen.

"Sure, my head knows it was half my lifetime ago." But she'd left him at the altar. Does anyone ever totally get over a rejection like that? Cliff had been a total goner over her. "Not only did she skip our wedding, she vanished."

For a long time, he'd wondered if she were dead, and they'd even sent out missing persons fliers and police alerts. Boy, he could've used a P.I. back then!

"I saw online she married that movie director. Doesn't that nail the coffin shut?"

"It should. Totally." But did it? Nothing about Kiva made sense. In her final text to him, she'd at least told him why she left.

You're a taker, Cliff. Nothing but a taker.

His soul had recoiled. Something about that false accusation, had wedged its way inside him and festered.

I won't be a taker. And yet, he'd accepted his inheritance when it came, proving Kiva right.

"You look like you just smelled rotten mincemeat pie." Andrew eyed him. "Kiva is married. Get over it. Date Jessamyn Fleet, like you've been destined to by Mayor Lang. I saw the two of you together at the Falls Overlook, remember? It looked like you were into her, even if she didn't give you a look back. Maybe you need a challenge in your dating life for once."

"We're not dating."

"Jessamyn Fleet is not a tourist, Cliff."

"She's off-limits." *Because I'm lying to her.*

"You're allowed to date a gorgeous woman. I've noticed she's movie-star-level attractive."

"You're really good at noticing stuff." Cliff glanced toward the door again. It was now ten minutes past noon.

"I told you, I'm working on being a private investigator. Observation of all types matters."

"Observe other people, not me." Cliff smirked and stirred his drink.

"Come on, Cliff. Embrace it! Embrace *her.*" Andrew slapped Cliff's bicep. "Anyway, I'm due in court."

Andrew went to the counter, leaned across it and kissed his wife.

Must be nice.

Meanwhile, Jessamyn still hadn't come. He checked his phone. No texts from her. Of course, he had her number and she didn't have his yet. He was about to shoot her a message, when an email notification popped up.

JW@giantmail.com: *I'll answer you not-vaguely about my business at some point, but right now, I have a fresh problem: I'm being manipulated by a well-meaning high-status lady into spending time with a man who either thinks of me as deeply emotionally unstable or as his business competition. Either way, he finds me disgusting. It's not awesome.*

Disgusting? Hardly! More like dangerously attractive when he should stay far away.

BUT, if my self-confidence can endure his repugnance and work together with him, I can potentially save my business. In the process, however, I have to stay off the matchmaker's radar. Which will be tricky, since she's forceful.

Right? Jessamyn could say that again about Mayor Lang.

Because of some very complicated reasons, I can't have the meddling lady, or the man himself, thinking a relationship is a possibility.

Just a cockeyed minute while he processed the three big revelations in her message.

One, Jessamyn didn't actually *want* to meet up with Cliff? And especially not date him? The no-look-back thing had been sincere and wholehearted? And spending time with Cliff was something she'd never do unless manipulated into it?

Ouch.

Two, she'd noted that he considered her unstable. Of course, that was before the note in the bottle thing became clear. She hadn't been jumping. She'd been throwing.

That must really hurt her—and he hadn't intended that. If only he weren't faking his identity, he'd shoot back a message clearing up his impression of her. *But I'm a fake.*

Three, she couldn't be with Cliff.

Double ouch.

No! Not ouch! Good!

If she couldn't picture herself with him, it released the pressure valve in some warped way.

He shouldn't continue this deception for a single minute.

Not even one more email.

Well, just one. He typed a quick response.

Hi, JW.

Give the situation a chance. It might not be as fraught with emotional danger as you seem to think. Unless he's the one doing the coercing, maybe see if he's willing to help you with your business dilemma. And make sure he knows a relationship isn't possible. Let me know how it turns out.

SC

Send.

There. He'd done it. The *last* email. For sure. Then, he'd come clean. Or at least stop playing Santa Claus. *If I'm actually done with this fakery, then why did I ask her to tell me how it turns out?*

Fine. He wasn't only lying to Jessamyn but also to himself.

Well, one bright spot appeared. At least this email exchange proved she wasn't technically standing him up.

Frankly, Santa Cliff had no choice but to encourage her to give Sweetwater Hotel Cliff a chance. Without Jessamyn, Mayor Lang's generous offer went nowhere—for either of them.

50

Until he could figure out where his hotel's financial ship leaked, Cliff needed to tread water any way possible.

The front door of The Cider Press flew open, and Jessamyn breezed in—bringing a blast of winter sunlight to his heart. He put his heart's sunglasses on fast.

"Hi, Jessamyn." He stood and went toward her, and as he did, she engulfed his senses. She smelled clean and like new-fallen snow, a fresh contrast to The Cider Press and its spices. "Everything all right?"

He helped her take off her coat and sit down. Her shampoo's scent bombarded him, weakening his resolves. Jessamyn Fleet had to be in the top three most beautiful women he'd ever seen. The other two, he'd only seen in movies—where the lighting and professional makeup played tricks on the eyes.

Jessamyn, in living color here, was the real deal.

"If you're asking that because I'm late, I'm really sorry." Jessamyn stacked her mittens and tucked them into her purse. "I'll be honest. I thought about chucking it."

"That's okay. So did I." Cliff explored the deep honey tones of her irises. "But I've known Mayor Lisa Lang too long to think I could get away with running off. It'd end up like Jonah in the Bible—running away only to get hauled back to shore by way of a whale's guts."

Did he just use the word *guts* in front of the most beautiful woman he'd ever sat across a table from?

Dingbat Cliff had supplanted both Santa Cliff and Sweetwater Cliff.

"That's a good analogy." Jessamyn drew a circle on the wooden top of the table. "In a weird way, it makes me feel better that you don't want to be with me either."

"Exactly," he said. *I only want to be with you enough to find out how I can help.* Just a second. "Sorry. That didn't sound very gentlemanly."

She pulled a wan smile, then it broke into something warmer. In its radiance, the smile made Cliff forget Kiva and his dumped-teenage-groom heart of Christmas past. That smile made him forget his lying, deceitful Christmas present—plus everything else.

I should make her smile. That might be more important than fixing her business worries and her messed up loan problems.

Poppy brought over drinks, and the apple cider with cinnamon, blackberry, and cloves steamed between them.

"This is delicious." Jessamyn closed her eyes after sipping. "I love that."

"Poppy is a mad scientist when it comes to cider."

"I believe it. Tell me what's first up on the Sugarplum Falls holiday event calendar. Since we can't get out of it."

"The Orchard Lights Walk I mentioned." Cliff sipped his drink, too. Berry essence and spice combined to heighten the moment. That magical cider made the gorgeous girl across from him even gorgeous-er. And made him think gorgeous-er was a word. "It's held every year over at Kingston Orchards."

"What date again?"

"Next Monday, but there's a preview for dignitaries tonight at six, and we should go so that we can get our pre-event articles written and sent to the mayor before it launches."

"Good idea." Jessamyn looked up from her cider. "That's smart."

The compliment swelled in him like a wave at high tide. "Thanks."

"How do we get into the preview?"

"On it. I called Owen Kingston, the orchard owner, to request us a spot. Luckily, he'd heard about what Mayor Lang was doing to us and sympathized with our plight."

"Other people know about our situation?" Jessamyn blanched. "Like who?" Her horror seemed overblown.

"It's a small town." Cliff tried to brush it off, downplay it, help her smile again. "Looking at the schedule, my last reserved VIP guest checks in at five. So, anytime after that I'm free, and we could head over together." The other staff could handle the walk-ins, but Cliff liked to be there for the annual regular guests he referred to as his VIPs. "I can pick you up."

"Five thirty works." The tension seemed to drop, and her shoulders relaxed. "Okay, so wear gloves and a hat since it's cold. What else do I need to know before we go?"

"When you see the orchard all lit up, we'll have plenty to smile about. Er, I mean write about." *Face, meet palm.* "I'll pick you up at five thirty."

Chapter 10

Jessamyn

Cliff's misspoken phrase about having something to smile about when seeing the lights had been unwittingly accurate. As they approached the colorful, glowing hillside, Jessamyn could not suppress a smile.

"It's amazing. It's a whole hillside turned to light."

"You like it?" Cliff parked in one of the few available spots. "The whole Kingston family comes from wherever they live in the world to work together and create the Orchard Walk. Plus, a few of the summer workers who live in Sugarplum Falls year round lend a hand. It's quite a family project."

"I am in love." Peace enveloped her. Light hadn't always brought her peace—stage lights and cameras and flashes had been her enemies. But these lights of Christmas and family had the opposite effect. "It's like a heavenly halo over the hillside."

"That's good. Put that in our article notes." Cliff opened her passenger door and let her out. They joined the throng of early-viewing visitors on the trail that led into the rows and rows of trees.

Music was being piped in—and while there was no snow on the ground yet, the current song's lyrics begged, "Let it Snow."

Yes, please.

Cliff walked beside her, his shoulder occasionally bump-touching hers. The narrow walkway through the trees forced them into close proximity.

But there was a definite upside: Cliff's warmth and broad shoulders seemed to block the cold wind.

"Owen Kingston's father started it, but Owen really bumped it up a few Christmases ago. The walking map tells us which fruit trees are which color." He pointed to the brochure.

"Pink for cherry trees," Jessamyn said as they entered the veritable *vie en rose*. "That's perfect for the blossoms. Green for nectarines, white for the apple trees, red for the peach branches." It went on and on, sweet and beautiful and light. "How special it must be to grow up in Sugarplum Falls, to have a childhood with this tradition. Have you always done this walk?"

She suddenly wanted to know Cliff better, his past, what made him want to run a hotel. But she shouldn't ask. It was better to lie low, keep her distance.

"Always," he said.

"Even when times were hard for my siblings and me, we made sure we did the Orchard Walk."

What did that mean, hard times for his siblings?

"Look out!" Cliff said, pulling Jessamyn to his side.

A ladder toppled right into their path, and Cliff clutched her close once again, just as he had at the Falls Overlook. Her traitorous heart raced—for multiple reasons.

"Help!" a guy in thermal coveralls dangled from an unlit branch. "Can you put that back up for me?"

Cliff was already on it. He righted the ladder, and the man climbed down, breathing hard. He had to be sixty. Why wasn't one of the younger workers lighting the orchard?

"Thanks." He placed a hand on his chest. "That spill almost gave me my second heart-attack in the orchard. My wife would've killed me if cardiac arrest didn't."

"Hi, Mr. Kingston." Cliff shook the man's hand. "The orchard looks like a fantasy land. It's better than any theme park or resort lights in big cities that I've ever seen."

"My family did it all." He looked upward. "There was a strand that went dark, though, and they've all gone inside to take a breather. They finished just before the gates opened, so when I noticed it, I didn't want to bother them. You know."

"Actually"—Cliff edged past him to the ladder—"can I get that for you? You're replacing a bulb, right? So the strand's current will reconnect and light up again?"

Three minutes later, Cliff had remedied the connection—and thereby lit the whole strand—and returned to the base of the ladder, shaking Mr. Kingston's hand all over again.

"Thanks, Cliff. You've always been a credit to your folks. And to the Houstons."

"I deeply appreciate that." Cliff sounded so modest responding to that high compliment. "They were good people. All of them."

It struck Jessamyn hard. No one ever called her a credit to her family. Instead, Jessamyn had been nothing but her family's source of heartache after her supposed happy engagement to none other than Douglas Queen on *The Queen of the Queendom* had ended.

Well, she'd blown that parental point of pride to smithereens.

Sorry, Mom and Dad. Someday, they'd understand. Someday, they'd forgive her. Wouldn't they?

Meanwhile, Cliff had stepped away to help someone unwrap their dog's leash from a tree trunk.

"Jessamyn!" Up jogged Esther Lang, dodging a few strollers. "It's so good to see you." She jutted her chin toward Cliff, who was still a few yards off with the dog. "Mr. Bingley, I presume? Taking a turn together about the room. Er, the Orchard Lights?"

He couldn't be Bingley, since Jessamyn hadn't turned into Jane yet. She still had one foot firmly planted in Kitty Bennet-dom, thanks to caving to Mayor Lang's pressure. "It's a work thing."

Esther looked around at the lights. "Rather blinding, aren't they?" She lowered her voice. "So bright they could make you miss the little pinpricks of light when *sparks* fly." She moved her elbow up and down toward Jessamyn's side. "But seriously. He's a good guy. As Charlotte Lucas would advise, *secure him.*"

"Oh, brother. Now you're Charlotte? I thought you were Elizabeth."

"Word to the wise, my mother won't stop until there's an official engagement. You might have to fake one to get her to relent." Esther looked up. "Oh. Hello there, Cliff."

Cliff had come back and stood protectively beside Jessamyn. "Hi,

Esther."

"Rather, call me Lydia-turned-Lizzy." Esther gave Jessamyn an exaggerated, annoying wink. "Bye, Jane dear." She sashayed away.

"What was that?" Cliff asked, as they started walking toward the apple tree section on the hillside that was glowing with so many white lights it could've been heaven. "Did I overhear references to *Pride and Prejudice*?"

"Stop the presses. A man who recognizes Austen references with nothing more than three names dropped?"

"And?"

"And, lots of men think they'd have to rescind their manliness card if they made an Austen reference. Not that you're not manly."

Oh, brother. Had she darted a glance at his biceps when she said that?

Bless him for not pointing that out. Instead, he said, "My sisters watched the five-hour version about fifty times one summer. I should've spent more time outside, but I hung out and challenged myself to see how many of their popsicles I could steal and eat right in front of them without their noticing."

"But you were secretly watching the show." She fell into step beside him as they passed through the apricot orchard's yellow lights. "How many popsicles did you get, on average?"

"What can I say? It has a good storyline. Though, I do sympathize with Wickham more than some people do."

"Hold up a second!" Wrong thing to say! "Wickham is a two-faced villain."

"Yep. And I lost track of the popsicle count after about thirty."

He'd probably earned a stomach ache to go with his Mr. Wickham misinterpretation. "Explain your sympathies for the bad guy, please."

"Wickham?" He steered her out of the path of a double-stroller holding two golden retrievers. "Most villains are the heroes of their own stories. He's doing anything he can to exact revenge on the guy he's most jealous of, and does he get it? Yep. And he even achieves it by being smart—and taking the path of least resistance, which is via marrying Lydia. I have no choice but to admire his resourcefulness, even if I think his character is abhorrent."

"Abhorrent is right."

"You have to admit on some level, he's a sympathetic character. We know his motive for being two-faced."

Ouch. The two-faced thing she couldn't condemn, under the circumstances of living her life as both Jessamyn and Sammie.

"Well, I *will* admit, you do know your *Pride and Prejudice*. Impressive."

"I'm impressive in a lot of ways." He sent her no flirtatious glance, but the words set off a flurry of flutters in her belly. "I didn't mean that like it probably sounded."

"I think you did." Helpless in the moment like a true Kitty Bennet, she sent him a flirtatious glance. It hung in the air between them as they reached the green lights of the nectarine orchard.

"Esther called you Jane. As in Jane Austen herself, or her character Jane Bennet?"

"The character," she said, still under the spell. "Probably like a lot of women, I wish I were a Jane Bennet type."

"To have your mother say, 'I knew you couldn't be so beautiful for nothing?' and marry a wealthy neighbor?"

"Naturally." Too bad some of that fit her actual, non-Jane life. "Other than I absolutely never want to marry the man my mother would've picked for me. No matter how wealthy."

"Independent minded. That's more of a Lizzy trait."

"True, but Jane is still my spirit-literary-figure."

"Well," Cliff said, "the Lydia-into-Lizzy thing for Esther I do get." Cliff looked over his shoulder, and compassion laced his tone. "She had a rough time of it back a few years ago. At first, I was pretty annoyed with her for ditching Fargo at his Christmas wedding." His voice sounded actually pained.

"But wasn't he a well-known louse?"

"Not until later. He hid his lousiness well."

"Some do." The image of Douglas Queen's face popped up like a jump scare turn in a haunted house. She shuddered.

Cliff went on, "And, like Esther, sometimes only the person in the relationship figures it out while everyone else blames them for the failure."

Jessamyn's heart pounded. Cliff couldn't have had any clue how pointed a statement he'd just made, lancing her soul.

After Jessamyn had fled Douglas's demands, not one person in her life had understood or been the least bit understanding. Not her mom, her aunts, her cousins, her so-called friends, no one. Jessamyn had been forced into solitude and self-sufficiency back in the city. Going it alone, making *all* the stupid mistakes, with no one to guide her.

Neither of them spoke for a few paces, and they entered the red glow of the peach orchard.

"I owe Esther a lot, and I'm sorry she suffered," Jessamyn said, not telling much about her past, but coming dangerously close to doing so. "Esther is the one who told me to check out Sugarplum Falls. She promised me I'd love it here."

"How does it rank compared to the other places you've lived?"

"It's climbing the charts."

She'd fallen hard for Esther's enthusiastic description of the small-town joys, but all these months later, Jessamyn was still living with the consequences of those mistakes, albeit incognito.

In Sugarplum Falls, no one knew much of anything true about her. No one would offer that forgiving *her fiancé was a louse* wince on her behalf. Because no one was a confidante.

Well, no one but potentially her new emailing friend, Santa Claus of Billionaire Island.

I can trust him. He will never know I'm Sammie or that I'm Jessamyn.

Thus, she'd been ridiculously forthcoming with him in their email exchanges.

Was that safe? Of course! She'd obviously never meet him in real life.

A child fell off a swing and started wailing. No parent appeared, so Cliff jogged over to right the little girl.

Jessamyn gazed after him. Cliff helped the child back onto the swing, and then gave a few pushes—which turned into more, which always happened with little kids and swings.

It could be a minute. Jessamyn took her chance. She pulled out her phone and typed a quick email to Santa Claus.

You were right. It wasn't as bad as I feared. Ready for a compliment? You're really wise and intuitive. Thanks for choosing me as your project and giving me that advice. Glad I took it. Good on you for a job well done.

Bye now. It's been nice. I hope you have a Merry Christmas.

Send.

That ended that.

It was for the best. Falling for someone whose character she knew little-to-nothing about had not worked out for her in the past.

Besides, as the woman formerly known as Sammie Westwood, Jessamyn had no right to get hopes up of any kind.

Her hopes needed to die of lack of oxygen.

Right now.

Chapter 11

Jessamyn

Later that evening, back at Gingerbread Inn, Zinnia greeted Jessamyn with a haggard look. "It's hard to make everyone feel loved when they're in bad moods."

"Our guests are unhappy?"

"Not with their accommodations—with other stuff. Politics, religion, family strife. You name it. But not with Gingerbread Inn."

"When folks are down, they need hospitality the most."

"I know, I know." Zinnia slapped her employee lanyard down on the lobby counter. "But at this point, the only person I feel hospitable toward is myself. I'm going to take a hot bath."

Zinnia waved goodbye, leaving Jessamyn to finish up the evening's duties.

That was fair.

After she'd wrapped up all the loose ends, Jessamyn paused at the front desk to power down the computer for the night.

However, curiosity about her personal email hooked her, and she opened it. *Had Santa Claus answered me? Even though I gave him the cut-off switch?*

A new, unread message flashed up in bold type in her inbox—from Santa Claus!

You're welcome. I'm glad it worked out. You implied that you're done communicating with me, and that's fine. However, if there's anything else you need related to your business, or anything else, please ask. It's not quite Christmas yet. I'm still in project mode.

Project mode. As much as she despised the idea of being someone's project—*again*—Santa Claus seemed blessedly chill about it.

Plus, he could have absolutely nothing to gain from her or from helping her. Unlike Douglas Queen.

Frankly, her money situation did have some monstrous tremors shaking the ground she stood on, quakes that could cause financial avalanches.

Fine, maybe keeping up a correspondence with rich ol' St. Nick, just through the holidays, wasn't such a terrible idea.

Okay. She sent the single word, and then squeezed her eyes against the feeling that she may be making a terrible mistake.

"I'm not checking Douglas's website," she told herself aloud. A one-time guest on *Queen of the Queendom*, a psychologist, had told Douglas that a way to gain power over temptations was to declare intentions aloud. "I am turning off the computer and going to bed."

But—if she used a VPN, he couldn't trace her, right?

One look. Only one. To see whether he'd given up.

Jessamyn launched her VPN, putting her in stealth mode. Then, and only then, she navigated to Douglas Queen's personal website.

When it popped onto the screen, she nearly swallowed her tongue. He'd doubled the reward for information leading to her whereabouts? Good night, nurse! It was up to six figures now.

Her heart raced like reindeer trying to pull a sleigh airborne.

In Sugarplum Falls, even if someone recognized her, there was a chance they might honor her privacy and keep her identity and location a secret.

No matter how high the reward.

Right?

Why had she looked! She was being Kitty Bennet again, falling prey to her past.

But the truth was, Jessamyn must face the reality that at some point, Douglas's offer would soar too high for some desperate Sugarplum Fallsian to resist. And her ex-fiancé would find her.

Chills climbed her spine. Jessamyn shut off her computer and went to bed, but even the electric blanket dialed to high didn't warm away the ice in her veins.

Chapter 12

Cliff

A live string quartet offered instrumental versions of Christmas songs while oregano and garlic wafted through the air of Mario's Italian restaurant. Cliff and Tarquin had parked themselves at their usual place for their weekly business powwow. The table even had a red candle perched in a wreath.

Looked like Mario had already leveled up for the holiday season, even before the storefront window painter came through town and before the Waterfall Lights event. He must have been bucking to get the state tourism website to choose his eatery as their featured restaurant.

Not a bad idea. He whipped out his phone and, in his notes app, typed, *String quartet or pianist at the grand piano in the lobby. Playing Christmas music. Setting the mood.*

"Leave those worries to me, Cliff." Tarquin waved his forkful of linguine, continuing the touchy subject of hotel finances. "I'm doing a full audit, like we said. Some outstanding invoices are holding me up." He grimaced, moving his already low hairline even lower toward his eyebrows. "But I'm sure we'll have good news soon. The holidays are coming! It will snow, and skiers will flock to Sweetwater Hotel."

"It hasn't snowed yet." Add that to the list of concerns Cliff couldn't control.

"Either way, no panicking." Tarquin took his next bite and chewed deliberately. "Not until we have solid numbers."

Cliff had been waiting on those solid numbers for weeks, and Tarquin had been promising they'd be forthcoming. But, the accounting software had crashed, and then they'd both been swamped—literally and figuratively—by the plumbing disaster.

"What percentage do you think the competing hotels contribute to the problem?"

"First off, I'm not ready yet to define it as a problem, per se. It's ... well, maybe that's it." Tarquin placed his hands together and steepled his fingertips. "Quite a few new lodgings options have cropped up locally. I'm not going to say they're cannibalizing our occupancy rate, but ..."

"But you're going to say that places like Gingerbread Inn have been posing a threat to Sweetwater Hotel's bottom line all year." They'd done the rounds on this topic before. Truth was, the first rumblings of financial struggle began the same month Gingerbread Inn opened its doors. He'd not pinpointed that before now, but it seemed like a neon Las Vegas sign, now that Cliff noted the time correlation.

"I can't quantify it precisely ..." Tarquin collapsed his steeple-fingers. "And we'd be cowardly if we blamed other hotels entirely."

Ouch. Cliff wouldn't shift blame. "The bottom line is we need to get more guests in our doors." Cliff set down his breadstick, suddenly not that hungry for anything with the word *bread* in it, gingerbread or otherwise. "So, I'm on it. I'll focus on getting that website placement."

"Good." Tarquin sipped his water glass. "Meanwhile, I'll keep hunting for financial leaks. Beyond the known maintenance issues we already battle."

Maintenance issues! Cliff ran both hands through his hair. Maintenance had been the bane of his hotelier existence all year. If it wasn't roofing, it was electrical. If it wasn't electrical it was plumbing. So much plumbing! He should place Porter's Plumbing on retainer.

"Maybe we've been running in the red, but I predict good things for us, Cliff. You deserve them." Tarquin's slicked-back hair reflected the Christmas tree's lights from where it stood in the nearby corner. It was weirdly festive. "When year-end numbers come out, the overall result will be black-hole black. Especially with the massive influx of holiday guests you'll be getting from the state tourism website. It'll blow both our minds."

Cliff didn't point out that the timing of the website placement hadn't been mentioned yet. It might not even happen until next year.

If so, would that be too late to save Sweetwater Hotel?

"Hey, it's going to be fine." Tarquin pushed a basket of bread his way. "These past three quarters have been anomalies, right?"

Right. And miracles had happened for Cliff in the past. Not just hotel-owning type miracles. Others too, but the hotel miracles had been too plenteous to name.

"To the future!" Tarquin lifted his glass to toast, and Cliff raised and clinked.

"To the future." Cliff sipped, but aspirated a drop and started coughing.

Tarquin's phone rang.

"Excuse me." Tarquin twisted around in his chair, as if that gave him privacy.

"What do you want, Nardo?" Tarquin said as he answered. "I'm at dinner with my business partner. Make it quick."

Cliff tried his best not to eavesdrop. Who was Nardo? A relative? A distributor?

Checking email would help. He'd sworn off opening his secret San Nouveau email account, and that might have engrossed him, but Tarquin's voice was loud, and he couldn't help but overhear.

"Come on, Nardo. We're not talking about rocket science here. Pick up the package. She's half your size." He placed a hand over the receiver and spoke to Cliff. "I ordered a whole case of Clorox bleach at a discount, enough to last us all next year. I thought our deliveryman would be willing to bring it specially from Darlington, but he's being difficult. Excuse me while I argue with him over the numbers. We'd better keep an eye on every penny at this point."

Tarquin walked out of the restaurant, the door slamming behind him.

A message notification blinked—from his San Nouveau email. Just reading what she'd sent wouldn't hurt, would it? One last one—for the road?

Last night, they'd exchanged a couple more emails. Well, quite a few more. The thread had become a rope, then a cable.

At one point, very late, Jessamyn had opened up to Santa Cliff about her work worries.

JW@giantmail.com: *I'm good at my job, and I know it. I had a brilliant* *tutor in my grandmother, God rest her soul. In fact, she's the reason I am desperate to repay my creditor—I'll disgrace her legacy if I lose my business. She deserves to have her legacy live on. It can't be at her original place of business, since my uncle sold it when she died. I was crushed, honestly. Cried for days—more than when my romantic relationship imploded and my disappointed parents basically disowned me for it.*

So candid, so vulnerable, the message had bored a hole in Cliff's heart. What could make parents be so unfeeling?

SantaClaus@SanNouveau.SN: *Venturing a guess, but I believe your grandmother would have been very proud of you, JW. What is the situation with your creditor? Do you need money?*

But she must have fallen asleep because there'd been no response.

Until now. Finally, it loaded.

JW@giantmail.com: *Well, if you're obliquely offering me money, don't. I got myself into this mess when someone "helped" me by offering money. Now, I have to face the consequences of that so-called help. I'm sure you mean well and that you're acting as a knight in shining armor. If you're not offering money, please forgive my mini-rant.*

She'd said those same words about being a knight after he'd tackled her at the lake. Cliff absolutely did, but apparently, some other person hadn't meant well at all.

Face the consequences? That sounded ominous. Cliff's abdominals tensed. To whom had she gone for aid and been trapped by?

Did she have a past relationship with the lender? If so, was she physically safe?

Cliff typed, deleted, and retyped. Someone was obviously threatening her. How could they? Jessamyn was a good person! Fury surged, and he typed and sent.

SantaClaus@SanNouveau.SN: *Let me help. Not by giving you money.*

Since he didn't have money …

Someone was obviously breathing down her neck. Who?

Dang. Cliff's shortcomings were everywhere—but he would do anything he could to safeguard her.

Without wealth or influence or power, what could he do? What were his resources?

A crumbling hotel and a lot of grit.

Well, grit could take a person pretty far in life. He was living proof of that.

Cliff pushed his phone aside and picked up a breadstick. Even Mario's didn't taste good right now. He set it down and sipped from his water goblet, fuming. What kind of a monster would prey on someone as good-hearted as Jessamyn Fleet?

It had to be an angry ex.

SantaClaus@SanNouveau.SN: *How long ago did you break up with your controlling ex?* Stab in the dark. Where would it land?

JW@giantmail.com: *How did you know my ex was controlling?*

Bull's-eye.

JW@giantmail.com: *Hey. Who are you? Never mind—Santa, right? Santa knows if you've been bad or good so be good for goodness' sake, right? Then you know not to worry, since I'm physically safe, for now.*

Physically safe! *For now?* He shot to his feet, convulsing his water glass and sloshing water over its rim. He stomped over to the men's room and back while he collected his emotions. The string quartet playing "Holly Jolly Christmas" didn't help.

SantaClaus@SanNouveau.SN: *Lucky guess.*

His brain rattled for her safety. Who was she really, and why was she at Gingerbread Inn? And again—what kind of jerk would threaten the life of a nice person like Jessamyn Fleet?

Is her last name actually Fleet? Or did she have a different last name, one that started with W?

She didn't respond to his *lucky guess* email, and Tarquin didn't return.

Cliff whipped out his debit card to pay the bill.

No question, he'd need to do more than weakly emailing her, if he were actually going to protect her from the threats.

It wasn't enough to piece together the big picture through the scant drizzle of facts she shared with her fake Santa Claus pen pal.

He pulled out a napkin and a pen. He made two columns. First, *Things I Know*.

One, that she was trying to fulfill a legacy left by her grandmother.

Two, that it was being threatened by someone with a financial choke-hold on her.

Three, that the villain was likely an ex-boyfriend.

Then, he labeled the other column's heading *Things I Don't Know*.

The glaring blank beneath that column heading encompassed a whole world of facts.

Cliff would have to dig deeper.

But how, without tipping her off that he, Cliff, was her Santa Claus of San Nouveau—and that he'd read her letter?

Wow, he'd opened a can of worms. Just what everyone wants for Christmas.

Well, he was determined to solve those worms and make Jessamyn's life exponentially better—by Christmas. No matter what.

Chapter 13

Jessamyn

"**H**eavenly halo of light," Jessamyn typed into the shared document she and Cliff had been creating for reviews to submit to Mrs. Lang. "Family love and warmth embodied in a beautiful ..."

Dots appeared on the screen and then words. "See you in five. I'm on my way."

Cliff! Jessamyn jumped up, whipped off her ugly sweatshirt and found her favorite red sweater. Was it too form-fitting? There was no time to dither.

Since, there was only one showing of the town Christmas play, she and Cliff had no choice but to attend this performance, whether the writing assignment for the Orchard Walk had been submitted or not.

"You look nice." Cliff stood on her doorstep. He took one quick glance across her figure.

Dang. Too form-fitting. Her face probably went as red as the wool of the sweater. All that cooking and baking for guests had brought back some of the femininity to her body, after too long being starved while on camera. The sweater proved that much.

"Are you"—cleared his throat—"going to grab a coat?"

"Yes." She picked it up and hugged it over her curves, but a little part of her smiled that a man had noticed this version of her. *Jess. Not Sammie, not Jessamyn. Me.*

"Let's get going." Cliff helped her on with her coat, and then left his hands resting on her shoulders a split second. "We want to make sure we get seats."

The orchestra's instruments tuned up as they entered the Kingston Theater, a harmonious and dissonant combination at once. Jessamyn and Cliff seated themselves halfway back in the center section, in two of the few remaining empty places.

"Fifteen minutes to show time," Cliff said, looking up at the clock, "and a sell-out."

Jessamyn settled in. The seats were narrow, practically antique, which added to the ambience but also to her closeness to Cliff. He pulled out his playbill and opened it to the cast list, his elbow crossing the armrest into her territory.

"Do you know any of the actors or actresses?" She looked across at his open paper.

"It's a small town." He named a few of the cast and how they were related to him or others. His voice soothed her, and she tilted her head toward him, mostly listening, but gazing off.

Heavy velvet curtains hung across the stage. Cliff's broad shoulder pressed against her arm, heightening her awareness of him. As the oscillating heater-fan breezed past them, his scent floated to her, causing even more havoc to her attention span.

The other night, Cliff had been like Superman, matching his looks. He'd helped fix the burnt-out bulb in the orchard and pushed that little girl on the swing. Then, the Jane Austen discussion, and his appeal had shot even higher.

And he'd started out at a very high appeal level.

Jessamyn leaned away from him, in an attempt to clear her mind. Didn't work. She looked around the room for familiar faces. Saw a few. Couldn't concentrate.

At last, she lowered her voice, in case any moms of actors or director sat nearby. "I've heard this play is awful. Are you sure it's a good idea for us to write up a review for the town's website if it's as bad as everyone warns?"

Just when Cliff couldn't get any more attractive, he handed her a Delacourt Dark Chocolate Truffle he'd bought in the lobby.

"You're sharing?" She held it to her nose. It smelled heavenly. The recipe for chocolate must have been downloaded from angels.

"There are always more where that came from." He opened the wrapper of his own, and then, when he spoke, his breath was chocolate-laced.

Good grief, he was not only pheromones-heavy, but cocoa-infused. *I'm going to lose it unless I quit breathing near this man.*

"The rumors about the stinkiness of the play are both true and false. Fact is, it *used to* be awful." He offered her another piece of chocolate. "A couple of years ago, it got a major rewrite and it's pretty good now. Still cheesy, but in a good, holiday-magic kind of way. Everyone likes cheese now and then, right?"

"Personally, I like cheese every day." Jessamyn closed her playbill and opened the Delacourt Dark Chocolate Truffle he'd handed her. It melted against her tongue. "Chocolate and cheese are two of the major food groups of my life."

Cliff took her tinfoil wrapper and folded it up. "I approve of those food groups." He mimed a stamp of approval. "Where do you stand on maple syrup?"

"As close to the spigot as possible."

"Is that so?" He tilted his head.

"I'll basically eat anything maple-flavored."

"Where are you on maple bacon and maple sausage?"

"The two most controversial items? For me, the maple-ier the better."

Cliff gave her an enigmatic nod. Either she was attracting or repelling him with her maple enthusiasm. No matter which, she wouldn't deny her maple love.

"If you're trying to test me, I won't back down. Just like a Reedsville Rhinos hockey diehard fan never denied Dempsey Dean Davidson, I would never be disloyal to maple. Give me maple candy, maple add-ins for drinks, maple syrup on snow as a snow cone—all the maple, please."

"Okay. You can stay." Cliff laughed as he pulled his outstretched legs in so a kid could scoot past them. "How did you know I was testing you?"

"Probably because I have my own test—cinnamon, nutmeg, and cloves."

"Warm spices. I like it." His face pulled a little. "That's funny. I expected *Pride and Prejudice* as your litmus test."

"This is the *food category* of litmus tests." No, she didn't mention that these had always been her *dating* litmus tests. The red flags. The deal breakers. "I have a whole battery of them."

"Oh?" Cliff stretched his legs back out. "For instance? Must love dogs?"

"Meh, I'm mildly allergic, but I do like them, but it's not on my list."

"Is there an actual *list of litmus tests*, like a written one? I bet you have it on your phone. Show me."

"I—" She hiccupped. She did have it on her phone. "I'm not *showing* it to you!" She waved her index finger toward the stage. "The play is about to start."

"We still have two minutes." He proffered her his wrist.

The guy wore a wristwatch! How *retro*. Embracing retro was definitely on the list, but she was not showing him the test list.

"Their backstage clocks must be off. It's starting." She pointed at the velvet curtains, which were parting. The house lights dimmed, and the audience hushed. The curtains swished open, and the narrator walked out in a quite nicely designed Victorian costume.

"Welcome, friends," the actor in the black top hat called over the din.

The play launched, the stage lighting came up and Victorian-clothing-clad actors filtered off and on, singing and speaking—with a love story at its heart. It was sweet, and Jessamyn might have been fully engrossed if it hadn't been for the sturdy breadth of Cliff's shoulder.

That broad shoulder encroached on Jessamyn's seat space. She leaned forward a little to relieve pressure, but it made her back ache after only a minute. Then, she angled a little to place her shoulder behind his. For some reason, at that point, she couldn't see the whole stage anymore.

"Are you okay?" Cliff whispered as a batch of tumblers performed choreography to the orchestra's rendition of "The Holly and the Ivy." "These seats are really narrow."

"It's fine." She leaned away from him, but she bumped into a little kid on the other side of her. He held up a half-eaten sucker which threatened to park itself in the fibers of her red sweater. She leaned away from him, and back into Cliff.

Automatically, as if it weren't the biggest deal in the whole world and a heart-stopping move, Cliff lifted his arm and placed it along the back of her seat.

Thud-thud. Thud-thud. A microphone on stage malfunctioned. Thud-thud.

No, that was her heart! It pounded so loudly in her ear that the players' dialogue disappeared.

Slowly, as if stealing something, she edged back into her chair, resting molecule by molecule against Cliff's arm. With a simple shift, and no other reaction on his part, he draped it along her shoulders, not just the seat itself.

He has his arm around me! her body shouted. He was touching her and keeping her safe and giving her literal comfort in an uncomfortable moment. She closed her eyes and drank it in, the chocolate and the masculine cologne and the pheromones and all.

So what if the embrace only sprang from necessity? Her body's chemistry certainly couldn't tell the difference. It rushed like Los Angeles freeways. She lost track of the play's plot. And her own while the axillary pulse from beneath his arm thudded in time with her own beating heart.

No! That meant nothing! There'd been that article that claimed listeners' heartbeats synced during storytelling. It was natural, evolutionary, not a sign that she and Cliff Rockingham were in harmony.

That was ridiculous.

Out of the question.

And yet, maple syrup. And warm spices. And *Pride and Prejudice.* And how protected he made her feel. And how kind he was to old men and to young children.

And geez, now she was making a new list.

An hour of a valiant battle against surging attraction later, Jessamyn clapped as the play ended with a chaste kiss between the two main characters.

Deliciously, slowly as an eroding glacier, Cliff removed his arm from around her shoulders and offered some applause as well.

Exposed—that's how she felt. Like she'd lost her shield against danger. Like her electricity had gone out and she was plunged into aloneness.

"Did you like it? What can we write about it?"

"Um." *That it's a good place to get closer to those you care about.* "That was pretty good."

"Yeah," he said as they exited with the crowd. "It's a far sight better this year than I remember."

Because he was there with me? Shush that wishful thinking.

"So, how do you keep Gingerbread Inn's parking lot so constantly full?" he asked as they headed down the cold sidewalk and around to the parking lot behind the Kingston Theater. "I've never seen your vacancy sign lit."

"It's been consistent." She glanced around, looking for his truck. "But, money is always on my mind. In fact, I borrowed some money to get it up and running. Unfortunately, the note is due." Putting it that way sugar-coated her situation, but his protectiveness during the play seemed to have oiled her jaw.

"Honestly, I'm dealing with some financial things myself. My business partner is handling them, but I can't help feeling the pinch. Tell me more about your situation."

His openness made her even more candid. "It boils down to a foolish bargain with an unscrupulous creditor."

Whoosh! A huge weight lifted. Mentioning it aloud to a living person, not just to someone on the other end of a computer connection, gave her soul flight.

"Debts?" Cliff looked almost too interested. "Who's your creditor?"

"Trust me, they're not people you want to borrow from. He's a shark." He'd even nicknamed himself *Shark*. How meta of him.

"But, can you at least warn me who I shouldn't deal with?" Cliff pressed her arm.

"Umm." *Nuh-uh.* No way would Jessamyn mention the name of the lender. Cliff would never be so unfortunate to stumble across the guy by accident, and ignorance was bliss.

"Jessamyn!" Esther rushed across the parking lot and gave Jessamyn a huge hug. Bless her for showing up at just the right moment. "Did you watch the play? You should've seen it the year my bestie Portia starred. She was the most angelic thing you've ever seen. Don't you agree, Cliff?" She didn't wait for Cliff's affirmation but continued talking to Jessamyn. "You guys going to the spelling bee here next week? It's the most suspense we ever get in Sugarplum Falls."

When Esther left, they climbed into Cliff's truck.

"Spelling bee? Is that next on our list?" Cringe. The word *list* harked back to the test list.

"We have the Christmas tree lighting at the rec center, the Hot Cocoa Festival with its karaoke night, and a ribbon cutting thing before the spelling bee, and then the Waterfall Lights after that. This town does love its holiday festivals."

"Is the spelling bee a Christmas thing?" That seemed unlikely.

"Holiday-related words."

"Ah. So, Cliff?" Jessamyn wrung her hands. This next thing she needed to say would either sound full of kindness or full of hubris. "You asked how I keep the Gingerbread Inn full. The answer is, that my Grandma Ginger had magic when it came to creating a guest experience. She could've tutored the Imagineering staff at Disneyland."

With a heavy sigh, Cliff pulled onto Orchard Street, heading back toward their hotels. "I wish she were here now to give me some pointers."

The financial struggles must be even bigger than he'd let on.

"This will probably sound like so much *newbie nonsense,* since you've been in business successfully so much longer than I have." Jessamyn mustered the courage to be bold. "But would you be interested in letting me tour Sweetwater Hotel? I'd try to look at it through Grandma Ginger's eyes and tell you what she'd say."

He glanced over at her, his face betraying nothing. He returned his eyes to the road.

Quickly, she backpedaled. "You can ignore everything I say. You know your hotel best. Just forget I offered."

The truth was, however, her comments wouldn't be ignorant. Grandma Ginger knew people, and she knew hospitality, and she knew her world. Jessamyn had soaked up pure knowledge while staying with Grandma. *I miss her so much.*

"Your place is doing well," Cliff said, stopping for a light. "Even though it's newly established. Your grandma clearly taught you principles of success."

"I haven't been able to implement everything she taught me yet."

If only that goon with the soul patch hadn't kept showing up and demanding money, Jessamyn would've been able to add even more amenities to make the guests feel Grandma's wise influence. Like offering those Christmas-print caftans for every guest, like Zinnia wanted.

"Thanks, Jessamyn. I'll consider it seriously." He moved forward when the light turned green and took her home.

***

That night, Jessamyn sat at the computer monitor at the front desk of Gingerbread Inn. All the guests were settled in for the night, and Zinnia had gone home. It was a good time to send an email to Santa Claus of San Nouveau, her own Mr. Darcy.

JW@giantmail.com *I made a major blunder today—socially, not financially. Do you also give relationship advice? I need honest feedback.*

Chapter 14

Cliff

Cliff pulled on his jacket. If he didn't quit staring at Jessamyn's email and leave now, he'd be late picking up Jessamyn for the big annual Sugarplum Falls Spelling Bee.

How was he supposed to respond? He'd left it unanswered for days while they attended all those other events and wrote up the reports together for Mayor Lang.

But it had eaten at him constantly.

"Heading out, Tarquin." Cliff buttoned the jacket at his neck and looped his scarf an extra wrap. The weatherman called for a deep freeze and strong winds, but no snow yet. The worst combination. "Back after the bee with Jess."

"Jess? As in Jessamyn Fleet, owner of Gingerbread Inn?" Tarquin emerged from the room behind the check-in desk. "This is bad timing, I know, but the plumber billed us more than I expected."

"Plumber?" Another bill? This was getting out of control. "We paid Porter's Plumbing in full."

"That was for the leak in the main water heater. This is about the pipes on the third floor. Remember?"

Honestly, the sheer volume of repairs swirled like a tornado in Cliff's memories. No way could he keep all of them straight. "Pay him. I don't want to be dishonest in my affairs."

It bugged him though. Why was the plumber billing them again and again? Cliff would have looked into it closer, but Tarquin handled those things, and Cliff should stay in his lane. It was the only way to keep a business partnership healthy—don't step on each other's toes.

"Okay. From which account?" Tarquin lowered his voice. "The maintenance account is ... low."

"As in the payment will bounce?" This was worse than he'd feared. For the past three quarters, Cliff had successively doubled his maintenance budget. "Then use the rainy-day fund." It was the only option at this point. Cliff's fingers tightened over the truck keys in his coat pocket. "Look into the plumber, Tarquin, would you? See if he's purposely sabotaging us, as in fixing what we request then breaking something else before he leaves, so we have to call him again."

"Sure. Good idea."

Cliff had known Draven Porter, the only plumber in town, since he was a kid. He'd never seemed like the dishonest type, but people sometimes fell on hard times and made out-of-character decisions, like gouging customers.

Tarquin would handle it discreetly. Unlike Cliff, who'd better not run into Porter anywhere socially, lest Cliff drop a hint of suspicion like a boulder on Draven's foot.

The whole money situation had put him in a crusty mood for the Sugarplum Falls Spelling Bee, even with the prospect of sitting beside Jessamyn at the Kingston Theater again. All week he'd been dreaming of placing his arm around her again—or more.

But now, *the plumbing*. And *the money*. And *that email from Jessamyn*. It all clattered in his ears like emergency vehicle sirens heading to a crash scene.

"The kids are all wearing reindeer antler headbands. Check it out." Jessamyn settled into a seat next to him as the theater filled with guests—parents and teachers and townspeople. Everyone came to support the spellers. "That's cute."

"It's new this year." Cliff glanced down at the printed program for the first time. He needed to get his head in the game here. "Looks like they keep the antlers on until they misspell, and then they have to take them off. Last one with antlers wins. Well, that's embarrassing. I'd probably misspell just to get them off my head."

Whoops. Had he said that aloud?

"What's with the Grinch thing today?" Jessamyn offered him a Delacourt Dark Chocolate Truffle from her purse. "Sugar crashing?"

"Something like that." He thanked her and ate the chocolate, and the

77

event began—while his thoughts raced.

He could barely grunt when Jessamyn made cute little comments to him between rounds.

With just two kid-spellers wearing antlers remaining, Jessamyn rested a hand on his knee. "I hope one of them gets the word *distracted.*"

Ah, he caught her drift. "Sorry. I'll pay better attention." To the bee so they could write up the article for the website, but also to Jessamyn. She didn't deserve his sour grapes. He placed his arm behind her, draping it across the seat but not against her shoulders.

That second part ought to be easy. But the email he'd read from her the other night had thrown him off, too. The request for honest feedback shouldn't have been such a jarring phrase. But the word *honest* cut him to shreds.

I'm lying to her. He pulled his arm from the back of her seat, chilling him.

The final two spellers stood side by side at the microphone, their antlers quivering with tension.

"The word is *yuleshard.*"

Yuleshard! Cliff sat up straight. "Why are kids being asked to spell words no one has ever heard of?" His dam cracked. "This is ridiculous," he whispered too loudly. A parent in front of them turned around and shushed them.

"Origin?" the kid at the microphone asked.

The judge gave it. "From Scandinavian and Old English."

The kid shifted his weight, and his antlers slipped to the side. "Definition?" It came out with a squeak.

"Also called yule-jade, someone who leaves a lot of work still to be done on Christmas Eve night."

"Y-U-L …" The kid misspelled it, took off his antlers, and the final kid got it right, plus the required bonus word, *doniferous,* which, according to the judge's requested definition, means, *carrying a present.*

Jessamyn surged to her feet. "Bravo!" She turned to Cliff, pulled him to his feet, and said over the din, "We should've been doniferous tonight and brought flowers or chocolate or something for the winner."

"What's *doniferous?*"

"Weren't you listening? What's going on with you tonight?"

"Nothing. It's nothing." As in, he had nothing to pay the plumber with, nothing to offer in the way of honesty, and nothing to solve his problems. "Let's head out to the lobby." Maybe he could breathe better there, where it was less crowded.

In the red-carpeted lobby, a very small kid stood in the corner, crying loudly and rubbing his eyes.

Cliff's instinct was to leave the poor non-winner to his own sad moment, but Jessamyn ran to the child.

"Are you all right?"

The little boy dropped his hands and threw his arms around Jessamyn. "I had to take off the antlers on my first word." He cried into her shoulder, probably ruining her cashmere sweater, blubbering as he told his sad tale. "It was an easy one, too—cinnamon. Everybody knows how to spell cinnamon. I just started wrong with S, and then I was out. And now I can't find my mom."

Hugging him, Jessamyn rubbed a circle on his back. "It's okay. It's just one day of your life. Things get better."

That was good advice. Where had he heard it before? Oh, right. He'd given it to Jessamyn at the Falls Overlook during their misunderstanding of a first meeting. Frankly, on a day like today, he should take it himself, eh? Cliff went and stood by them as they continued to chat for a minute.

"We're Cliff and Jessamyn. What's your mom's name?" Cliff asked, crouching down to meet the kid's eyes. "I'll go look for her."

"Trissa Thompson."

Cliff knew her. "I'll be right back."

Before Cliff could get three steps away, Trissa came dashing out of the auditorium into the foyer.

"Trey!" she ran over and hugged the kid. "I've been looking everywhere for you. You weren't with the other students."

"Mom!" Trey hugged her back.

"Were you all right?"

"I was fine." He wrested out of his mom's hug and pointed to Jessamyn. "That lady's name is Jessamyn."

"I think you mean *Miss Jessamyn,* Trey."

"Yes, ma'am."

"Jessamyn Fleet." Jessamyn held out a hand to shake Trissa's. "This is Cliff Rockingham."

"I know Cliff." Trissa pulled Trey back into her arms. "It's a small town."

"Miss Jessamyn said you and me get to come to her hotel tomorrow morning and she'll make us some gingerbread oatmeal for a special breakfast before school."

Trissa clutched her son one more time, and then she stood up and faced Jessamyn. "That's so generous of you! I have been dying to tour Gingerbread Inn ever since it was remodeled. It's so cute and charming and irresistible. I booked a room for my parents to stay there when they come out to visit us at New Year's. The other hotels in town seem so *soulless,* you know?"

Soulless! Cliff's shoulders bunched. Sweetwater Hotel was not soulless. It was classic, time-tested. It met guests' expectations.

Whether on purpose or by accident, he didn't know, but just then, Jessamyn touched Cliff's hand, merely a soothing graze. His hackles relaxed.

Hmmm. Maybe he should let Jessamyn tour it and give him honest feedback.

Not that phrase! He bunched again, but Jessamyn was focused on Trissa.

"Thanks again for the oatmeal offer." Trissa shook hands with Jessamyn. "Trey does love gingerbread men, and gingerbread man oatmeal sounds delicious. What time?"

They settled on a time. Wow. Jessamyn had worked magic for that heartbroken kid, turning his saddest moment of grief into something good and warm and comforting to hope for. Even if the hope involved oatmeal.

"Oatmeal?" Cliff asked, falling into step beside her, as they headed out. "You healed him with hot cereal?"

"Trey told me oatmeal and gingerbread men were his two favorite foods. I figured they should combine pretty easily, and voilà. A new breakfast food is born—for both Trey and my hotel guests." Jessamyn buttoned her coat as they exited the theater into the street once again. "What's the matter, you don't like hot cereal?"

"Please! It's one of the finest, most delicious heart-healthy foods on the planet. Oatmeal, cracked wheat, grits, Malt o' Meal, and the granddaddy of them all, Cream of Wheat—you name it, I'm there. I just didn't think a seven-year-old kid would be cheered up by it."

"Do you want to try my invention tomorrow morning when Trey comes?" Jessamyn asked.

For a second, he gazed into her honey-brown eyes. They were soft, calming, and beautiful. "Sure," he found himself saying. "It's a date."

To his shock, she didn't argue with his word choice—and neither did his spirit. He took off in his truck.

**

That evening, Cliff stood in the grocery store checkout line.

Three shoppers ahead of him stood Wyatt North, future Vice President and heir-apparent of North Star Capital, talking on his phone, apparently unaware—or just not caring—that all Sugarplum Falls could hear Wyatt's side of the telephone conversation.

"Mom, I might have other plans." A pause. "Yes, it's for Christmas Tree-O. Heath is only in town for a few days, and we have to practice before we start our holiday gigs." Another pause, with some indistinguishable words but a definitely distinguishable angry tone. "Sorry, gigs is the only word I could think of for *bookings* at the second. Lots of people in the Sugarplum Falls Chamber of Commerce are counting on Heath, Chelsea, and me, Mom. We can't let them down. It wouldn't be good for North Star's reputation." A little hint of triumph laced his tone at what he must have considered the *coup de grâce*. "No, I'm not letting Chelsea *weasel her way* into my affections. Please, Mom. She's Heath's little sister. We're not dating." A mumble that sounded a lot like *if only*. "Fine. I'll see if I can move the trio's practice back a couple of hours. Yes, I'll go to dinner with your sorority sister's daughter—but that's the last time until after the Christmas *bookings,* okay? I'm hanging up now."

Tough luck for Wyatt. Cliff had never known him back when they were growing up, and their societal paths never crossed now, except at the occasional Chamber of Commerce meeting. But Cliff pitied the poor little rich boy on some level. His own mom, if she'd been alive, would never have been pressuring Cliff into dating someone he wasn't interested in.

The line moved forward. Wyatt paid for his items and left. Cliff tightened his grip on the stems of the roses, crinkling the cellophane.

"Yo, Cliffie." Andrew Kingston strolled up behind Cliff, pushing a full grocery cart, sans Beast. "You decorating the front desk with red roses for the Christmas season? Good idea. You'll probably get points toward the state tourism board contest with that. Classic. Classy. Just like your hotel."

"Classic? You think Sweetwater Hotel is classic?" They were actually for his breakfast with Jessamyn. His *date*. Plus, there was the whole rule from both Mom and Mrs. Houston—never attend a meal as a guest empty-handed. That was it. Not that the red rose was a symbol of ... Never mind.

"Sure. I said so, didn't I?" Andrew snorted. "I was standing there in the lobby at the spelling bee when Trissa said your hotel was soulless. Flowers should help."

"You disagree with her, then." Cliff adjusted the stems in their plastic cone to keep them from dripping.

"Well, I mean ..." Andrew's head tilted and he lifted a shoulder. "I would've used the word *generic* instead."

"Dude! Generic?" Cliff hip-checked Andrew's cart. "Kick a guy when he's down, why don't you?"

"My wife runs a drink shop—a successful one. She's forever telling me people don't want *generic* these days, they want an *authentic experience*. To feel something when they go somewhere. To connect with the owner's heart and soul."

Oh, brother. "That's asking a little much of a mere place to sleep, isn't it?"

Connection with my heart and soul? Seriously?

Andrew shrugged, and Cliff used his debit card to pay for the flowers. It got denied.

The system was probably down.

He paid with cash.

Man, all manner of bad luck dogged Cliff.

Outside, Cliff glanced up at the dark clouds. Maybe Andrew wasn't wrong. Maybe people did want some kind of unique, connection-filled experience no matter where they went these days. No, maybe they *needed* it.

He pulled out his email and typed a request: *I'm up for the walk-through. You can tell me what your grandma would say about Sweetwater Hotel if she were here.*

He checked spelling. All good. His finger hovered, until—good grief!

Curse that Santa Claus of San Nouveau!

He deleted the email, tap-tap-tap, letter by letter. Geez! What an idiot! He'd meant to text Jessamyn as *himself*, not email her as Santa Cliff.

The narrow escape shook him. He had to quit emailing Jessamyn as Santa Claus! He never should've started in the first place!

Or, should he quit?

Real-life-Cliff and Jessamyn were getting emotionally entwined. They were going on a *date,* for heaven's sake. He'd bought her red roses. He'd told her about the financial woes of Sweetwater Hotel. She'd admitted to his face that she'd borrowed money from a crook.

Meanwhile, she opened up to Santa Claus about things she wouldn't have told real-life-Cliff. For instance, the key fact about the scummy ex. Worse, she'd taken the advice of Santa Claus to give Cliff a chance.

Oh, the duplicity!

Blast it, but Cliff needed that other guy.

Cursing again, Cliff switched his phone over to his texting app.

I'd love some help diagnosing the illness at my hotel. Does the offer still stand?

Jessamyn's response came right away. *How's tomorrow right after oatmeal?*

Good. The sooner the better. He could use all the honest feedback he could get.

Come to think of it—when they were talking in the grocery store, Cliff should've hit Andrew up for investigating the shady plumber. Tarquin had other duties, and Andrew could use the practice.

Next time he saw him, he'd do that.

Things at Sweetwater Hotel definitely smelled fishy.

Chapter 15

Jessamyn

An early-morning stint in the kitchen gave Jessamyn too much time to think about her emailing friend. "Santa Claus" hadn't responded even after a couple of days. She really should stop messaging him, especially since—cringe—he'd been clear as clear could be that she was nothing but a project to him. A way to pad his service hours or whatever.

And yet, he gave good counsel! When he deigned to do so, that was. It had all been so valuable, including the advice to give Cliff a chance. Besides, she'd shared so much with him about her financial situation, things she'd been unable to divulge to anyone else. The only other person who even knew a thumbnail of what she was going through was Cliff Rockingham.

And I shouldn't have told Cliff what I did about my bad borrowing decision. Why had she let that spill?

Because he talks about Jane Austen, and he helps little kids, and he cares enough about strangers to stop them from jumping off ledges, and he is steady, and he is vulnerable enough to tell me he's facing some struggles of his own, and he isn't annoyed by newbies offering help, and he loves hot cereal and maple, and I feel this irresistible urge to comfort him when he is struggling. I want to lift him up, like yesterday, when something was obviously wrong. That's the only reason I said this morning was a date. He seemed like he could use some good news. Was I egotistical to think that he'd view an official date with me as good news? I just ache to connect with him.

Her soul tore in two. Jessamyn should not connect with anyone—because Sammie Queen wasn't allowed to!

Enemies potentially lay in wait everywhere. Honestly, Douglas could appear any moment. And then what?

The only person worse than Blue Soul Patch was Douglas. And Blue Soul Patch had to be due for another visit.

Jessamyn shouldn't—couldn't—drag anyone else into her swirling vortex of chaos. Not even Santa Claus Billionaire, and especially not the very steady Cliff Rockingham whose real life could be affected or endangered.

No, the disaster she'd made for herself, she needed to repair all by herself.

She switched the hand-mixer's motor to high and spoke aloud, "If I'm ever going to believe in myself fully, I need to take full responsibility for fixing my situation. A hundred percent responsible. Period."

Maybe this *speaking aloud* thing worked. She did feel stronger. That, or else, stress was slowly driving her to a state of talking-to-herself-level insanity.

Jessamyn placed four steaming-hot bowls of gingerbread oatmeal on the table in the breakfast room of Gingerbread Inn. Atop each bowl, Jessamyn rested a cute mini-gingerbread boy, fresh from Sugarbabies Bakery's earliest morning batch, since she hadn't had time to bake any herself.

Perfect!

The Swiss-sourced cuckoo clock above the mantel sang seven times, and Trey dashed through the front door of the Gingerbread Inn, followed by his mom.

"I'm sorry for just barging in," Trissa said, removing Trey's coat as he tugged ahead.

"See? I told you she'd make us the oatmeal." Trey plopped into a chair. "It even has the awesomest ginger-man ever on top." He picked up his spoon, but Trissa swiped it, still holding his jacket.

"*Most awesome*, not *awesomest*. And, hey. Manners, kiddo." She hung his coat on the chair's back and took off her own, then sat down. "Wait for everyone, please."

"But it smells so good!" He looked up at Jessamyn, his eyes bright with excitement. "Thanks for making me this cool breakfast, Miss Jessamyn. Did you really invent it just for me? Or did that Cliff guy who follows you around want some too?" His happiness and sweetness infused the air—and Jessamyn.

"Yep." She poured him a glass of milk. "Just for you." Who could worry when a darling kid like Trey looked on in adoration?

"Can I marry you?" Trey asked.

Trissa gasped. "Trey!"

"Trey, are you proposing at this early hour?" Cliff strode into the breakfast room, unwrapping his scarf, mirth lighting his face. "Early morning proposals are rare."

Cliff's jet-black hair was glistening, as though he'd come fresh out of the shower.

Hmm. Jessamyn went into a momentary stupor.

No! No lingering on that image!

Eyes! Think about his eyes! Cliff's blue eyes were clearer than ever, awesomer than the awesomest gingerbread oatmeal!

"Good morning." Cliff handed her a bulky item wrapped in tissue.

When she took it, cellophane crinkled. She peeked beneath the tissue. "Red roses? I love red roses."

"Not too cliché?"

"Never! Grandma Ginger's bed and breakfast was covered in climbing roses. Red. Thank you."

"Just a second. Is *he* proposing too?" Trey harrumphed and folded his arms over his chest. "I asked first."

"And thank *you*, Trey." She crouched down beside him and looked him in the face. "If you're still available when I'm finally old enough to get married, we'll talk." She beamed at him, and he reached for his spoon from his mom.

"Can we eat now?" He batted his lashes. "Pretty please?"

"We're all here now." Including the roses. Jessamyn couldn't take her eyes off them. She grabbed a vase from a cupboard and placed them inside.

Truth was, she adored roses, and red were by far her favorite. The TV producers had declared Sammie Westwood a fan of a sponsored flower brand—a bulb company—and for all the time she starred on *Queen of the Queendom*, she'd ostensibly loved hyacinths that sprout and bloom and die in a plastic pot on the kitchen table.

Fake. Her whole public life had been faked.

Red roses were the true flower—and somehow Cliff had sensed that.

Cliff sat down and led them in grace. He was so real and so present and so intuitive.

I'm starting to fall for this guy.

"Amen," they said together, and Trissa finally gave Trey the go-ahead to start eating. Trey dug in like he'd been starved for months.

"You should wait for me to get married." Trey grinned at her between bites. "You can make me oatmeal every morning."

"What about Cream of Wheat?" Cliff asked, picking up his own spoon. "If you have oatmeal every morning, when will you have the finest hot cereal?"

"For lunch," Trey said without missing a beat.

After a couple of bites, Trissa looked around the breakfast room, as if taking in all the details.

"I love what you've done with this place. The storybook mullioned windows, the old-world charm of the low, beamed ceiling, the cozy feel of the plush carpets. It's magical. I want to splash it all over social media, if that's okay?" She picked up her phone and snapped a few pictures. "I have a few followers."

"Sure! That would be amazing." Free publicity for the Gingerbread Inn? "Thank you!"

"Don't let Trissa fool you with her modesty," Cliff said. "She's got a following in the tens of thousands."

Sammie Westwood had tens of millions, but Jessamyn Fleet had zero. Jess preferred it that way. "Thank you so much."

"Cliff, let's not mention that." Trissa took about a hundred pictures very quickly. "Truth is, I do have a pretty fair following on the picture site, so I hope it helps get the word out." Then, she turned to Jessamyn. "And how about one with Trey and his future wife?"

Instinct made her palms fly in front of her face, blocking the shot. "No pictures, please! Please!" She was shouting. It was irrational. In an instant, she was back to the talking-to-herself crazy version of Jessamyn.

Everyone froze and stared at her.

Sharp intensity crackled in the air.

Finally, Trissa broke it with a laugh, as if assuming Jessamyn was being coy. "Fine, I get it." She put away her phone. "You like your privacy."

The tension only dissipated a small degree.

"Yeah," Jessamyn exhaled now that the camera was gone. "I'm not big on photos."

"Forgive me, but that's kind of insane, considering how pretty you are," Trissa said. "I bet you could get a job as a model, if you wanted."

"No. Not for me." A thousand times no. "That's nice of you to say. Do you want more oatmeal, Trey?" Jessamyn rushed to the stove with his empty bowl. "I'll put two gingerbread men on top this time, since it's your second serving."

"Yep!" Again, the kid gobbled the meal. This time he finished at the same time as his mom and Cliff completed their first servings. Jessamyn couldn't take a bite, after that spike of fear-induced adrenaline.

He ate a third, and then it was time for school.

"See you later," Trey said, hugging Jessamyn's waist. "You make the best gingerbread man oatmeal in the world. Thank you."

"I think it might be the *only* gingerbread man oatmeal in the world, but I appreciate the compliment anyway."

Trissa smiled at her. "Thank you—for everything." They left.

Jessamyn headed back to the kitchen with the dishes.

"You really made him feel important." Cliff picked up a dishcloth and started to dry the clean utensils. "It was cool to watch."

"Oh, brother. Grandma Ginger would have wanted to chew me out. Did you see how rude I was to Trissa? I'm so ashamed."

"She will forgive you. It's too small of a small town to hold grudges here. Besides, she cares about Trey to the moon and back—and he loves you. If she's upset, it will melt as fast as frost on the tree branches on a misty morning."

"Thank you." And what a nice image. They washed and dried and cleaned. "You know, your undeserved compliment of me hit the nail on the head. Making people feel noticed and important is basically the whole key to my grandma's hotel success formula."

"There's a formula?"

"More or less."

They'd finished cleaning up everything but the remains of the spiced oat porridge, when Zinnia arrived.

"Who do we have here? I didn't see *you* check into a room last night, Mr. Rockingham."

"I'm just here for a breakfast date with Jessamyn." Cliff shook hands with Zinnia. "Nice to see you."

At the word date, Zinnia's eyes landed on the roses. "Breakfast date, hmmm?" A slow smile spread, and her white teeth gleamed. "Isn't that interesting."

Jessamyn had already been gauche enough today without adding a protest against public knowledge of their dating status.

"I wrote down a few things I hope you'll have time to do today while I'm out, Zinnia." Jessamyn gave her the instructions for the day. "But before you start, would you like to try my new invention? I created it for Trey. I saved you a bowl."

"Trissa's son?" Zinnia asked, taking a heaping bite. "This is great. The guests will love it."

"The guests are getting blueberry-and-nutmeg muffins, today, while we did a trial run of gingerbread man oatmeal. Do you think it's good enough for our menu?"

"It's good enough," Cliff said. "Trust me."

"Yes," Zinnia chimed. "Trust Cliff Rockingham."

Multiple layers of meaning vibrated in Zinnia's statement. Jessamyn hung inside them for a moment.

"Okay, this goes into the breakfast rotation." Jessamyn clapped and readied herself to leave things in Zinnia's capable hands.

"Are the red roses part of the breakfast rotation as well? They do class up the place."

"They're because of the breakfast date." Cliff took Jessamyn's coat off the rack and helped her into it. "Jessamyn is the best. She deserves to be treated like it."

Now *those* words resonated in the air.

Finally, Zinnia said, "Truer words were never spoken in Sugarplum Falls, Mr. Rockingham. Now, you two go enjoy. See you soon?" Zinnia asked. "Or, will you be on an all-day date? Or longer?" She raised her brows up and down.

Um, the rest of the day wasn't a date, was it? The oatmeal had been a date, but this next part, the tour of his establishment, was business. *Or was it?* If he held doors, it would feel like a date. If they stayed for lunch, it would feel like a date. If he touched her, it was definitely a date.

"I'll let you know if I'll be gone past noon."

Outside in the cold morning air, Jessamyn and Cliff walked the two blocks that separated Gingerbread Inn from Sweetwater Hotel. Clouds gathered, but they left a few openings of blue sky, the color of Cliff's eyes.

"So, here goes." He held the door for her at the hotel entrance. One point for *this is a date.* "Ta-da!" He waved an arm to showcase the room as Jessamyn stepped inside.

The lobby's ceiling stretched two stories. The all-white room had shiny marble floors and a seating area with streamlined black sofas. A gas fire blazed blue in the black marble hearth. A Christmas tree to rival the Rockefeller Center's, every branch meticulously spaced with blue lights, dominated one corner. Poinsettias in pots wrapped with blue cellophane ringed the base of the tree like toy soldiers in a line. The front desk was draped with a garland of beautiful evergreen boughs trimmed to perfection with blue metallic ribbon.

"It looks like a catalogue."

"My business partner hired a professional decorator from Darlington to set this up, you know, for the state tourism website."

"I need to set up a tree in Gingerbread Inn."

"Really?" Cliff tilted his head. "I thought you had one already, but come to think of it, I didn't see one. I guess it just feels Christmassy there as a default setting." He gave her a blank stare. "I just figured out something important, didn't I?"

"Grandma Ginger would say so."

"Do you want the full tour?" Cliff took her coat and hung it on a coat tree near the front desk, which was manned by a girl wearing a tight bun and a starched uniform. "I'll be showing Miss Fleet around, Nan. Hold my calls, please. I'll be gone until after lunch."

Lunch? It's-a-date point number two.

"Yes, Mr. Rockingham."

So formal! "Zinnia and I just call each other by our first names."

"I noticed that." He touched her hand. "Let's go."

He touched me. It's-a-date point number three.

That would make this tour their *second* date. Flutters danced in her belly the way visions of sugarplums danced in children's heads on Christmas Eve night—anticipation of sweetness to come. *I like this dating-Cliff thing.*

People who dated also kissed.

Chapter 16

Cliff

Cliff showed her the grand piano, the grand staircase to the second floor, the balcony overlooking the lobby, and the indoor swimming pool with its heated floor and the steam rising from its clear blue surface. Next, they checked out the workout room, the guest laundry area, the vending machines.

"No breakfast nook?" she asked.

"We discussed adding breakfasts, but my business partner determined it didn't provide strong enough ROI."

"ROI?"

"Return on investment. Food handlers' permit, inspections, all that type of thing."

"But—but, the investment is in people."

"According to Grandma Ginger's formula?" Tarquin would never stand for those computations, but Cliff was keeping an open mind. Touching Jessamyn's hand a moment ago had opened his mind to all kinds of things with her.

I want to show her the roof.

He never showed anyone the roof. It was *his* place. Where he could think.

"Let's take the elevator." Cliff inserted a special key, turned it, and pushed the button labeled *Roof*.

When they stepped out, the world opened up. Jessamyn shivered and hugged herself.

"It's cold." Cliff took off his sport coat and offered it to her. "Do you need this?"

"All I need is this view!" Jessamyn raced to the railing at the roof's edge. Cliff came and stood beside her. "It's gorgeous, Cliff. Beautiful. It clears the mind and the heart."

Precisely his reaction to it—every time. "I come up here to think things through."

She looked up at him. "I can see why. I bet on a clear day you can see clear to the other side of Lake Sugar from here."

The three-sixty view from atop the Sweetwater Hotel showcased Lake Sugar, the waterfall, the orchard, the ski resort, the shops of the town—all of Sugarplum Falls. Cliff placed his jacket over Jessamyn's shoulders.

"I feel like a bird, soaring over the most beautiful village on earth," she said, breathless.

"You like it that much?" Why did it matter so much to him whether she liked it or not? *Because I'm falling for her. I want to include her in all my secrets.*

"Are you kidding? I could throw my arms wide and spin like Fraulein Maria on the mountaintop above the abbey."

"In case you're wondering whether I caught your reference, my younger sisters also binge-watched *The Sound of Music*."

"I like your sisters."

"Well, you haven't met them yet. They're pretty intense." But she should. How could Cliff make that happen? Would Lark and Swan take to the idea of Cliff bringing a woman to meet them? He'd never done that before. "Would you like to?"

Jessamyn's head snapped toward him. Cliff's question zinged in the air between them. *Meet my family? I'm getting serious about you and I haven't even kissed you yet.*

But the longer she gazed into him with those honey-colored eyes, the more desperately he wanted to kiss her.

"I'd like that."

She said yes! *She's into me too.* He could've fist-pumped the air, but he was too hypnotized by the depths of her irises, by the soft parting of her full lips.

Jessamyn leaned slightly forward. Cliff moved toward her.

His phone rang, breaking the spell. "I'm sorry." He might've been on a date with the most gorgeous woman he'd ever seen, but these were working hours. "Just a second."

Speaking of … "Hi, Lark."

"Annual Christmas party next week. Don't forget."

"You could've texted that."

"I know, but I'm driving, and I have voice commands so I can be hands free while I have babies on board my awesome minivan of mom life."

"Got it. I'll be there. Can I bring a guest?"

"Only if she's special. If so, I'll count it as your Christmas gift to me."

"She is."

Chapter 17

Jessamyn

He was going to introduce her to his family next week? That was a huge step most of the time, but with Cliff it felt like the natural progression of things.

"I don't really know much about your family."

"We should go back inside and finish the tour so you can give me your grandma's analysis." They entered the elevator to take it down to one of the floors with guest rooms.

"I'm the oldest of five," said Cliff.

"And your parents?"

"That's a long story. Can we save it for another time?"

"Sure." *There will be another time.* Hope of another get-together prior to the family Christmas party he'd just invited her to filled her mind with third-date kiss visions again. Sweeter and more natural than cane-sugar candy—kissing Cliff might become plum upon plum of sugary deliciousness. In fact, here they were alone on an elevator together, with a key that could stop it, and they could have this moment all to themselves, and—

The elevator doors opened, and her sugarplum vision popped but lingered, like a dream suddenly awakened.

"Are you okay?" Cliff asked, waiting outside the elevator for her.

"Mmm." She stepped off and followed him for the rest of the tour of the guest rooms.

"No fireplaces?"

"In every room? There's one in the lobby."

"The gas one with the blue flame?" She pivoted. "I like the stark white linens. They look really ... clean."

"You say that like it's a bad thing."

"Not at all! But there's definitely a theme here. Of cleanliness."

"Isn't that what guests want most?" He closed the guest room door as they left. "I'm guessing your grandma would say no. I'm ready for Grandma Ginger's feedback whenever you want."

"Should we go sit somewhere?" Even the sofa beside the gas fireplace with the color-changing flame didn't feel warm in Sweetwater Hotel. "Somewhere cozy we could talk?"

"Cozy talking does sound good." He leveled a gaze at her for a split second.

"Yeah." She tore her eyes from his and looked up and down the balcony and across it into the lobby below.

Cliff's eyes darted back at the second floor's guest room hallway. It was replete with bright white sconces and shiny white terrazzo flooring. He pursed his lips and moved them to one side.

"Ah, I think I get what you're saying." His voice dropped to a dejected level.

"The hotel is beautiful, top to bottom, Cliff!"

"No, you're right. Sweetwater Hotel doesn't have anywhere that *feels* cozy. That's why you asked about fireplaces and mentioned how relentlessly *clean* it feels. As in antiseptic."

"Cliff, I wasn't going to say—"

"You didn't have to. Now that I've experienced the lobby and breakfast nook of the Gingerbread Inn, there's a glaring difference. I feel it too. They're vastly different effects."

"Well, some people *want* classy, sparingly decorated spaces. The modern vibe. Stark colors and straight lines. You see it everywhere in the books about design."

"Yes." Cliff ran a hand through his hair, ruffling it and letting one fetching, dark curl land in the center of his forehead. "But they want the modern vibe in fast-paced urban settings, not when they come to Sugarplum Falls."

Grandma Ginger's wisdom sparkled in the air all around them. And Cliff talked as though he were channeling her words directly.

"This is Sugarplum Falls. I run Sweetwater Hotel. They come to town craving someplace *sweet*. Like warm honey." His eyes darted to hers. They lingered there a moment, until Jessamyn's heart and throat constricted together. "Sweet," Cliff said, his voice low. "Like brown-sugar-laced oatmeal with a gingerbread man on the top."

Like you, he seemed to be saying.

Jessamyn's heart sprinted like the gingerbread man of fairy tales himself.

"Sweetwater Hotel could fashion its own brand of sweetness." She willed her tone to not be as breathless as she felt in the intensity of his stare.

"Right here might be the best location I can offer for cozy conversation." He swallowed, his Adam's apple bobbing and giving Jessamyn's heart one pronounced thump. "I can take the bad news."

"There's no bad news, Cliff." Jessamyn touched his forearm in a gesture of comfort, that discombobulated her further. *This is definitely a date.* "I'll just tell you her philosophy, and then you can decide if any of it applies to Sweetwater Hotel."

"Lay it on me." The words sounded hungry, and maybe not just for information.

He closed the distance between them, and she didn't drop her hand from his arm.

"Grandma would say that the word *hospitality* shares a root with the word *hospital*. People come to us needing healing, renewal, rest. We give them that, and they'll come back again and again."

"Healing, huh?" Cliff stepped closer, gazing down into her eyes. "I can see that happening at Gingerbread Inn. I can see it happening with *you* as their host."

Her knee quivered as he came closer, closer, the tension taut as a wire.

Then, Jessamyn's phone rang. *Blast!*

Zinnia—who would not interrupt anything she perceived to be a date unless it was an emergency.

"I'm sorry, Cliff." Jessamyn answered the phone. "Zinnia? Is everything all right?"

"You have a *visitor*." By her tone of voice, the visitor didn't sound welcome.

It had to be Bluebeard. Jessamyn dropped her hand from Cliff's arm, and hugged her chest, trying to keep her thudding heart from being heard everywhere.

"I'm sorry, Cliff. I have to go. Now."

Chapter 18

Cliff

"**J**essamyn, wait!**"** Cliff paced after her, but she was faster than she looked. Jessamyn raced down the stairs from the balcony to the lobby, racing away before he could stop her or ask questions. Cliff had unintentionally heard Zinnia's phone call.

Whoever her visitor, Jessamyn had turned into lightning as she raced away.

She still had his coat, which gave him a good excuse to follow her and spy to see who was terrorizing her.

"Cliff? Hold up." Tarquin sauntered over in his smooth way, the quintessential concierge, but he still managed to stop Cliff's progress after Jessamyn. "Is everything all right? I came to find you because I think I spotted the leak in our finances."

"I'll look at them later, Tarquin." Cliff edged his way around and headed for the door. Jessamyn was long gone, but Cliff knew where she was going, and—

"I specially wanted to tell you we just had an unusual guest register for the presidential suite. Booked it for a month. Promised to book the whole top floor if I'd arrange for her to see you immediately. She said she knew you *very* well. Redhead. Candy-apple lipstick. Legs from here to Darlington. She's waiting for you in your private office, insisted you'd definitely remember."

Oh, Cliff remembered all right.

Kiva.

Chapter 19

Jessamyn

"You've got to stop doing that, Miss Jessamyn."

"I know."

"Do you?" Zinnia lowered her chin and gave Jessamyn a death-ray-like stare. "You can't just keep giving that thug all the money in the till. For one, you'll never get rid of him. He's like a kid who never gets told no, and he will think he's always gonna be able to get whatever he wants whenever he wants it."

"But I'm the one who borrowed money, Zinnia. I have to pay it back."

The bell sleeve of Zinnia's snowflake-print caftan wafted back and forth as she waved her pointer finger *no* at Jessamyn. "For another thing, it's terrible accounting practices. Do you even count those dollars before you hand them over?"

Jessamyn looked everywhere in Gingerbread Inn's lobby *except* at Zinnia.

"That's what I thought." She shook her head and mashed her lips together. "If Soul Patch guy doesn't get you, the IRS will."

Oh, no! Jessamyn hadn't even considered what the tax liability of repaying a loan shark would be. She flumped down onto the desk and pushed the sides of her head with her palms.

I should just turn myself in to Douglas and ask for the reward money for finding Sammie. Er, myself.

A clink sounded near Jessamyn's head.

"When are you going to see that nice Cliff Rockingham again?" Zinnia had placed a plate of oatmeal applesauce cookies beside her. "Eat one of these and tell me about your date."

"It wasn't a date."

"Did he hold your door?"

Jessamyn stayed quiet.

"Did he do nice little things for you?"

He'd given Jess his coat when she was freezing on the roof, but she didn't mention that aloud.

"Did he touch you?"

A cry of anguish left Jess's lungs. "I touched him, actually. I held his forearm after only wanting to touch it but it felt like carved marble and I kept touching it when I shouldn't have."

One long nod from Zinnia. "I'm going to let that weird part pass on by and just tell you that I can see plain as the ice on Lake Sugar that you're attracted to him. Why don't you just let yourself, you know, see how it goes?"

"I can't. It's not possible."

"Because …"

"Because a thousand becauses." Jessamyn took a big bite of the oatmeal cookie, which was studded with dried cranberries and gave off tart pops of heaven as she chewed. "Because he's a business competitor, on the level of Goliath and I'm David. Because he's too good-looking, and I don't trust good-looking men anymore. Because"—*Because I don't trust myself to not be manipulated and used again.*

"That's not a thousand. But I can see you're feeling anxious. What about going with the flow?" She floated her arms back and forth, and the bell sleeves demonstrated *flow*. "Relax. Let life take you where it goes. You might be pleasantly surprised when you quit fighting against it so hard."

But Jessamyn had to fight. "For me, life has handed over big piles of men with blue soul patches and sharp teeth."

Zinnia's eyes popped. "Bluebeard has sharp teeth, too?" She shuddered. "It's unnatural."

It was. "You're right. I need to at least count the money in the till and keep close tabs on it so I know what I'm handing over."

"We were *talking* about Cliff Rockingham." Zinnia harrumphed and took the plate. "I know you're going to keep thinking about him. Me, I'm going to send up all those prayers to my mama for you. She was a matchmaker extraordinaire in her day. Do you know how many Christmas weddings she ended up arranging? Dozens." One nod of satisfaction, and Zinnia was gone.

Christmas wedding!

Just the word *wedding* turned Jessamyn's heart to steel. No weddings. Never again.

The front door jingled and in walked Cliff.

"Are you all right?" He glanced all around the lobby. "Am I too late?"

Maybe he was. Douglas's destruction had made everyone else too late to put Jessamyn back together.

Chapter 20

Cliff

"Did you come to get a more personalized version of Grandma Ginger's advice?" Jessamyn asked him, her face pale and her eyes still wild. "I'm sorry for running off."

He waved that aside. "What's going on, Jess?" Cliff stepped nearer, but Jessamyn had visibly closed herself off.

Curse Kiva for her horrible, selfish timing! The ten minutes he'd spent with her had ruined his shot at helping Jessamyn with whoever the guy was.

"It's fine. I took care of it."

"But—" But she didn't look fine. "Whenever you're ready to talk about it, I'm ready to listen."

Her shoulders dropped, and a little color returned to her cheek. "I appreciate it. Can we finish talking about ... *things* later? Like at the next event we have to attend?"

Back to assigned friends status. Great.

Everything in him longed to race over and gather her in his arms, but just then, some guests appeared on the stairs and asked to check out.

Cliff loitered a minute, waiting for another opening, but more guests came down, and it was clear their date had ended for the morning.

At least he'd avoided a longer meeting with Kiva.

For now. She'd sworn that he would hear her out sooner or later. *Sorry to disappoint you, lady.* That wouldn't happen. Kiva could have nothing to say that he cared to hear. Ever.

He paused at the door and waited for the guests to finish, but a few lingered.

"The Waterfall Lights at the base of Sugarplum Falls are tomorrow night,

Jessamyn. I'll pick you up at eight?"

"Waterfall Lights?" a guest piped in. "I've heard they're very romantic. We should go, too, dear," the woman said to her husband.

Jessamyn nodded. "Eight sounds good. I'll order mulled cider from Poppy's shop."

And Cliff would order an ideal place for conversation.

I might even tell her about what happened to my family, if she wants to hear.

Chapter 21

Cliff

"Is this cozy enough?" Cliff tucked the blanket around the sides of her legs on one side, and then around his on the other. The stack of flattened-out sleeping bags beneath them gave a nice cushion to sit on the steel truck bed, and he'd set up a space heater that he'd hooked to the converter from his truck's engine. "Are you warm?"

"This is the coziest outdoor space I can imagine." Jessamyn sipped her cider and gazed upward. "Look at all the stars!"

"We could do with a few more clouds—and some snow—but you're right. They're spectacular. Mayor Lang always tries to schedule the Waterfall Lights on the night with the new moon, so it's as dark as possible for the light show."

"Is there going to be music?"

Cliff sipped the berry-spiced cider. "Mm-hmm. As you'd guess, jazzed up versions of favorite Christmas songs."

Other cars lined the area, mostly trucks, with passengers in much the same setup as Cliff had prepared for Jessamyn to view the Waterfall Lights for the first time.

"Since you declared this place cozy, can we continue our conversation from the other day?" He couldn't stop looking at her, despite the night sky's appeal.

"I'm afraid I lost the thread."

"You were telling me about Grandma Ginger's theory."

"I think I said everything I wanted to about that." She gave a little shrug. "I could go on, but the night is too beautiful to talk shop."

"Then, I want to hear about your life. What was life like in high school for you?" He half expected her to clam up, like she had anytime the subject of her past came up. "Did you earn all A's and B's? I bet you did."

"I did. What about you?"

Yep. Just as predicted, she had deflected. "I was a straight-C student."

"But you're so well-read and bright. At least, you've watched a lot of classic movies. That's my modern equivalent of well-read."

Cliff had a good excuse. "Too many part-time jobs for top marks."

"Like what?"

"Restaurant work, yard work, anything I could get." He told her about the time he'd accidentally dropped the mop into the grease pit in the restaurant where he worked as a janitor, and the time as an apprentice landscaper he'd clipped all the lady's rosebushes down to the quick right before the county fair where she was going to show her blooms, and the time he and his fellow waitstaff in the Mexican restaurant sang happy birthday to the wrong table and handed out too many dishes of fried ice cream and nearly got fired.

"Wait a minute. How did you have that many jobs? Did you get fired from one after another? Because you don't seem the type to get fired."

"I'll take that as a compliment, and they weren't successive. They were simultaneous during my sophomore and junior years. By my senior year, I didn't have to work that much."

"What? Really? While you were in school?"

"Uh …" Someone had had to provide for the Rockingham kids at the time. "It was only a few hours a week for each of them. Mostly weekends. Weekdays I worked at Pine Cone Cabins, where my siblings and I lived. You do what you have to do."

"But why did you have to do so much?"

"Um," he cleared his throat, where the secret pain of his youth was stuck. "It's a long st—"

"Hey, you two!" Mayor Lang stood at the tailgate of the truck.

"Hi, Mayor Lang," Jessamyn said. "We're on the job! Watching all the events!"

"I've been getting your articles. They're well-written. Glad to see you two enjoying yourselves while on duty. You are, right? Enjoying yourselves? Together?"

Cliff looked at Jessamyn. They were getting played by the mayor, but was she okay with that? With every passing day, Cliff was more and more okay with it. *I want her to know everything about me and vice versa.*

"It's a beautiful night." Jessamyn waved at the stars. "Can't wait for the show to start."

"Me neither." Had Mayor Lang winked? "Okay, then. What better location than here for the task I need from you two next!"

"What do you need next?" Cliff was ready to shoo the lady off, no matter how important the website placement was to both him and Jessamyn. "We're pretty swamped with what you've assigned us so far."

"Oh, pish. You'd be going to these things anyway. Might as well go together!" A gut-guffaw. "Now, since the two of you are serving as the de facto cub reporters for the town, and since your articles are going to be featured all over the Sugarplum Falls official website, I'd love to get a photo of the two of you together. You know, in front of the light show." Mayor Lang lifted a very nice camera to demonstrate.

Jessamyn grabbed Cliff's hand and squeezed hard enough to crush his metacarpals.

"We can put it on the site," Mayor Lang continued, oblivious to the bone-breaking nearby. "We'll feature both of you beautiful people, get people connected to your brands. It'll be fantastic marketing for you, not to mention for the town. It's that time of year when the world falls in love." A cackle.

Meanwhile, Cliff might need to go to the ER. This hand smash thing was as violent a reaction as when Trissa Thomas suggested putting Jessamyn's face on social media to advertise Gingerbread Inn. Trissa could be dealt with, but how could Jessamyn stand up to the steamroller that was Mayor Lisa Lang?

"Say cheese!" Mayor Lang aimed the camera.

In that micro-second of the camera's flash, Cliff dove in front of Jessamyn, contorting himself to face her, and successfully blocking her face from Mayor Lang's shot. He wrapped his arms around her protectively, and put his face as close to Jess's as he dared.

Their noses touched. Their breath mingled, hers with a fragrance of cider and cinnamon.

Frozen, Jessamyn stared at him, wild-eyed, her breathing fast. With her pressed this close to him, he sensed her heartbeat even through their parkas.

"Stay close," he whispered. Then, he placed his hands on either side of her face, pulling her hair down to cover any features that might still be visible. In the quietest whisper possible he said, "I'll protect you. Even from her."

Jessamyn blinked once.

They stayed frozen for a long moment, until Mayor Lang started to laugh again.

"I get it, I get it. Well, I wasn't expecting the bonus of a romance shot, but thank you. This makes the two of you even more intriguing, since we've only got your broad shoulders, Cliff, and Jessamyn's fabulous blonde hair." She cackled into the night. "The visitors to the website will eat it up, wondering who the mystery man and woman are and what they look like. It's great. Brilliant marketing! I owe you both so much!"

"Then arrange to put both of our hotels on the state website," Jessamyn said, still not moving from the near-kiss.

"Wish I could promise that." Mayor Lang's boot steps crunched away on the gravel. "Bye, now, sweethearts," her retreating voice hollered.

"Quick thinking for the win," Jess said, still a fraction of an inch from Cliff's lips.

"Yeah. Thanks for playing along." His palms and fingers rested on the soft skin of her face, his eyes so close to hers and open that the stance should've been uncomfortable.

"I find I like playing this game."

"Yeah?" He didn't move, didn't want to stop falling into the sweet, golden depths of her gaze. His upper lip twitched, demanding that he kiss her, but he stayed statue-still, not wanting to lose this moment. Not even for a kiss.

"What is this, anyway?" Jessamyn asked in a breathless whisper.

"Keeping the camera off you," Cliff said. "I saw earlier that you don't like to be photographed."

"Not that." Jessamyn's breaths were shallow, quick. "This ... thing happening between us. It scares me. But I can't seem to stop it."

"Same." He brushed his fingers down her cheek, and she shivered visibly.

He swallowed. "I meant that. I'll protect you—even from her."

"Thank you," she said. "For everything."

"It's nothing."

"It's everything."

Music filled the air from the sound systems of the surrounding vehicles.

"Light show time." He let his hands fall from her cheeks and pulled back a little. He could look in her eyes this way, and see her lips that were so full and tempting.

"I like it." She didn't look away from him. "I like everything I've seen so far."

"Me too, Jess."

"I like when you call me Jess."

"Yeah?"

"Grandma Ginger called me Jess."

The light show began. Blues, reds, greens flashed up on the frozen, contoured wall of ice, creating prismatic arrays, timed with holiday music. Even Las Vegas or Disney couldn't have dreamed up or created anything better.

But Cliff couldn't pay attention to it this year. He only saw Jessamyn. "I want to tell you about my family."

She maintained his gaze but gave a slight nod. "Should we watch the show while you talk?"

"Yeah." That might help. He rearranged, and they leaned back. Jessamyn nestled against him, her head on his chest, her shoulder beneath his. Nice fit, carved perfectly for one another. "I like this."

"Yeah." She snuggled closer while the light show continued and music played. "I'm listening."

Those words served as the key to the floodgates. His past burst from him in all its dreariness.

"My parents died when I was twelve."

"Twelve? You were so young!"

"Looking back, I see that. But at the time I felt instantly transformed into an adult."

"How did it happen?"

"Accident. They'd gone hiking on an anniversary trip into a wilderness area, and they didn't come back. Search and Rescue couldn't access the trail well, due to the legal wilderness designation and some bad winter weather. Everything got placed on hold. And I was responsible, as the oldest child."

"What about extended family? Grandparents? Anyone?"

"Not at first."

"Why not?"

"Both sets of our grandparents had died, and our parents were both only children. Which is why they had wanted to have five kids—so that we'd never be alone. They probably would've had more, if …"

"And you're the oldest?" she prompted.

"A younger brother and three sisters—the Austen-obsessed sisters. I've got quite a few second cousins, so I do have family. They just didn't show up for about a month back then. It was being kept out of the news while the search continued."

"Why?"

"The government didn't want the area overrun by amateur rescuers." Looking back, that seemed ludicrous. Mom and Dad might have lived if they'd been found sooner, whether by pros or novices. As an adult, that fact angered him now and then, but it was also water under the bridge, never to flow back to him.

"What did you kids do while waiting? Did you all just hunker down at home?" Jessamyn placed a hand across his heart.

"That was the thing. Our house had just sold. Crazy timing. Papers had been signed. All us kids were making an adventure of it at home, sleeping-bags-on-the-floor style, while Mom and Dad were on their long-planned trip. We had to be out the following Wednesday, and they were in the accident on a Saturday. Everything had been packed and placed in storage to move into our new house. But that, obviously, fell through."

"So—wait a second. You were homeless? Five kids with nowhere to live?"

"Basically." Of course, their parents had had assets—vehicles and bank accounts and life insurance. But at twelve, he'd been clueless about those things. "As the oldest of the five kids, I took on the weight of responsibility." An iron-core meteorite weight. "Somehow, we fell through the cracks with the authorities. Looking back, that seems impossible. However, I found us a spot to camp in the woods." The story tumbled out.

They didn't have access to the storage units. There'd been weeks of camping, scavenging for food. Cliff had left during the days and found odd jobs, earned a little here and there to buy stuff from the grocery store deli, since that was prepared, and they didn't have any way to cook, other than a fire, and that year there was a drought, so no fires were allowed in the area.

"Someone spotted us after a couple of weeks, took us in—the owners of a small hotel, Mr. and Mrs. Houston."

"Oh, I'm so thankful for good people!"

Cliff, too. But accepting help had been hard at first. "In my warped, overactive sense of responsibility, I told them no. We were fine. I thought accepting help made me weak. That doing so would be like failing my parents."

"But you did accept their help, finally?"

"Yeah. Once my siblings and I had beds to sleep in and food to eat, I exhaled. A hot meal and a good night's rest did a lot to reset my brain into right-thinking, it turned out."

"That sounds a lot like what Grandma Ginger would say." Jessamyn tipped her head onto his shoulder. "I know she would've liked you, Cliff."

Warmth spread through his veins. Not fire, not like earlier when he'd been breath-to-breath with her, but a deeper connection, something on an atomic level bound him with her, as if their spiritual electrons were covalent, creating a new type of molecule, uniquely *Cliff and Jessamyn.*

She shivered, and Cliff reached into his tote bag and pulled out a hand-warmer. When he gave it to her, she set it aside, and instead, she placed her hand in his.

Speaking of electrons! Zillions of them shot through every part of Cliff, electrifying him, or so it felt even if that's not what they actually did. He buzzed with energy, fully awake and alive for the first time in as long as he could remember.

"I don't really know what to do about you, Jessamyn," Cliff found himself saying. He took her hand. "So, I'm just going with the flow."

He took their hands beneath the blanket, and interlaced their fingers. His stomach tipped over and back.

"I think that's a great idea." She drew closer to him, and tilted her chin upward. "I've been feeling that way, too. Whenever I'm with you."

"It's a good feeling." Everything about Jessamyn gave him a good feeling.

"So, you stayed with the Houstons for a while," she prompted, and he refocused on the conversation—instead of what his instincts were telling him to do.

Kiss the girl. It was as if crabs and fish were singing it all around the truck.

"Yeah, they let me work for them. They had a little hotel, Pine Cone Cabins."

"They're why you decided to get into the hotel business." She seemed to see him as transparent as glass. "Family helped you after that?"

He poured out the rest. In a nutshell, they stayed a couple of months with the Houstons. They let Cliff work with them that summer and every summer until they sold the place and moved to the coast to be nearer their children. During the school years, he and the other Rockingham kids bounced between relatives. Some of the family had wanted to split them up. The same members of the family who'd accepted the life insurance payouts to ostensibly raise the Rockingham kids but who bought boats and jet skis instead.

Cliff had forgiven them a long time ago, and Aunt Irene had stepped in to rectify all that.

"I pushed to keep us together, even if it meant we moved a lot. Luckily, we got to spend most of our growing-up years in Sugarplum Falls, with only a few stints with out-of-town relatives. Everyone was really good to us. Especially one great-aunt. Aunt Irene. She helped each of us immensely." More than he would've accepted, but he couldn't think about that now.

"Your sisters are all here? And your brother?"

"My sisters live in Sugarplum Falls. Married, kids, happy and busy lives." He traced the back of her hand with his fingertip. "You'll like them when you meet them."

"I think I will."

Over in the distance, the show's song changed, and the waterfall lights shifted to muted colors. The mood shifted, too. Closer, quieter, deeper.

Cliff's belly jittered—and not due to the cold. *She really likes me.* The sides of the truck bed protected them from the wind.

"Thank you for sharing some of your soul with me, Cliff." One side of Jessamyn's mouth lifted in a smile that stopped Cliff's breath. Her gaze darted to his lips, a clear invitation—or at least a clear indication that she was thinking the same thing as he was. "Grandma Ginger would've liked you a lot," she said again, her chin lifting and her lips parting.

"I know I like her granddaughter." Cliff closed the scant distance, his lips brushing hers, the touch exploding not just with physical sensation but with an emotional blast big enough to crumble all memories of past failures, fears, and hurts.

He took her face in his hands, pressing his lips to hers more firmly. She hesitated, her eyes flying wide, but they closed and soon she returned his kisses, pass for pass, pressure for pressure, passion for passion.

Cliff flew, rocketing through space. Kissing Jessamyn brought all the stars down out of the sky, injected them into his mind and all over his skin with sparks and supernovas. She was light and life and freedom. Her kiss unlocked all the iron doors, setting him at liberty to love and to soar.

He kissed her deeper, and the rest of the world, waterfall lights and all, mingled into one swirl of light and hope and truth.

I'm falling for the girl I'd intended only to help—and she was helping him far more than she could possibly know.

Chapter 22

Jessamyn

Kissing Cliff was so wrong, and yet it felt more right than anything she'd chosen to do in months. Years. Ever.

He was definitely a Mr. Bingley to the better version of herself as Jane. He was generous and alert and open-hearted and good. And what was more, his touch expanded her soul, making it rise and expand like baking dough in a hot oven. His kiss was ginger and cinnamon and cloves, molasses and brown sugar and goodness.

Comforting.

Filling.

Delicious.

Best of all, in all her life, she'd never received a kiss so laden with sincerity, with truth, or that made her trust the message the kiss communicated.

She luxuriated in him as the moment stretched.

After some time, the music around them stopped, but his kisses didn't. Cliff continued kissing her, his arms around her, warming her, keeping her safe, letting her into his world kiss by kiss by kiss.

He was kissing her into falling in love with him.

Some time later, curled up in his arms, looking at the stars, his warm breath brushed her cheek. She could stay like this forever in his arms. Cliff was so human, and yet had risen higher during his trials, and had allowed them to turn him into a great and generous person.

"Tell me about your family," he whispered.

Ooh. That. "I love my grandma?"

"I know that much. Do you have parents?"

"Biologically, it's a given."

"So, they're not more than that to you?"

"We've both lost our parents. Only, with yours it was by accident."

"No wonder you felt such a bond with your grandmother. You needed her."

"So much."

Telling him, telling *anyone*, would endanger the safety of her current identity.

She'd grown to trust Cliff Rockingham far more than Mr. Email, in whom she'd confided far too much. She longed to trust Cliff fully. He wouldn't tell anyone, would he? About who she was. He'd keep her secret, surely.

But with the way things stood in Jessamyn's life—ambiguous, danger-fraught, shadowed—

Sitting up, Jessamyn withdrew from his embrace. "I heard the Angels Landing bookstore is open late for holiday shopping tonight."

"What?" Cliff opened one drunken, sleepy-happy eye. "You need to go shopping?" He sat up beside her and placed a tender kiss on her forehead. "I get it." He gave her one last embrace, as if regretting their embrace couldn't last forever. "You can't talk right now. But I hope you'll be able to share it all with me. Someday. When you're ready."

Oh, bless him.

Wow, she could totally fall for this man.

All the other cars were gone now.

"We should … yeah." He scrubbed the side of his face. "Anything you want to confide in me, Jess. Anytime you want."

Jess. The name settled over her like a downy-soft blanket. A reminder of her deepest self.

"Thank you," she said. For so much more than the kiss or the blanket or agreeing to take her to the store on a late-night whim instead of kissing her again. *Thanks for all you are, Cliff.*

Maybe soon, she could tell him about Douglas Queen.

But if she did, he might hate her, might never speak to her again.

"Let's go. I have a present to buy for Zinnia."

And a decision to make about what to tell and what to keep secret.

***

Angels Landing bookstore was packed. Late-night shoppers teemed between the shelves, laughing and filling their shopping baskets with new and used books of all kinds.

It was a reader's paradise—a party of like-minded friends, all chatting and laughing in the light-filled room, the air wafting with pine-scented candles and instrumental holiday songs coming from the sound system.

Once inside the shop, Jessamyn made a beeline for the cookbooks. Behind her, Cliff kept pace, and he reached for and caught her hand, lacing his fingers between hers.

"Can I help you find something?" A lanky-limbed older man's cragged face pulled into a giant grin. "I'm George Milliken, second in command here. If we don't have it, we can get it ordered and into the store by Christmas. Name your book."

Jessamyn smiled back. "Holiday baking for beginners?"

George directed them to an aisle with no other customers. The shelves stretched high, hiding even the tall frame of Cliff Rockingham. They had their own aisle all to themselves, when George slipped away.

"Beginners?" Cliff asked.

From the shelf, Jessamyn plucked two books. "For Zinnia, my front desk clerk who's been asking me to teach her to bake." She held them out for Cliff to see the covers. "I'm sure these would be better teachers than I would be."

"You're pretty instructive." Cliff raised a brow. "You tutored me, for sure."

"Cliff!" She swatted his arm.

Oddly, the packed shelves created a sort of sound-proof barrier, muffling the sounds of the other shoppers and even the holiday music. At the far end of the row, two armchairs sat empty in front of a fireplace with a blaze in the hearth. He took her hand and led her to them, where they sat across from one another.

"I'm being serious." He placed his feet on the ottoman between the chairs. Jessamyn stacked her feet on top of his. "I spent the whole night talking—"

"I wouldn't call that talking. More like non-verbal communication."

His eyes crinkled a second, and then he said, "I mean it. I hogged the conversation, and you didn't get to tell me anything about yourself."

During the storm of chemistry between them, she'd longed to share all of herself with him. Telling someone *real* would've been such a relief. Make that, telling *Cliff* would have been wonderful.

Could she? The secret of her famous past had been locked inside her for so long. Maybe she could let a small portion of it out.

Mr. Milliken leaned around a bookshelf. "You folks doing all right?"

Jessamyn's heart clutched. *I can't tell Cliff about Douglas here. Not in a store. Not in public.* "Great," she managed. "We're almost finished." She waved, fingers only, at him.

"If you need anything, holler."

She gave him a thumbs up, and then turned back to Cliff. "What did you want to know?"

Don't ask about why I'm in Sugarplum Falls.

"You were going to show me that litmus test list." A glint lit his eye filled Jessamyn's tummy with flutters.

"But I deleted it!" She shook her head fast.

"Then it will be in your device's recycle bin." He held his open palm upward. "Hand it over."

She pressed a fist to her heart. "You're killing me." She pantomimed death. "Fine. It's lame, though."

"I'm sure it's not lame. Besides, lists like that reveal things that we hold dear."

"I made this list before—" *Before I met Douglas, before I realized what I really didn't want in life.*

He bounced his arm, insistent with that open palm.

Sigh. "Fine. If I show you, will you tell me one of *your* secrets?"

"What do you want to know?" He raised a flirtatious brow.

She bit her lower lip and thought. What *did* she want to know about him? *Everything. I want to know his past, yes, but also what he wants for his future.*

"Your wish-list for Santa for Christmas this year." *Let me be on it!* She placed the phone in his hand, screen open to her holiday-related litmus test for someone she was dating.

Must love warm spices.

Must be better at wrapping gifts than I am.

Must be willing to watch three cheesy Christmas films a year.

Must enjoy hot cocoa slowly and not guzzle it—or if a guzzler, must pour a second cup.

Must be willing to sing in public at nursing homes during the holidays.

"Uh." His face fell, and it turned a little green. "Nice list." He took a cursory glance at it. "I like it."

What had she said wrong? Was there something horrible on that list?

"What's wrong? Do you hate hot cocoa?"

"Nope." He looked like he'd gone into a dark tunnel. "They're holiday-related."

"It's my …" It was her holiday-related litmus tests. She had other categories, like she'd said—food, clothing, values. She'd junked all of the lists except the values one. *Must care about family. Must help me care more about my family. Must love people and use things—not the reverse.* And so on. "Never mind. Are you okay?"

"I'm fine."

He was clearly not fine. She'd better change the subject.

"I shared my list, so how about you tell me something. What about your great-aunt Irene? You mentioned how much she supported you and your siblings, but you didn't say how."

If anything, this question made him worse! His face scrunched, and he flinched as if he'd been stabbed.

I don't know what's happening all of a sudden.

Cliff handed her phone back, sober as a judge. "Jessamyn, tell me why you're in Sugarplum Falls."

Chapter 23

Cliff

First, she'd slammed him with the *wish-list for Santa* question—reminding him that *he* was Jessamyn's secret Santa Claus. Lying to her, manipulating her, and then *kissing* her.

Just when his head was slamming with those sirens, she delivered the *coup de grâce*—a pointed question about Great-Aunt Irene, on the very day Kiva had reappeared in Cliff's life.

You're a taker, Cliff. Kiva's words echoed in his head. She'd said it to him the day she walked out on him.

On one level, Kiva was completely right. Cliff *had* accepted that inheritance, money he hadn't earned, didn't deserve. Kiva had demanded he give her some, but eighteen-year-old Cliff had been so unsure and had believed Aunt Irene would hold different ideas about what the money should be used for.

He'd been obligated to honor those wishes of the aunt he'd never known—and it had lost him the only woman he'd ever loved.

A wounded animal in spirit, out of patience with himself, he lashed out at Jessamyn. "Jessamyn, tell me why you're in Sugarplum Falls."

However, instead of looking stricken at his demand for information about her past—and about the situation that pummeled her in the present—she looked relieved.

"Can we talk about it somewhere else?" She stood up and took his hand, her touch calming him. "I think I'm ready to tell you."

What? Really? That was unexpected. He forgot his pain almost instantly. "You're ready?" he asked, taking her hand, letting her touch reset all his emotions. "Okay. Let's go."

His step quickened, and they bought her book and then left the bookstore.

He drove them past the Falls Overlook—which didn't feel right. Where should they be? What was a good place to hear whatever troubles of her life she was willing to share with him?

Finally, he knew. He steered them toward the hillside below the Orchard Lights Walk.

"Does this feel right?" *Safe?*

"It's the heavenly halo." She nodded. "It's perfect."

He idled the truck, keeping the heat on. He touched her hand. "It's okay if you don't want to talk about it."

"No, I want to. I need to." Soon, she dropped her eyes, her lashes brushing her cheeks. "I can't be too specific, but here goes." She took a deep breath.

"I was younger. He was famous—at least in certain circles. We met by chance in the city. A mutual friend introduced us. Instantly, I got swept up in his charm and in how fascinated he seemed with me."

"Well, you are pretty fascinating." He shouldn't have made a light-hearted comment, but he couldn't help himself. She deserved all the compliments.

"I'm just plain me." She shook her head, giving him a quick glance then looking back at the lights on the hillside. "I don't want to be anyone but plain old me."

Plain old Jessamyn was neither plain nor old. But he didn't want her to be anyone but herself either.

"So, you fell in love with him?" His fingers flexed involuntarily. Even his subconscious didn't want her to fall in love with someone famous or unkind. Or both.

"Did I? I wonder." She tilted her head, then righted it. "Not at first. More like the charisma sucked me in. Then, he chose me as his protégé."

"I'm not sure I understand." The vagueness left him in the dark, but he didn't push.

"He was good at making people over in his own image of them. It might not sound like a skill, but it is. At the end, I guess it was impossible for him not to fall for his own creation."

"But you fell for him first?"

"I thought so at the time. Now, I'm not sure in what order things happened. What's clear is he lavished tender attention on me, a previously unnoticed girl. I had never meant anything to anyone before, you see? I really wasn't anyone to anyone."

She would've been someone to Cliff. "You just let him mold you as he wished? Is that what I'm hearing?" That didn't gel with the personality of the Jessamyn Cliff knew. She'd never stand for manipulation like that. Then again, she did bend over backward to be kind to people, no matter who they were.

She nodded and drew a sharp breath. "It was a mistake. I'd like to think I wouldn't do that now."

Cliff was getting a blurry picture of what had happened to her, and it sliced him like hot knives. "What about your family? Did they just stand by and watch you go through it?"

"My parents adored him and the effect he had on my self-image. They loved my so-called newfound confidence, thought he was *so* good for me."

"But?" Cliff's frown grew deeper, as did his concern about the situation both back then and now. "He wasn't, I take it?"

"It's complex. Yes, they were right that I blossomed, but in the process …"

"In the process you also completely subjugated yourself to this person." Cliff huffed.

"Exactly." She looked his way, slowly shaking her head. "In the process, I lost myself." Her voice was a thread, barely perceptible.

Cliff gripped the steering wheel, wishing it was that guy's neck. "Did he hurt you? Physically?" he ground out.

"Oh, no. Don't misunderstand! My values and my virtue stayed intact."

Cliff exhaled, and his fingers loosened a little. "That's at least something."

"Not that he appreciated my fierce determination about that."

It was such a good thing the guy was nowhere near Sugarplum Falls right then. Cliff could've gone from friend to felon in two seconds flat. "Does he know you're in Sugarplum Falls?"

Jessamyn pressed her lips together and shook her head. "And that's why I'm here."

And she clearly hopes he never finds her.

"Exactly who is this guy?"

"Sorry, I can't—"

He hadn't intended to push her. "It's okay." Someday she'd tell him.

"If I said his name, you'd recognize it." Her lips mashed together and she breathed once through her nose. "Just when I'd resigned myself to unrequited love, out of nowhere, he proposed to me. In a fantastically fairy-tale-esque way. The prince declaring his intention to stay by the sweet little pauper forever. I couldn't believe it, and I tumbled into believing he loved me."

"That's only natural." Cliff's temple pulsated, suddenly flashing back to his own proposal and acceptance and subsequent events. "When a guy proposes, it implies he's in love. And when the girl says yes ..." *It implies she loves the guy back.*

But that guy should never assume. He's a fool if he assumed.

But this wasn't about Cliff. This was about Jessamyn—and some kind of danger she faced. "Then what?"

"Wedding plans progressed. Let's just call my fiancé Pygmalion—proved more and more egotistical."

"I'll call him Pyg for short." Cliff thought he was funny.

Jessamyn didn't miss a beat. "The wedding grew and grew, the guest list stretched a mile, and he never once asked me what I wanted. It was going to be"—she hiccupped—"televised, and the last thing I ever wanted was making those precious promises to each other in a spotlight's glare."

Televised? That sounded horrible. "What did your parents think about the elaborate plans?"

"That was the worst part. They got caught up in the whirlwind. When I told them I wasn't sure about the marriage anymore, they claimed I just had cold feet. Couldn't I see what I'd be giving up? They outlined all his good qualities. Told me I was being unreasonable. Insisted I'd feel better after the vows were said."

"They didn't support you at all?" Cliff's parents, from what he remembered of them, would never have abandoned support of any of his sisters in that kind of situation.

"To put it mildly," she said, screwing up her lips and face.

"And?"

"And I didn't marry him."

Cliff exhaled. The happy ending *for him* that he'd waited for, when it came to Jess. But his ears rushed again. How had that wedding's wheels come off? Who'd made the decision—and at what point?

If she'd left him at the altar like Kiva left me ...

Chapter 24

Jessamyn

"And I didn't marry him." Saying it aloud—to someone else, not just herself—lifted another weight. This whole coming clean about her past was incredibly relieving! She could get used to it.

Except—had she? Married Douglas Queen, in actual fact?

That was the huge, looming, dark-matter question up for dispute. Jessamyn certainly didn't *think* of herself as married. She'd never said *I do*. She'd never kissed him as her groom and she as his bride.

And yet, Douglas still to this day disagreed. Vociferously, according to his website.

The reward he offered for information leading to her whereabouts kept her in the public consciousness, even when all she'd wanted to do was disappear forever.

"He's why I'm in Sugarplum Falls." Now, the worst thing, the hardest thing Jessamyn had ever admitted came out. "He's looking for me, Cliff. All the time." He had his dogs after her—and every one of his fans that was money-hungry became his dogs. Anyone could be her enemy at this point. "I can't let Trissa or Mayor Lang or anyone take my picture. I have to stay hidden, completely."

Jessamyn turned to Cliff, meeting his eyes, searching for safety.

"He won't hurt you." Cliff pressed her hands reassuringly. "I'll make it my sole project to protect you, Jessamyn."

Project. The word made her nerves stand on end, but then she saw the sincerity in Cliff's eyes once more. He meant those words, that promise, with love, not with some kind of self-interest.

Cliff is different.

Even Santa Claus of San Nouveau admittedly wanted to help Jessamyn for his own gratification—because he'd decided to do a good deed. But Cliff meant his kindness with a true and honest heart.

In the distance, the lights in the orchard winked out, and a man in a huge hat sauntered up beside the truck.

Cliff rolled down the window. "Owen Kingston, hello. Merry Christmas. We were enjoying your orchard's lights."

"Midnight, my friends." Owen Kingston, the orchard guy. Of course. "Gotta consider the electric bill, and not just all the sights for the local lovebirds." He winked at them, wrinkling the whole side of his face. "Merry Christmas, to you both. You know, the best Christmas gift ever is love."

He walked off, and the word *love* spun in the air like a glitter-covered Christmas ornament on a tree, catching the rays of a spotlight, sending showers of sparkles over everything.

Love. Was this love? He didn't raise red flags.

Cliff did love his family, and he might help her love her own. He did care about people and use things, and not the reverse.

He was honest about himself in every way—no masks, no ulterior motives. Sure, he'd called her his project, but not for his own aggrandizement.

He met all the other important parts of her litmus test, and probably some of the frivolous ones she'd deleted. He was even taking her to meet his family this weekend for their annual party—full of traditions and who knew what else.

Do I dare let myself love Cliff?

Chapter 25

Cliff

Cliff lived on the oxygen of his date with Jessamyn. Even the plumbing problems hadn't caused him grief. He'd let Tarquin manage them, and he'd just focus on making guests feel at home.

Was there a way to install fireplaces in each of the Sweetwater Hotel's guest rooms? How much remodeling would it require—and how much for renovating the lounge area into a breakfast nook? Guests in Sugarplum Falls could use a breakfast with warm spices. Gingerbread man oatmeal might be a good place to start.

But those ideas still aren't the authentic, restful, healing experience Sweetwater Hotel could be providing. He walked the hallways, the lobby, the balcony. *What could I give?*

Jessamyn would know. He counted the minutes until their date that night.

***

"You're not nervous to meet my sisters, I hope." He steered them toward Lark's house. "They'll love you."

The truth was, Cliff thrummed with nerves. The bigger question was, would she like *them*? It mattered. Cliff's siblings had been everything to him for years, ever since he was twelve.

Well, up to this Christmastime, anyway.

Now, he had Jessamyn, too. And she was filling holes he hadn't ever realized were so gaping.

On the doorstep to Lark's house, Jessamyn asked with a tremor in her voice, "Will they like me?"

Before he could take her in his arms and reassure her, the door flung wide, and Swan sailed out.

"Jessamyn!" She threw her arms around Jessamyn, not even acknowledging Cliff. "We're so glad you're here." She shuttled Jessamyn into the house, still ignoring Cliff.

"Hi, Swan," he said, coming inside the warm, holiday-dinner-scented house. Mmm. Turkey with all the fixings. "I brought rolls from Sugarbabies." He held up the bag from the bakery, to no effect.

"I'm Swan, by the way. I heard you run Gingerbread Inn. I planned us a fun activity in your honor." She dragged Jessamyn not only into the house but straight to the kitchen before Cliff could choke out a remark. "Gingerbread houses! Do you like decorating them?"

"I haven't done a proper one in a long time." Jessamyn walked a circle around the table where Swan had set up cookies, icing, and candy. "You went to a lot of work to prepare. Thank you so much!"

"I'll speak for Lark, who's not here yet, even though this is her house, but we're Cliff's sisters, and we owe him everything. So, we're happy when he's happy. And he's been so happy ever since he met you."

"Swan." Geez! He clicked his teeth. "Little sisters can be so—"

Swan kept talking. "He hasn't actually talked about you specifically, but it's a small town, so we knew you were together, and we saw him glowing like the Christmas tree at the rec center. His feelings cannot be repressed. That's a man who ardently admires a woman."

Geez again! "You all have watched too many Jane Austen movies."

At last, Swan looked his way. "Oh, Cliff, you know you love watching them, too." Swan turned to Jessamyn. "Do you read Austen? Or watch the movie adaptations? We're obsessed. Do you like Elinor Dashwood or Lizzy Bennet more?"

"I think I'm a Jane Bennet fan."

Swan threw her arms around Jessamyn. "I thought you looked like a kindred spirit."

"That's an *Anne of Green Gables* line."

"You like Anne, too?" A second hug. "We are going to be bosom friends."

He was in danger of losing Jessamyn to Swan for the whole evening!

"About that gingerbread house activity. What do you say we make it a competition?"

"We do love a competition in this family." Swan rubbed her hands together. "We can make it a couples thing." She made kissing lips.

This was all to get under his skin. It was working. "Where's Lark?" he asked.

Just then, Lark bustled in through the back door, bearing huge shopping bags. "We had to use Bobby and Bubba's mom's oven, since ours went out."

Lark's husband Bobby followed, his arms stacked with casserole dishes. "Did someone say competition?"

Lark stopped short and backed into Bobby, her husband. "Whoa." She gave Jessamyn the top-to-bottom scan. Then she blinked but not enough to clear the flustered air. "Sorry. That was rude. I'm Lark."

Something must have been wrong. Lark never lost her cool.

"You all right, babe?" Bobby took her dish after placing his on the countertop. "You look like you've seen a ghost."

Something must have *really* been wrong. Bobby never noticed other people's emotions. He was an alpha man, all logic and straightforwardness all the time.

Lark's weirdness beat went on as she said, "Nope. Yep. Never mind." She busied herself with arranging their items and removing tinfoil from the tops of dishes. "We're making gingerbread houses?" she asked without turning around.

Why so much reaction to Jessamyn? Were they secret college sorority enemies? Because Lark was usually the most tactful of all the Rockingham kids. But Jessamyn did nothing but smile in Lark's direction and continue making polite conversation with Swan.

After a bit, Lark came over to them—a fake smile plastered on. "Excuse me from a second ago. You must be Jessamyn. I'm Lark, and this is Bobby."

"Nice to meet you." Jessamyn pulled strands of her blonde hair in front of her face momentarily, then cleared them. "You have a beautiful house."

Luckily, Swan took charge. "You heard right about the competition. Cliff launched it." She moved everyone toward a place at the table. "Bubba and I are going to beat the socks off all of you. Watch."

"Bobby and Bubba?" Jessamyn sat down beside Cliff. Just then, Swan's husband strolled in and was introduced. "Twins?" she asked, apparently noting the resemblance.

"The Sutherland brothers fell in love with the Rockingham sisters." Bobby took a seat between Cliff and Lark. "And we're all pretty competitive, so you'd better bring your A-game to the gingerbread house decorating contest. Pass me that tube of royal frosting, stat."

"Can we play?" Three little faces peeked through the kitchen door, with the oldest as spokeskid. "Mommy? We want to make a gingerbread house."

Cliff's two nieces and nephew—Isla, Flora, and Julian—all looked utterly forlorn.

"Are there enough for us, too?" Isla begged.

Jessamyn leaned in, whispering to Cliff. "They can have ours, if they need one."

"Nah," Swan said before Cliff could consider anything but how good Jessamyn's heart was. "I got them one." She turned to the kids. "It's all set up for you in the laundry room. Go on."

They shrieked in delight and disappeared.

"That way, if they make a mess, it's only on a tile floor, not hardwood."

Smart. Mom-wisdom for the win.

In the end, the kids did make a mess of theirs. But so did Jessamyn and Cliff. The walls kept collapsing.

Swan and Bubba won because they plastered the whole thing with colored candies, which worked like an extra brick-and-mortar support that kept it from falling over.

"Winner eats all the houses." Lark pushed hers at Swan, slightly pouting. "Congrats."

Swan broke an edge off the roof and put it in her mouth, chewing. "I've been wanting to do this all night." She turned to Jessamyn. "I bought these at Sugarbabies, but Cliff says you're a great baker."

"Thanks. My grandma taught me." Jessamyn told them a little about Grandma Ginger.

"She sounds wonderful. I'd love to have met her." Swan took another bite of Lark's house.

"Yeah," Jessamyn breathed, and Cliff pressed Jessamyn's hand beneath the table.

Before either of them was forced to talk about Grandma Ginger's passing, however, Lark ushered them into the living room and whipped out some board games, beginning with Twister, the Rockingham family tradition.

"I'll be the spinner, since Cardinal isn't here."

"That's our youngest sister, who's working as an au pair in Europe," Lark explained. "I'll be the caller."

"Nope, me." Swan hogged the spinner. "Cliff and Jessamyn will start us off. Left foot on blue."

It went on, and the twisting began.

"Right hand on red."

They both went for the same red circle, their hands brushing, and Cliff getting the tingles of her touch. He chose another circle, but regretted losing the skinship with Jessamyn.

"Knee on yellow."

Call after call, Jessamyn ended up twisted around and over him. Eventually, they fell in a heap, ostensibly losing, but it felt nothing like a loss.

Mmm. Jessamyn.

All night long, Jessamyn continued to fit right in. They loved her.

Did Jessamyn love them, too?

Finally, the turkey finished roasting. Casseroles were reheated in the microwave, and dinner was served.

Lark's dinner table was as noisy as ever, with everyone talking at once.

"Your little sisters put on a spread!" Jessamyn took a big bite of potatoes and gravy. "It's all so good."

"Does your family do big meals like this?" Swan asked Jessamyn, but then got distracted and pushed back the green beans being shoved her direction. "Lark! You're trying to stuff me like you stuffed that bird."

"You don't get enough protein, Swan. You get any thinner and your neck will resemble your namesake's." Lark stood, taking her plate and her husband's. "Jessamyn, you stay put and talk with Swan and the family. I want a word with my brother about his eating habits, too. In private."

Cliff stood. Lark's topic of conversation with him clearly wouldn't be vitamins or minerals. He followed her into the kitchen.

Lark rinsed her plate in the sink and then set it in the dishwasher. She left the water running, as if that would muffle their conversation from those sitting in the next room. It might. The sink was pretty loud.

"You like her."

"Yeah, I do." *I've fallen in love with her.* "She's got a heart of gold. And she's good at a million things." Things beyond baking. Things like being kind to people, noticing their needs. Things like being a good businesswoman, having an understanding heart, writing.

Most of all, she made him feel alive.

"I like her a lot, Lark. She's the real deal."

"Real deal!" Lark yanked him by the sleeve into the walk-in pantry, leaving the water in the sink running at full blast, and shut the door.

"It's dark in here."

"Just a sec." She pulled a string on a chain, and the light came on. "Better?"

"You going to shut that off out there?"

"Please tell me you know who she is." Lark gave him an intense stare. "That you're aware she's Sammie Queen."

Sammie Queen? Ha. Hardly. "Her name is Jessamyn Fleet." What was Lark even talking about?

"Look her up, dingbat." She marched out, closing him in the pantry. Outside, the water shut off, and faintly, he heard Lark return to her party hostess duties.

Defying his sister, he kept his phone in his pocket and processed her words. Sammie Queen? What did that even mean? Jessamyn wouldn't lie to him about who she was.

I lied about who I was. Er, wasn't.

But that was different. Wasn't it?

Except—there was the fact she had admitted the other night at Angels

Landing bookstore that she was hiding from her fiancé, that he might be unstable. It made sense that she'd change her name if she hadn't wanted him to find her.

But—she definitely insisted she hadn't married him. Right?

I won't disrespect her privacy by looking up that other person. She's Jess. My Jess.

When she was good and ready, Jessamyn would fill him in on the rest of the details of her life. When she trusted him fully.

So far, he'd been able to earn her trust by simply being trustworthy. Well, mostly. There was the whole lie involving the email correspondence, but Jessamyn had divulged the troubles of her broken engagement to *Cliff,* not to Faux Santa Claus.

She hadn't told Cliff everything, though. She hadn't named all the circumstances, and she hadn't gone so far as to admit that the guy owned her.

Because—that fiancé had to be the person she owed the money to, right? For Gingerbread Inn? Or, wait. Was he? Cliff had made that assumption based on their email exchanges.

But, if so, her fiancé would have had to know where she was, in order to collect payments.

It didn't make sense.

Cliff definitely needed more information.

Regardless, how awful for Jessamyn to be so much in another person's power! Especially someone so controlling, and obviously someone who had even duped her parents.

Cliff might have lost his parents early, and, in that way, they'd abandoned him on some level—but never of their own volition.

His heart stretched out to Jessamyn, who'd obviously lost everyone in her former life, including that beloved Grandma Ginger she always talked about with so much longing. It crushed him to empathize with such social destitution.

No, he wouldn't search her online. *I'll be the one rock of safety for her, the person in her life she can trust fully.*

Finally, he did pull out his phone, but he didn't search Sammie Queen. Instead, he opened up his email app and sent a final message.

SantaClaus@SanNouveau.sn: *Signing off for the holidays. Gotta load the sleigh with toys now. To respond to your last question about relationship advice, trust your gut. How's that? Wishing you the best in the New Year.*

He hit send and shoved his phone in his pocket.

There. It was over. Done with, and yet he'd chickened out about cutting her off forever.

With enough time, he and Jessamyn would solidify their relationship. They'd determine whether they could make it work. No internet searches, no fake-identity email threads, no secrets, no lies.

Lark swung the pantry door wide. "Well? Did you do what I asked?"

Cliff pushed his way past her. "I'm giving her the benefit of the doubt. Just like I'd like her to give me." Even though he probably didn't deserve it, considering the wool he'd been pulling over her eyes, ever since he'd plucked the blue bottle from the base of the falls. "It seems like you aren't okay with that."

Pushing her short black hair behind her ear, his little sister lowered her voice. "There's a reward out for information leading to her whereabouts, Cliff. A huge one."

"She's wanted? By the law?" That was laughable. Cliff snorted.

"No, no. The reward was posted by Douglas Queen."

Suddenly, the air thickened. Douglas Queen? The famous guy from TV? Douglas Queen. Sammie Queen? Lark's words clicked into place.

The eyes—they were the same honey-colored irises.

But! No, she was Jessamyn Fleet! Sammie Westwood had brown hair, and wore too much glamour all the time.

However, from the first second they'd met, he'd felt like he'd seen her somewhere before, and that she was beautiful enough to be on TV.

No, it can't be true.

But, she had told him her wedding was going to be televised. A few other pieces of the jigsaw puzzle spun in the air, begging to be snapped into place to fill out the full picture.

"Thanks for all the advice, Lark." Cliff fought to subdue all emotion. "I'll do what I can to keep Jessamyn safe, no matter who you think she is."

"Cliff!" Lark grabbed his forearm, pinching hard. "Face reality. Open your eyes *to reality TV!*"

"Even if she is who you think she is, Jessamyn is not a threat to me." She had her own problems to deal with, including being hunted down by a wealthy celebrity and being forced into hiding.

"Cliff. I love you enough to tell you the cold, hard truth. You've been burned by women who only want money in the past. Need I say Kiva's name? Gouge-em-and-leave-em. You attract that type."

"That's not what Jessamyn is like. Please!"

"Well, Sammie Queen is. Like I said, look her up, dingbat."

***

Back at his place, midnight struck and Cliff still lay awake with Lark's words gnawing at him. He tossed and turned until the sheet wrapped around his legs like shackles.

Until the accusation was confirmed or denied, he might never sleep again.

One search. One. He opened his phone and filled in the search bar with the name Lark had used.

Up popped a dead-ringer for Jessamyn. Cliff sat up and flipped on the light.

The headline read, *Douglas Queen Doubles the Reward for Information Leading to His Wife's Whereabouts.*

Wife! Wife?

Lark had mentioned the reward. Jessamyn had said her ex-fiancé was searching hard for her.

Cliff squinted to take in the small type of the ensuing article, soaking up every word, but the article told him nothing about Sammie's history with Douglas Queen. Since Cliff didn't follow the TV show, he didn't have the context.

What was he supposed to do with that scant amount of information? He'd promised himself to only do one search.

The only solution was to go to Jessamyn directly for confirmation.

But, how could he insist on the full truth, when he himself had a big secret about his own identity—one that impacted her trust in him and cracked the foundation of their relationship?

Yet, he had to tell her about Santa Claus of San Nouveau first, before asking for truth from her.

Period.

Then, the clock struck one, and with it, the demons of doubt were loosed.

That huge reward offered by Douglas Queen careened through his chest and skull.

Did the reward mean Jessamyn had taken Douglas Queen's money, skipped town, bought Gingerbread Inn with the ill-gotten funds, and now he'd set the hounds on her so she would pay it back?

Was Sammie a Kiva?

Was Jessamyn?

He shut off his phone and clicked off the light, lying there with his dark thoughts.

Money did ruin relationships. Notoriously. And love did blind people.

After all, Cliff had been completely blind to Kiva's ulterior motives. She'd somehow heard about Cliff's upcoming inheritance from Aunt Irene. She'd latched onto him. Kiva was a little older than Cliff's eighteen years, and she had possessed skills and beauty and wiles. Cliff had fallen for all of them, hard, like only a teenager can fall. First love can be all-encompassing, and he'd been fully wrapped.

When Kiva found out about the strings attached to the inheritance *on their planned wedding day*, Kiva had conveniently remembered her feelings for her ex-boyfriend in Darlington.

Ghosted.

At the altar. On Christmas Eve.

Wide-eyed innocent Cliff had been duped by a gold-digger who'd never cared about him in the first place, only about the six-figure cash infusion he received on his eighteenth birthday.

Most stymieing of all, she'd shouted that *he* was a taker not a giver.

Why did I ever listen to those toxic words?

Only because he'd worried they were true. He'd first taken help as a child from his parents, then far too much from the Houstons, and finally a huge amount from Great-Aunt Irene.

How could he disagree with Kiva's accusation?

After Kiva's swath of destruction, Cliff had sworn never to fall in love again, and certainly not with someone who only cared about money.

Had Douglas Queen fallen for a woman who only cared about money? Was Sammie Queen really like that, like Lark hinted?

Jessamyn certainly worried about money, if her emails were any guide. She'd stoutly refused to accept money that Santa Claus had offered—sort of offered—but was that to put him off his guard?

Jessamyn wouldn't have latched onto Cliff for his net-worth, would she? Done the same thing to him that Kiva had—and that Sammie had done to Douglas? Or so the gossip reports shouted at every check-stand magazine rack in the world.

The gnawing began again, especially the later the night stretched and the weaker his powers of logic grew.

No matter what he believed about her integrity and her character and even her identity, there was definitely more Jessamyn wasn't telling him about the man she claimed she hadn't married.

Chapter 26

Jessamyn

Jessamyn ladled the first spoonful of batter for the pumpkin waffles onto the griddle and closed it. Fragrant steam escaped, filling the air of the breakfast nook at Gingerbread Inn. A batch of applesauce simmered in a crock pot, which she had dotted with red-hot cinnamon candies. Guests would be down soon, but for now, she basked in memories of the previous night.

What would it be like to have sisters? What would it be like to have a family like that who loved games and competition and food and traditions?

I wish I could be part of them.

Jessamyn had fallen hard for Cliff—and now, she stood on the precipice of falling hard for his family. The way Swan had hugged Jessamyn was like a mother ought to hug a child.

My mom hasn't hugged me like that in years. With Grandma Ginger gone, Jessamyn hadn't expected a maternal hug ever again. Not that Swan was anywhere near old enough to be Jessamyn's mother. In fact, they might be the same age. But the maternal aura just emanated from Swan, creating a loving glow. And Lark's home felt like a *home*. It felt like Grandma Ginger had been there herself.

Jessamyn texted Cliff.

I had the best time. I love your family—all of them. Be honest with me. Every time you get together it feels like Christmas morning, doesn't it? She added a heart-eyes emoji, and a couple of Christmas trees and wreaths.

Zinnia sailed in, her caftan's bell sleeves waving. "Good morning. You look happier than I've ever seen you. Did he propose?"

Propose! "No." *Not yet.* But would he? "We haven't known each other that long."

"It doesn't take but a few minutes to know when all the stars have lined up, sugar." Zinnia wafted a cupped handful of steam to her nose. "Mm. This smells divine."

"How do you know? About the stars lining up?" It felt so right, both in her head and heart, to love Cliff, but she'd been wrong in the past. Dead wrong.

"One way is to contrast it with past experience. May I?" Zinnia took a plastic spoon and dipped it into the warm applesauce. "Delicious. That, my darling, contrasts mightily with applesauce from a can, let me tell you." She smacked her lips and went to start front desk duties.

Jessamyn didn't need to think deeply at all to draw the contrast between Cliff's tender attention and Douglas's hyperactivity around her, always going. The excitement of him had blurred her vision and given her a counterfeit of true feeling.

No more counterfeits. Only truth.

Jessamyn took the waffle from the griddle, plated it and brought it to Zinnia. "I've decided to love him. He's the most honest person I've ever met."

Chapter 27

Cliff

Cliff woke after a fitful night's sleep.

Before his alarm clock rang, a group text chimed.

Swan had looped in all the family—plus Jessamyn.

He groaned, opened the message, and rubbed his eyes to read it.

Monday night is the latest addition to the Sugarplum Falls holiday festivities lineup—the dance with the letters-to-soldiers project. We should all go together! Lark, line up a sitter! Jessamyn and Cliff, don't say no!

Way too many exclamation points for this early in the morning. But at least the content proved Lark hadn't poisoned Swan with her suspicions.

He'd have to attend with Jessamyn, if he wanted to get that website placement.

His ends frayed. *What am I going to do?*

Either way, it was time to get ready for the day.

At eight sharp, he marched to the front desk of his hotel, where he was met by Tarquin, who wore an apologetic grimace. One Cliff could read all too well.

"Not again," Cliff said. "Are you telling me we've got more …" He stopped himself, considering the handful of guests who milled near the huge, apparently soulless fireplace. *Another thing I have to make right.* He signaled for Tarquin to follow him to the room behind the desk. "What is it now?"

"Nothing new, sir. At least not maintenance-wise."

Thank heaven for that. "So, what, then?"

"It's the occupancy rate history report I promised to prepare."

"Show me the records, please?" Cliff stepped toward the computer that held their financial records and all the occupancy database for the past five years. Tarquin booted up a file, and the numbers were dismal.

"I knew it was bad, but I had no idea." The hotel had never seemed that empty, but the bustle of even a single guest check-in could mask truth. Hard numbers didn't lie.

And Cliff couldn't lie to himself anymore.

"I didn't mean to burden you, Cliff. The snows will fix this." Disbelief bled through the cracks in Tarquin's words. "It's not in the forecast yet, but …"

"No, I'm not depending on snow. I'm taking responsibility for the situation." It was more than maintenance and snow. It was on him, as the owner.

Other hotels were doing fine.

When Tarquin left the workroom to go help a guest at the desk, Cliff hit print on the report. As he read the printed version, he rubbed his cheek hard enough to leave a mark.

To whom could he even confide about this? The only person besides Tarquin who had any inkling of his financial woes was Jessamyn. But with his trust in her faltering, he didn't want to build something that might just crumble tomorrow. Throw good trust after bad.

I shouldn't think that way after one speed bump. But Lark's words had infiltrated his brain. And it wasn't a speed bump if Jessamyn was just using him.

And yet, the weight of the hotel's demise was suffocating. He couldn't lose Sweetwater Hotel, not after all he'd done to build it. Not when the money had come as a sacred trust from Aunt Irene. Not when the Houstons' legacy depended on it.

Bless Tarquin for shouldering the burden thus far.

Until it was solved, he might have to walk away from all distractions.

That night, with the report draped over his chest like a pall, Cliff weakened, and his heart's ship sank. In what felt like an inebriated mode, though brought on by no sleep the night before and without a drop of real alcohol, he drunk-typed an email to her:

SantaClaus@SanNouveau.SN: *How do you figure out whom you can trust?*

Luckily, he stopped himself before hitting *send.*

He'd give her one more chance to tell him the whole truth. At the Christmas dance.

Chapter 28

Jessamyn

All the guests were checked in, and the gingerbread cheesecake had been cut and plated and was waiting in the refrigerated case for guests who wanted a late-night snack.

Like Gingerbread Inn, Jessamyn's head was fully occupied—but with thoughts of the upcoming holiday dance.

Yes, she would attend, but would Cliff ask her, as though it were an official date?

In high school, she'd been a wallflower and avoided dances, had never gone to a prom or any other date dance.

Sugarplum Falls seemed to be filling in all the blanks on her *must experience in this life* card. Dances, holiday parties of all kinds, small-town traditions, family dinners, kissing under the stars.

A year had passed now, and no matter how large the reward, Douglas hadn't found her. She might get to exhale.

I might actually be safe in Sugarplum Falls. I might get to live and love and be myself.

Her insides buzzed with the thoughts, best of all, that they included Cliff.

And yet—her closet boded ill.

What was she supposed to wear to that Christmas dance? She didn't have a single thing the right level of *nice* for a small-town holiday party. Everything was either too casual, or else it was a glitzy holdover from her famous days.

In fact, why had she even kept that sequined gown from Douglas?

She shoved it deeper into the back of her closet.

"Jessamyn!" Someone knocked hard on her door. "Can you come out here? Please? Right now?"

Jessamyn threw the door open, and one of the housekeeping staff,

Breanna, bounced up and down, her jingle-bell necklace ringing. "Can you come to the front desk?" Tears welled in her eyes, and she was patting her cheeks. "Right now? Please?"

"What?" Jessamyn grabbed her sweater and followed Breanna.

Breanna dashed ahead to the lobby, and Jessamyn broke into a jog, but the hallway teemed with guests.

"Beware, Miss Jessamyn. It's bedlam," called back Breanna.

When she set foot in the lobby, Jessamyn's socks soaked. The floor was an inch-deep in water!

"Sorry, folks. I'll be right back to help you. I'll see what's going on."

"Zinnia!" Jessamyn rushed through the hallways. "Where are you?"

Finally, she found Zinnia in the janitor's closet, huddled over and crying. "I couldn't fix it."

Water gushed from a splotch in the plaster of the ceiling like a highly localized storm.

"What happened?" She pulled the older woman into her arms, patting her puff of hair in its wild bun. "You should've called me."

"I know!" She heaved a sob. "It started last Friday when you were at Cliff Rockingham's family dinner."

"It's been going on for days?" Good heavens.

"I didn't want to bother you, so I stuffed a sock in it, which seemed to solve it at the time. Then I forgot about it until everyone freaked out. I'm so sorry."

"Why didn't you let me know right when it happened?"

"I couldn't interrupt that seminal event. It was a potential milestone in your life."

"We played Twister and ate turkey. You should've called!" But how sweet of Zinnia to consider Jessamyn's future.

"You played Twister?" Zinnia brightened a little. "How romantic."

Sure, but now was not the moment to discuss romance. "Show me the leak."

In short, another pipe had broken, possibly weakened by the original break. Now, not only the bathroom upstairs but the guests' rooms downstairs were flooded.

An overwrought guest had accosted Zinnia, and then more people came, and everyone got upset, including Zinnia.

"I failed you. All I could do was tell them to eat anything they liked from the refrigerator in the breakfast nook, and I ran to hide in here."

Jessamyn had to get everyone somewhere else to stay—and solve this horrific problem. "I'll take care of it."

However, Zinnia had more trauma to process. "Then, while everything else was happening, that creep showed up. He asked where the owner was and demanded his money." She shuddered.

"Bluebeard?"

Zinnia winced. "He has beady, greedy eyes."

"And he left?"

"I think he saw the flood."

An upside to a flooded hotel. Jessamyn pressed her palms together and looked heavenward, thankful for the Christmas miracle.

Zinnia rubbed her forehead. "Jessamyn, why are you involved with that man?"

"I—" Telling her, or anyone, anything about the man behind Soul Patch would endanger them. "I appreciate all you've done for me today. We've got to deal with the water. Look, you gather your wits, put on a dry caftan, and I'll go start putting out the fire."

"There's a fire now?" Zinnia gasped.

"It's figurative." Jessamyn hugged her and left.

Back out in the lobby, Jessamyn channeled Grandma Ginger. "Hi, everyone. We are going to get you safe and dry as fast as possible."

First, she called Cliff's hotel and got the clerk. "Can you make room for thirty extra guests tonight? Gingerbread Inn is flooded and will pay the cost of the rooms." With what money, she had no idea.

Next, she dialed Porter's Plumbing. "I'm so sorry to make an emergency, after-hours call." It was only six thirty, but business closed at five. "And on the night of a town celebration."

"Don't worry about it. I get that your business can't operate unless you have plumbing." Draven Porter, the owner, sounded completely sympathetic and promised to be over in thirty minutes, if not sooner. "I can arrange for a carpet cleanup crew first thing in the morning, if you want. A Chamber of Commerce discount will apply."

"That's amazing of you, Mr. Porter."

"We Sugarplum Falls businesses have to stick together."

"Sugarplum Falls is the best place in the world."

"Merry Christmas," he said. "And keep praying for snow." Within twenty minutes, Draven Porter and five more plumbers had arrived.

The crew set to work.

Mr. Porter took Jessamyn aside, asking in a low voice, "I've seen you around a few places with Rockingham, the Sweetwater Hotel owner, so I assume you're close. Is he, you know, all right?"

"As far as I know. Why do you ask?" And why so discretely?

Draven shook his bald head. "I just get a strange vibe lately anytime I run into him around town."

Jessamyn's senses switched to high alert. "What kind of strange vibe?"

"Look, it's none of my business if he decides to hire a different plumber. And it's probably unethical of me to try to pump you for information about it."

The plumber didn't seem to notice his own *pump* pun. "I wish I knew anything and could help you out."

"Don't worry about it. I just happened to hear he'd had some issues with pipes, and then he didn't call me, and we'd been working together since the days when he owned the Pine Cone Cabins, so … anyway. Honestly, I'd love to know whether I offended him. I guess I should ask him directly."

"You definitely should ask him directly. I don't think he's the type to hold a grudge or to refuse to answer if you just ask."

Draven Porter rubbed his shiny head. "You're right. Sorry, it just feels so safe in here, and I feel like I can ask or tell you anything. I bet you get that a lot."

"I'll take it as a high compliment." Grandma Ginger would have been so pleased! "Your worries are safe with me."

"Thanks." Draven headed off to go examine the plumbing disaster.

Within a couple of hours, the guests had all been re-homed, and the pipes were repaired. Draven had brought in huge fans to dry everything out—even the Christmas tree skirt.

Best of all, Zinnia had calmed down—having allowed herself to get too hungry and her blood sugar to drop, so she hadn't handled the situation as well as usual.

Everything was okay. Or it was going to be. Soon.

With a whoosh of relief, Jessamyn sat down at the table with a cup of hot cocoa and some leftover pear-and-apple bread, and checked her phone.

A message was there from Cliff.

Christmas dance tomorrow night. Swan and Lark want to go full-Hollywood. Are you up for that? They insist that spangles and rhinestones will be fun. Like many other times in my life, resistance is futile. Are you up for it? Or is it too cheesy? Are chocolate and cheese still your two favorite food groups?

Aw, he remembered. Cliff was quickly becoming everything on her every Christmas wish list.

She typed out a truthful enthusiastic reply.

We're going with your family? Awesome! Can't wait!

And, she had just the dress if their group was going all-out sparkle.

In fact, she might even do her makeup and hair for the night. She had the skills to look upscale, even though she never used them. The one good remnant of her life with Douglas.

Out of nowhere, a wave of sickness hit her—the one she'd felt when she first met Douglas and he'd told her she was captivating and asked would she like to be part of his TV show.

That same warning voice screamed at her. *Don't go!*

But—she'd already said yes. And Cliff's family was expecting her. The last thing she should do would be to brush them off.

Besides, Mayor Lang demanded it. If Jessamyn didn't go, Mayor Lang would be justified in giving the website placement referral to someone else.

Jessamyn had no choice but to attend.

***

The night of the event came all too soon, and Jessamyn still felt all wobbly, like her innards were a bowl full of jelly. She arranged her hair in a classic up-do—no plain ponytail for the dance. She slipped in a sparkly clip that matched the metallic notes of her smoky eyeshadow.

What would Cliff think when he saw this version of Jessamyn? Would he be impressed or wonder what stranger had tried to supplant the woman he'd been dating?

"Hey," Cliff said when he pecked her on the cheek. "Ready to go?"

No comment on her transformation? "Yeah." She grabbed her coat and told Zinnia goodbye. "I hear it is going to snow."

"I hope so." Cliff held her door, and they headed for the Frosty Ridge Lodge at the base of the mountain. "The ski resort we're going to tonight needs it more than any of us. Not saying we don't need it too."

He gripped the steering wheel, occasionally flexing his fingers, as he drove them up the winding road, past Kingston Orchard and into a canyon.

"Did Draven Porter talk to you yet?"

"Draven Porter?" Cliff shot her a glance. "What about?"

Oh, so he hadn't. And now she'd opened the can of worms. Great. "He came and helped me after the flood at Gingerbread Inn."

"What flood?"

He hadn't even heard about the flood? "We had a pipe break and flood the lobby. I thought you would've heard. Anyway, Draven mentioned to me he'd heard you had pipes trouble lately but that you hadn't called him about it."

"Why would he tell you that when I've been paying him hand over fist?" Cliff gripped the wheel. "I'm sorry. It sounds like I need to have some conversations." He blew out a breath, his eyes on the road in front of him.

Now she was sorry. Maybe this was why she'd had the premonition not to come tonight—because she'd say all the dumb things and ruin things between Cliff and her.

"Is this where they're holding the dance?" Along the towering peak and down the edges of the lodge's A-frame, lights twinkled everywhere, almost as many as at the Orchard Lights Walk. "How did they even get the lights up there? A cherry-picker?"

"Jordan, the owner, hired some rock-climbers."

Rock-climbers with a death-wish? "Terrifying, but beautiful results. Ten out of ten for the holiday vibe."

"Jordan saved the Frost Ridge Lodge from a state of decrepitude." Cliff parked. "He did a lot to help bring Sugarplum Falls up in the world. I admire him." He got out to get Jessamyn's door. "We all owe him."

Inside, the giant ballroom of the lodge at Frost Ridge Ski Resort buzzed with Christmas energy. A live band played "Happy Holiday," couples and children danced, and the air smelled like a mix of pine and fresh-baked chocolate chip cookies.

"It's Christmastime magic," she breathed. "This is wonderful." Twinkle lights dazzled from the Christmas trees that lined every wall of the large room. Everyone wore red or green—right on theme. Jessamyn's deep red dress with sequins and her bedazzled shoes and rhinestone necklace were on-point.

She wouldn't have missed this for all the bad, gut-feelings in the world.

Cliff deposited their coats at the coat-check.

"Cookie?" a greeter held out a plate. "They're freshly baked by Sugarbabies Bakery."

Jessamyn bit into it. Toffee bits and chocolate chips and dried cranberries combined with the brown-sugariness. "No, *this* is Christmas."

Cliff had eaten his in one wolf-like bite. He brushed the crumbs off his hands and touched her arm. "Can we talk about the other night?"

The icky feeling in her stomach sloshed and heated. She set the rest of the cookie aside.

"Okay." Her knee trembled. Was it something bad? Had she said stupid things to his sisters, or …

Draven Porter crossed the room toward the punch bowl, his shiny bald head impossible to miss.

"After you talk to Draven?" She squeezed his hand. "Christmas gives us a chance to reset and clear the air with people."

"You're right." He gave her cheek a soft peck. "I'd better catch him." Cliff hustled off.

Swan raised a hand and beckoned for Jessamyn to join her and her husband.

I can't. Not yet.

Ducking into a corner behind a wall of Christmas trees instead, Jessamyn pulled out her phone, launched a VPN, and opened Douglas's site.

Maybe the gnawing feeling had something to do with Douglas—and not Cliff. *Please, don't let it be Cliff.*

The screen flashed up. Jiminy! The reward for information leading to Sammie's whereabouts had doubled. Again! Now, it neared seven figures.

Her breath came in great gulps.

Douglas could more than afford it. He could keep doubling and doubling, until someone, even a kind-hearted Sugarplum Fallsian wouldn't be able to resist.

She pressed her palm to her forehead, checking for fever.

Jessamyn should get out of here. She shouldn't have come. With great strides, she headed for the coat check.

"Hi, Miss Jessamyn!" the little boy from the spelling bee, Trey, blocked her path and hugged her legs, nearly tripping her. "Are you having fun at the party?"

"It's a beautiful party." Jessamyn pressed her mouth into a smile. "There's a whole buffet table with snacks. Will your mom let you eat some?"

"Yeah, but they don't have gingerbread oatmeal. Hey. You look like a princess! The gingerbread princess from that video game I was playing. But you need a crown."

She smiled and gave an eye-roll of agreement. "You're so right. I totally need a crown."

If my last name is Queen, like Douglas seems to think ...

Trey high-fived her and ran off to the sweets buffet table.

But I don't want a crown. Douglas insisted I wear a tiara for our wedding. I only wanted a veil.

She steadied herself, moving toward the coat check with more grace this time. "I don't need a crown," she whispered. "I only need Cliff."

"Did I hear you mention Cliff's name?" Swan swooped in and enveloped Jessamyn in a warm hug. "It's gorgeous in here. But not half as gorgeous as you."

The hug made Jessamyn's heart rate return to normal pace. "Thank you."

She pushed Jessamyn out to arm's length and looked her over. "Look at you! That dress is amazing on you. What did Cliff say? Doesn't matter what Cliff said, you objectively look amazing."

"You look beautiful yourself."

"Thanks. We try to gussy up once a year. Glad there's a chance now in Sugarplum Falls." Swan did a twirl and a curtsey. "Has anyone ever told you that you look like someone famous?"

"Me?" Jessamyn's mouth went dry as a Christmas tree cut in August. Her pine needles might fall everywhere. "Is Lark here?" Shameless redirect. "I thought I saw her writing cards to soldiers."

"Yes, she's over there. I bet she's written ten cards. Or more." Swan laughed. "She'll try to write the most of all of us, guaranteed."

At the letter-writing table in the far corner, Lark looked up, and she gave Jessamyn a deep frown. Like, a suspicious one.

Swan waved. "I'm going to write a few, too. Bring Cliff and meet us over there."

"Sure." But instead, Jessamyn saw her opening and whirled around to head toward the coat-check again. *If anyone sees me all glamorized like this, they'll ask if I'm famous again, and they won't be as charitable about it as Swan.*

It was a huge mistake to think she could safely show up in her Sammie garb and not be recognized. Fool! She hoofed it for the exit.

"Jess." Cliff swept up to her. "I am sorry I left you. I talked briefly with Draven Porter, like you suggested, and then I couldn't get hold of my business partner. Have you seen my sisters? Oh, there they are. Let's go write letters. Maybe that will take my mind off things until I can get some stuff straightened out."

Cliff grasped her hand, taking her toward the table.

Barely registering his words, Jessamyn took up pen and Christmas card, continually glancing toward the door. That nagging feeling grew stronger and stronger.

Jessamyn finished her card.

At the same time, Cliff asked, "Would you like to dance?" and pulled her to the floor to the strains of "Have Yourself a Merry Little Christmas."

It was a sweet song, but after a minute or so, Jessamyn told him the truth. "I'm not feeling quite right."

"Same. Let's go as soon as we've finished making our appearance. I told myself one card, one cookie, one dance."

"Good because I need to talk to you about something, too." It was time. Cliff really needed to know the whole truth about Douglas Queen.

Maybe that was the dark, looming feeling—that this was my moment of Big Reveal, just waiting for Cliff's reaction, for better or worse.

How Cliff responded to her confession could determine Jessamyn's whole future.

He groaned. "I'm sorry. I can't take this." Cliff suddenly maneuvered the two of them off the dance floor and down a dim hallway. "Being two people at once isn't good for the psyche."

Jessamyn shriveled. He knew! He knew about Douglas, knew she was Sammie, knew she'd lied about everything. "Cliff, I'm so sorry. I shouldn't have …" Pretended? Lied? Hidden?

But what choice had she had under the circumstances? Heat and cold prickled across her face, tightening her throat. "Go ahead. Say what you need to say."

Cliff shifted his weight and looked anywhere but at Jessamyn. "It's about that day we met."

"Oh!" she gasped. He couldn't have told her anything that would've taken her by greater surprise. "What about it?"

He shifted his weight, blocking her view of the rest of the guests dancing or hunching over the letter-writing tables. "Jessamyn, what are your initials?"

Was someone playing a prank on her? She looked back and forth for the TV cameras—the ones that used to dominate her life when she'd been with Douglas Queen as his protégé and show pony.

A moment passed, and Cliff's brow wrinkled. "Are they JW?"

"Why do you ask my initials?" A mouse had possessed her voice box.

JFW. Jessamyn "Sammie" Fleet Westwood. "My name is Jessamyn Fleet." Her first and middle names. Fleet after Grandma Ginger Fleet's maiden name, a name she'd never divulged to Douglas, so she'd been able to hide so well.

You mean JFWQ, Sammie! Douglas's angry voice—the one he never used on camera—shouted in her head. *You're a Queen and you know it! I have the documents to prove it!*

She ached to trust him, and for him to believe in her, too. But, he'd caught her off-guard, and she was stumbling. "What's this about, Cliff?" Her voice quavered.

"Have you ever heard of the Channel Islands off the coast?"

"Which coast do you mean?" she barely managed. Her stomach muscles started shaking uncontrollably. The foreboding resurged, spiking like a sudden illness. Her head swam. "Cliff, I don't feel well."

"Excuse me." A loud voice interrupted them, as a man tapped Cliff's shoulder in the semi-darkness of the hallway. "I need to speak with this woman, sir."

That voice! Now Jessamyn's stomach twisted like a used rag.

"Douglas!" With a gasp of horror, Jessamyn grabbed Cliff.

She'd been found.

Chapter 29

Cliff

Douglas? As in Douglas Queen?
Lark was right.
Cliff pulled Jessamyn to his chest, but inside, conflict raged. Was she really hiding from Douglas because of something innocent, or had she absconded with his funds after breaking his heart?

It doesn't matter. I swore I'd protect her. Nothing this guy said or did would change that.

"Do you have something to say to my girlfriend?" Cliff squared his shoulders. He stood six inches taller than the famous man. They always said people looked taller on TV.

"Jessamyn? Are you ready to leave?"

What? Leave without Cliff having a chance to come clean about being her mystery pen-pal, that was. The lie was eating a hole in him. "I'm sorry, sir, but we are in the middle of an important conversation." He edged between them, but Jessamyn's face looked horror-stricken, and he held back.

"Cliff, I was going to tell you, I swear. My situation was the very next thing coming out of my mouth."

Douglas stepped closer with perfectly coiffed hair and designer clothing. His cologne eclipsed the pine balsam and even the chocolate chip cookies.

"Legally, you have to relinquish her." He used a commanding, stage-presence-type voice.

"What does that even mean?" Cliff was not cowed.

Douglas held up a sheet of paper. "We're married. She's my *wife*."

Cliff froze.

Douglas's voice boomed louder than the bass beat of the music. "Sammie, it's been too long. Let's go." He grabbed her arm and pried her from

Cliff's paralyzed arms.

Cliff couldn't stop him—he'd been shocked into inaction. Wife? Jessamyn *was* married, after all?

His lips burned. He'd kissed a married woman, committed an immoral act.

This is even worse than what Kiva did to me. Jessamyn made a sinner of me.

His head throbbed, and his heart pounded as Jessamyn slipped away.

Going after her would be wrong, no matter what his heart shouted.

"Cliff?" A woman stepped toward him. "Cliff! I hoped you'd be here." She raced into his arms, her red curls brushing his chin and neck. She embraced him, pressing her soft curves against his chest. "Oh, I am so thankful for this moment. I've been praying for it for months."

"Kiva?" Cliff's spine stiffened, and his ears rang, as a millionaire celebrity stalked away with the woman he'd trusted until ten seconds ago.

Chapter 30

Jessamyn

Stares of every person in Sugarplum Falls weighted Jessamyn down, as if the spangles on her dress were lumps of lead.

She affected a bright voice, the one she'd used so often for the TV cameras as Sammie.

"Douglas!" The name scratched her throat as it escaped. "Why are you here?"

"Thanks to someone calling himself *A Friend in Sugarplum Falls,* who counts himself a very rich man tonight."

"Where are you taking me?" Jessamyn tugged to get her hand away from his grip, but Douglas squeezed tighter, pulling her tightly to his side as they wound their way across the dance floor toward the door.

"I'm not letting you go. Not again. I've been through too much." He raised his voice so that everyone listening could hear. "I've missed you so much, Sammie."

It was all a show.

With Douglas, it was always a show.

Jessamyn could go quietly, attempt to resolve this with Douglas out of the public eye—or she could send up a cry for help.

Why wasn't Cliff following her?

"I knew it." Lark came up and stood in their path. "I knew the second his heart opened again, he'd go right back to Kiva." She shook her head, jutting her chin toward a couple coming their direction.

A gorgeous redhead clung to Cliff like a baby gorilla.

"Excuse me, ma'am. No autographs." Douglas pushed past Lark.

"Didn't ask for one," Lark said with a huff. "All of you are fakes."

The words lanced Jessamyn's eardrums. "I never meant to lie to you,

Lark. Not to *any* of you, I promise."

"It was only a matter of time before you went back to this phony. I read all the articles, *Sammie*."

But—but … "Lark, it's not like that. I love all of you."

"What do you know about love? Cliff is the best man you'll ever meet, and you used him. I'm never letting you near him again."

"Don't worry," Douglas said, pulling Jessamyn to his side like a Siamese twin. "I'm never letting her go." He pressed a kiss to her forehead and pulled her forward again.

Now, the band even stopped, and all the gossip skittered in their wake.

That's Douglas Queen. Is that Sammie? I thought Sammie was lost. No, that's Jessamyn Fleet, owner of Gingerbread Inn. Was she dating Douglas? I thought she and Cliff Rockingham were together. I'm sure that's Sammie. Jessamyn is Sammie! I knew it!

Out in his sports car, Jessamyn went limp, inhaling his familiar but unwelcome cologne.

It turned her already distressed stomach.

He started the engine with a flick of his wrist and jammed the car into gear. "I knew if I made the reward for information high enough, someone would eventually reach out to me with the truth. It seems the price of someone's integrity is just about a million dollars. Enough for a down payment on a hotel of his own."

Gravel spit behind the car's tires as they entered the highway.

"The tipster was using the reward money for a hotel?" The mouse returned to her vocal cords.

Not Cliff!

It all clicked into place.

The money troubles.

The weird nervousness he'd exhibited all night.

The insistence that he needed to tell her something important.

He took the reward. He saved his hotel with it.

That's what he'd needed to admit to her, why he'd been so insistent they talk. He'd known she was Sammie, and he'd been powerless to resist the golden parachute for his financial troubles.

I can't blame him.

Jessamyn sent a pleading look back at The Frosty Ridge Lodge. But there was no reason to look back. Not now.

Lark hated Jessamyn. Swan would too, any second now.

The whole town scorned her for being Sammie and leaving Douglas who, according to his press agents and all the tabloids, loved her to the point of infinite sacrifice, and could do no wrong.

Cliff had gone back to that sexy ex-girlfriend whom Jessamyn could never compete with.

A thick, poisonous fog settled over her. She was alone. She'd created this situation, and there was no one to save her.

"I knew I'd find you." Douglas placed his hand on her knee. "It was only a matter of time and money. What do you say we go have our honeymoon at last, sweet wife?"

Chapter 31

Cliff

Kiva draped herself over him. "Let's go somewhere we can talk."

In the stupor of the aftermath of the confrontation, Cliff shuffled along beside Kiva. She led him up the stairs to the lodge's hallway of guest rooms. "I got a suite, since it was the only vacancy." The door swung wide, and inside the room glittered with familiar décor.

"I hope you don't mind, but I had all our wedding decorations stored all these years, and I thought today would be a good time to revisit the memories and make a new one. A big new one."

"What?" Cliff snapped to attention. "What are you doing, Kiva?"

"Cliff." She pressed herself against him. "I'm here to tell you the most important thing I've ever said to anyone in my life."

Cliff looked wildly around. The whole room was strewn with olive green and rust red ribbons and floral junk. "It's not a great moment for whatever you think should be happening here."

"I'm not the same person I was when we were young. You were still a teenager, for heaven's sake. I was not much more than one. Can we agree we've changed?"

"I know I've changed." For one, he saw nothing about Kiva that appealed to him. Well, other than the obvious attraction of her contrived looks. "I can't say I care whether you have or not."

She crumpled. "I hurt you. I knew it at the time. I'm so sorry. Can you ever forgive me?" She took both his hands and pressed them to her heart. "That's why I'm here—it's why I came two weeks ago. I won't give up, Cliff. Not until you say what my soul desperately needs to hear."

Her full lips were turned upward, a few inches from his face. The muscle memory of kissing her beckoned, the strains of first love tugged. His chemical makeup knew everything it needed to know about what *could* come next.

Jessamyn was a married woman. Bereft of the woman he'd thought he loved, Cliff ping-ponged for somewhere to turn.

But to Kiva? Willing, repentant, gorgeous-lipped Kiva?

It would be so easy. So, so easy.

"I had this fantasy, Cliff, of our first Christmas together. I was so young and naïve, and I ruined everything."

"Agreed." His voice was gruff. "What you did was harsh." He'd been an orphan—and the naïve one of the pair of them. "You called me a taker."

"That's rich, isn't it? When I was the taker? Now that I'm older, I want to give you something extremely valuable. My *trust*."

Trust. The word ricocheted around the high-ceilinged suite—off the olive and rust ribbons, off the draped wedding dress over the chair, off the king-sized bed.

"Please, Cliff." Her words enticed, wrapping slowly like silken strands around his will. "Forgive me?"

Chapter 32

Jessamyn

"It's all right here in the documentation." Douglas unfolded the parchment again and flashed it at her. "Married. Legally."

"Let me see that?" she reached, but he pulled it back. "We didn't stand before the judge. We didn't make the vow."

"In a lot of countries, all that's needed for a marriage to be official is the certificate. No ceremony required."

"This isn't *a lot of countries*."

"Maybe you've forgotten. We went to the courthouse and procured the certificate. Your parents were there, watching. My agent Larissa was there, and so were Ghizelle and Frances." Sammie's handlers. "Cameramen documented it. Do you need me to show you the footage? Clips went viral. Everyone knows you married me."

But that wasn't the same!

Her mind swirled. Douglas always spoke with so much authority, Jessamyn had always simply accepted his statements as fact. The spell was starting to weave itself over her again.

"Where should we go so you can pick up your belongings?" He eyed her. "I'm glad to see you haven't tried to do a glow-down since we were together. You're really quite beautiful with makeup and the right clothes."

He steered them back toward the town proper of Sugarplum Falls. "It's charming here. Maybe we should shoot a Christmas special—that's it! We'll do a *reunion* episode, where I show up and you admit you've been planning a special surprise for me all this time! That place will do. I'll buy it and we'll have a big show there." He pulled into the parking lot of Sweetwater Hotel. "Oh, yes. This is exactly the type of place I could own. Perfect side-business to keep back some of the tax collectors from barking at my heels." He actually barked. "With the right decorators from the city, we could make this place a modern-style palace. More glass and steel. More sharp shine."

"You're buying Sweetwater Hotel?"

"Of course! The owner can't say no to my offer."

"Was it one of the stipulations of handing over the reward money?"

"How did you know?" Douglas laughed. "But if you don't want to go in yet—if you want to wait until I've finished sprucing it up, that's fine. Do you want to show me the town, or should we just get back to our lives together? I can't wait to tell the world I've found you, Sammie!"

Chapter 33

Cliff

Cliff stepped away from Kiva's embrace. "Are you ... Are you trying to get back together?"

Kiva sprang backward. "Back together? No! I just want you to know I'm sorry. That's the big message I needed to deliver. My counselor said I need to start making restitution for the bad things I've done so I can forgive myself."

"What's all the wedding decoration about?"

"I guess I wanted to return it. Wasn't some of it from your mom's storage unit? I felt bad keeping it all these years. Maybe one of your sisters could use it for her wedding."

"There's only one sister, Cardinal, left to get married by this point." And she was living in Europe as an au pair.

"Oh." Kiva walked to the window, which opened to a view of the snowless mountain slope. "I'm sorry if I gave you the wrong impression. I guess hugging you that way was bad communication. I've always had a knack for doing the wrong thing at the wrong time. It's like I don't know how to express feelings without being overtly affectionate. My counselor says I need to work on boundaries, too."

Kiva sat down on one of the sofas with a huff.

For the first time, she looked like a sad, broken little girl—not the vampiress he always pictured her as. "Is it something you want to talk about?" He sat on a separate sofa, across a large ottoman from her.

"I wanted to tell you why I used you, and apologize for that, and then explain why I left. And what happened after that."

She broke into a story about being penniless as a kid. *You're too beautiful to be poor*, her mother had always said. "So I tried to live up to that."

"I didn't have money."

"You did, though! We all knew it! We knew about your aunt's legacy, and we knew it was huge. Your brother and sisters each got one too. You were the richest kids in town."

"We weren't allowed to spend a penny on anything but a business that would make the world a better place."

"I didn't know that at the time, but now that you say so, it makes sense." She rubbed her temples. "All I heard when you said I couldn't spend any of the money was that you didn't love me enough to take care of me. That I wasn't beautiful enough. That *I* wasn't enough. It spooked me, and I invented an ex-boyfriend, and I left for Darlington. Then, I made my way to the coast, tried to get a job in the movies, failed, and then realized I'd been chasing the wrong things. That's when I found my counselor. She's been helping me become a better person. I have to do that before I start any kind of a relationship again. Sorry if I gave off a different impression."

For a long moment, Cliff soaked up the explanation.

Finally, he let all the old feelings of rejection and disgust—for her and himself—float off like so many sparks up a chimney.

"It's all right, Kiva. We were both young. It's been too long to let this torment either of us for another second."

Kiva's head popped upward, and she met his eye. "Really?"

"Really." A knot in his belly unraveled. Another one in his shoulders loosed. Knots all over him came free.

I'm free.

"That's the best Christmas gift anyone could ever give me. It's the best *gift* anyone could give me. My counselor says ..." She said some more things.

Cliff only heard the first ones—forgiveness.

If only he could forgive Jessamyn and not stand here a man twisted like a used rag in his grief and betrayal.

I wish I knew why she did what she did.

But she was gone—*with her husband*—and Cliff would probably never see her again.

Chapter 34

Jessamyn

Douglas steered them down Orchard Street and into Sugarplum Falls proper to swing by the downtown area out of curiosity.

"I'd drive us back to the city tonight, but I have a video call with some high-paying VIP fans of the show scheduled in an hour, and I want to make sure I don't have a five o'clock shadow for that. What do you say we get a room, babe?"

He knew she hated it when he called her babe.

"Sure." Jessamyn's head throbbed. The shoes hurt, and this dress was ridiculous. At least if Douglas took her to Gingerbread Inn, she could change out of this getup he liked so much.

Instead, he pulled into the parking lot of Sweetwater Hotel.

"Why here?" she asked, gripping the armrest. "Are you sure?"

"Babe! It's the best hotel in town. You deserve the best. Have you seen the lobby? So modern."

"Yeah." And she'd seen the owner. "I've toured the whole place."

"Then you know why we're staying here. Let's go." Douglas got out and headed off.

Jessamyn waited, but he didn't get her door. *Cliff always got my door.* That had been so polite, and so pleasant to become used to.

Now, his ex would be the recipient of all Cliff's politeness. It was stunning how quickly everything had shifted, reset to years-gone-by. Her ears rang.

"Are you coming, or what?" Douglas had opened her car door at last. "What happened? Did living in Podunk make you forget how to get your own door? Come on. It's freezing." He stalked away. "I already reserved us a room and had Priscilla handle check-in." He waved a room key.

He'd planned everything, down to assuming Jessamyn would be powerless against his insistence.

But, was she powerless? They crossed the lobby, her dress swishing against her legs. The sound system piped-in "Baby, It's Cold Outside."

"Come on, babe." Douglas beckoned from the elevator. "The night is ours. Well, after my video call. I need to get that set up, but then I'm all yours, wife." He pulled a folded document from his jacket pocket and held it up.

The certificate. Was it valid? Enforceable?

I feel like Princess Buttercup—I didn't promise aloud. But I just don't know the law!

She stepped onto the elevator, the fight going out of her. For now.

"That's a good girl, Sammie, babe." Douglas put an arm around her shoulders. Stiff, not comforting, it crunched her. They swished upward to the top floor.

Douglas fumbled with the room key, and then threw the hotel room door open. "Enchanting!" he said—his attention on the room, and not on Jessamyn. He took off his long wool coat, and then his suit jacket. "I'll just get ready for the call, and you can get ready for *us*." He gave her a quick smolder, and then disappeared into the bathroom.

A corner of the document stuck out of the jacket pocket. She tiptoed over and pulled it free, scanning its contents fast—before Douglas saw. Her heart thudded and her fingers trembled.

Marriage License. Their two signatures at the bottom, and that of the officiant.

"Whatcha looking at, babe?" Douglas peered over her shoulder, wrapping his arms around her waist. "That's proof. We belong to each other. You're mine."

"Why do you want me so much?" It took effort to not sound like this came through clenched teeth. "When I'm so obviously avoiding our relationship?" Enough to go into hiding, enough to borrow money from an unscrupulous source in order to disappear?

Douglas pulled her tighter in the back-hug. "Sammie, I've never had anyone I wanted so much."

"Because you couldn't have me?"

"Maybe that's it. We always want the unattainable. And now that I have you again, I have never felt so accomplished. It's a major rush, and it was worth every penny of that reward."

The reward. "Who told you I was in Sugarplum Falls?" *I hid my identity so cautiously! Only Lark figured it out.*

"Does it matter? We're together now."

It mattered. If it had been Cliff, in whom she'd confided a few sketchy details that he'd be able to piece together easily, given the incentive, it mattered very much. *It would kill me dead if he took the reward, dropped me, and went back to his sexy ex.*

"Oh, that's my alarm. If I don't get shaved, I'll be off-brand for my VIP fans. They're going to be the first to hear that I found you and we're back together!" He squeezed her and disappeared into the bathroom again—blasting his fight song that he used to psych himself up for public appearances.

The marriage certificate lay at her foot. She picked it up again.

Then, as if her angel grandma whispered pure intelligence into her ear, Jessamyn refolded the marriage certificate, and grabbed her coat.

Need to change clothes and freshen up my makeup. Back in fifteen. She placed a note atop Douglas's jacket, in hopes he'd buy it. When she'd been Sammie, she'd forever used that excuse. People in Douglas's world valued a change of clothes. Aha. *Or an hour, if I decide to do a quick bleach on my teeth. For the cameras.*

With as much stealth as possible, she sneaked out of the hotel room and took the elevator to the lobby. Douglas wouldn't be finished with his grooming routine for at least an hour.

Only a clerk stood at the check-in desk, and Jessamyn hurried past it. No Cliff.

Cliff is still with her. It sliced deep, but if Cliff didn't want to belong to Jessamyn, now that he'd possibly accessed the money he needed to save his hotel, she would just have to find the strength to let her hopes of him go.

But in the meantime, she would figure out a way to get herself free of Douglas.

She just needed to get changed at Gingerbread Inn first.

But, when she'd hustled the two blocks through the cold and raced through the entrance, Zinnia was not at the front desk. In her place, a cold, steely stare met Jessamyn.

"Well, if it isn't the absent owner." Bluebeard cracked his knuckles. "Your payment is due. In full."

Chapter 35

Cliff

Once he'd closed the door to his past with Kiva, Cliff rushed back to Sweetwater Hotel. Something about his conversation with Draven Porter registered in his brain at last.

I haven't been fixing your plumbing—not since mid-summer.

Then, who had? Cliff needed a hard look at the books.

Tarquin stood at the front desk, singing "Santa Buddy," the part where the singer asks for a Rolex watch.

Jessamyn might approve. She was all about the money.

"Hey, Tarquin." Cliff headed past the check-in desk toward the workroom. "Did you change plumbers like we discussed?"

"Oh, hi." Tarquin looked up. "Why do you ask?" He was more guarded than usual, and he looked disheveled. His hair was normally slicked back, but a section had fallen over his eye. "What's going on?"

"Nothing." Cliff's senses went on high-alert, and caution kicked in. "It's late. Why don't you head home. You look wiped out."

"I am. Did you hear about our high-profile guest? I am doing everything to keep the rest of the top floor silent."

"What high-profile guest?"

"Douglas Queen."

He was here? Was Jessamyn—er, Sammie—with him? "Is that right? That should be good for publicity. Maybe even as good as placement on the state tourism website." Cliff kept his voice light, measured.

"That's only if he has a good stay." Tarquin rose. "I think I'll check with the concierge and make sure everything is copacetic for Mr. Queen."

"Maybe I should pay him a personal visit."

Tarquin balked. "Are you sure?"

"I'm sure." Cliff had to get a better look at that marriage certificate. He checked the computer to find out which room, and then rode the elevator and knocked on the TV star's door. "Mr. Queen." He stuck out a hand to shake.

"Sammie's Podunk boyfriend." Douglas Queen smirked at him. "Forgive me, but I don't have time for whatever confrontation you think we're going to have right now. There's a TV network waiting to interview me about how I pried her loose from your controlling prison here. How you all gaslighted her and convinced her I didn't want her. Then again, if you stay, you can explain your reasons for kidnapping her to all the breath-bated world." He jutted his chin. "It'll use up your fifteen minutes of fame, but what better cause than Sammie's ultimate happiness?"

Half of Cliff wanted to splutter in disbelief, and the other half wanted to make a fist and see if the guy had a glass jaw. "You're insane."

"Crazy? Crazy in love with Sammie Queen, *my wife*."

The facts didn't gel. Jessamyn couldn't have gone willingly with this guy. She'd been hiding from him. "If she's your wife, why did you have to offer a reward to learn where she was living?"

"Like I said, you kidnapped her and brainwashed her. She's been living as a total victim of Stockholm Syndrome. The world *loves* a good Stockholm Syndrome scenario. Come on in, we'll put a face to one of her captors." He beckoned Cliff toward a setup with studio lighting.

"Where's Jessamyn?" Cliff leaned into the room, craning his neck to see any sign of her.

"Oh, right. You've been calling her that. Jessamyn. Jess-SAM-myn. Sam. Sammie. Get it? We had a great time coming up with her brand. I'm disappointed she went back to her original hair color, when she looks so much better as a brunette." Douglas looked at his nails.

"You didn't answer me, but while I'm at it, here's another question. If you have a million bucks to throw away to a snitch about where she is, can't you just forget about the fact she *borrowed* money from you to start a business? She's honest and would've paid you back. You didn't have to terrorize her."

"What are you talking about? Sammie didn't take any money from me."

169

Cliff staggered and had to grab the door frame. "No?" Then who'd loaned her the money and pushed and pushed for her to repay, ruining what little peace she'd enjoyed in Sugarplum Falls? "Then who gave her the loan?"

"How should I know? Unless it was Tark the Shark. I mentioned him a few times, and she might've heard me."

"Who is that?"

"You should know." Douglas rolled his eyes. "My filming is starting."

"I repeat, where's Jessamyn?" Cliff stuck his foot in the closing door, stopping it.

"She's freshening up for the cameras." He held up a note in Jessamyn's handwriting.

She's really going back to him.

Or was she?

Downstairs, Cliff bypassed Tarquin, who was directing the staff about how to treat VIPs.

In the back office, he opened the business computer and did a search for *Porter's Plumbing.* Several files appeared, all familiar.

Then, a weirdly named file came up. *Backup of the Backup.* He clicked it.

Numbers in larger and larger amounts flashed as Cliff scrolled through the spreadsheet.

There was no way to absorb all of this in the amount of time he had. He sent it to his printer.

The town's clock tower struck nine bells. With a roar of furious blood-flow rushing in his ears, Cliff gripped the edges of the printout of the financial records of Sweetwater Hotel. None of them could be accurate! They all screamed falsification. And Cliff could think of no other possible suspect.

His best friend and business partner was embezzling.

Or worse.

Fingers shaking with rage, Cliff texted Andrew Kingston. *Want a job? Private investigating?*

Then, he downloaded the suspicious records and sent them to Andrew in an encrypted folder.

Look into this, would you? I'll pay you overtime and a rush fee.

A few moments later, Andrew texted back: *Got the files. I'm on it.*

Cliff called Andrew and gave him account numbers, names, dates. Then, he took a big risk by giving the attorney the passwords for access to all his cloud-based records. The truth would come out. Although, Cliff was pretty sure he already knew a lot of it, if not all. It stung like a million scorpions.

Everyone betrays me. Everyone.

Except Kingston, apparently. Just five minutes later, he texted with news.

Got something right off the bat. There's a "Plumber's Fund" column, but it redirects to your business partner's personal bank account.

Warning bells clanged in Cliff's ears. Nothing made sense!

Draven Porter's insistence that he hadn't repaired plumbing at Sweetwater Hotel in months made more sense now. Tarquin had been hiding something—something huge.

Chapter 36

Jessamyn

Bluebeard sported a new item of jewelry: brass knuckles that reflected the lobby Christmas tree's lights.

"What are you doing here? Where's my clerk?" she asked, backing away from the counter, her spine whacking the doors that had swung shut behind her. "I'm extremely busy tonight." She looked everywhere for any sign of Zinnia as she walked forward again.

Please let her be okay!

The clock in the breakfast nook cuckooed nine times. Bluebeard glanced at it and then menaced Jessamyn again.

"The boss is done waiting, Ms. Fleet, or whatever your real name is." The brass knuckles smashed against the man's palm, and his soul patch quivered as he spoke. "You look a lot more like Sammie today."

"Bernard," Jessamyn said softly, hoping to quell his fury by using the name he'd given when he'd first slunk into her life. Maybe her stalling would give the police a chance to identify him based on the security camera's footage, if the Sugarplum Falls police ever investigated this incident. They seemed more the types to give parking tickets and to throw pancake breakfasts. "Please, Bernard."

"Name's not Bernard, but I can tell you *Zinnia's* name. She's hoping you'll come through for her, I can tell you that."

"You have Zinnia!"

"She put up a fight, but yes."

Jessamyn's knees buckled, whacking the side of the check-in desk. If only she'd had the foresight to place a distress call button beneath the counter. But this was Sugarplum Falls! Nothing bad ever happened here.

Well, until Jessamyn drew it here with her bad karma.

"Don't hurt Zinnia. She didn't do anything wrong."

"No, but *you* did. You haven't paid back my boss in a timely manner, Sammie."

He kept calling her Sammie! How did he know—? A lump in her throat the size of a golf ball swelled. She couldn't muscle it down. Tears formed, spilling from her eyes. Cliff must have searched for Jessamyn online, and then alerted someone, and her identity and location had spread everywhere like lightning and wildfire combined. Which one of them had outed her to Douglas?

"Where's the money, Sammie?" he sneered. "Or do you prefer *Jess* these days?" His soul patch twitched, a blur of blue. "Isn't that what Cliff Rockingham calls you? His pet name for you?"

No one knew that fact except Cliff. No one! It was their little thing. "I have the money in the safe. Don't hurt Zinnia and it's yours." Please say he hadn't hurt her!

My carelessness put an innocent person in danger.

Bluebearded Not-Bernard trailed Jessamyn to the safe.

There had to be a way to keep herself from shrieking.

Calm thoughts. Calm thoughts.

At least the disaster of the plumbing had forced guests from the hotel and kept them safe.

At least she had some money set aside to hand over to save Zinnia, even though no amount would ever satiate Shark's thug.

At least Cliff wasn't here to be harmed, or Douglas—no matter how much Jessamyn hated both of them right now.

At least Jessamyn had returned to Gingerbread Inn and had intervened before Bluebeard went off the rails and burned the place to the ground, likely with Zinnia inside.

Zinnia had to be in the building somewhere. He wouldn't have risked missing Jessamyn's return by taking her somewhere else, other than maybe his vehicle.

She pulled out the cash box and fiddled with the combination, purposely messing up as she stalled for more time. "Where's Zinnia?" It opened too soon. She fumbled for a bag of any kind, and found a Gingerbread Inn-labeled cloth tote bag. She added the currency to the bag as slowly as possible. "I'm not handing this over until you tell me where she is."

"Good luck with that." He placed a meaty fist on her shoulder and pressed it hard enough to leave marks. "Just make sure every penny is there. This had better be all of it. My boss isn't a patient man."

Jessamyn clutched it to her chest and turned around. "Where is she?"

"Every dollar of it had better be there," he growled. "Or my boss will send someone worse than me." He ripped the bag from her grip and headed for the front door. Jessamyn chased after him. "Please!"

"Check room twelve." The door creaked and slammed shut.

In a flurry of adrenaline, Jessamyn grabbed one of the keys to room twelve and raced up the stairs. "Zinnia! Zinnia!" Her fingers barely controlled the key, but she opened the door and found Zinnia with a piece of duct tape over her mouth and zip-ties keeping her hands and feet bound. "Oh, Zinnia!"

Less than a minute later, Zinnia was free, thanks to a pair of scissors and a swift removal of the adhesive.

"That guy is a big fat—" Zinnia used some off-color comparisons. "I hope his danky blue soul patch gets stuck in a threshing machine. I hope he makes close personal friends with a wood-chipper. I hope his next guest-pillow at a hotel is a prickly pear cactus!" She brushed herself off and stomped three times. "I hope you called the police!"

"Will you call the police and make the report, Zin?" Jessamyn made fists and loosed them, unsure what to do. "I have something I have to do right now." She needed to get in touch with a lawyer about the marriage certificate. Did Sugarplum Falls have any attorneys? Was there enough crime or discord to employ one?

"I hope whatever you're so anxious to do involves telling some people the truth about your real name and your actual situation, Sammie."

"What? How do you know that name?" Jessamyn gulped. "How long have you known?"

"Don't worry, your secret has been safe with me for months. The whole time we've known each other."

Jessamyn's spine turned to jelly. "Who all knows?" Her eyes darted back and forth. "Who all did you tell?"

"No one, sweetie. But practically the whole town knows." Zinnia rubbed her wrists. "But don't get all scared. We care about you. We wouldn't be telling that famous creep-o who you are or where, no matter how much money he offers."

"That's so sweet!" Jessamyn threw her arms around Zinnia's neck. "But Douglas found me. He's taking me back to the city."

Zinnia pantomimed twisting a rag. "What I want to know is, who *did* tell, and when I get my hands on her—or him—I'll be doing the Hokey Pokey and turn him inside out."

"That doesn't make sense, but I have to get back to Douglas before he gets done with his video call. I have to reason with him."

Zinnia rolled her arm as if to hustle Jessamyn along. "Why are you here? You gotta get yourself free of that—" More choice comparisons.

There was no time to explain. "Just came to rescue you."

"I hope you didn't give that thug your money again."

"I did, but it sounded like I've seen the last of him." Jessamyn needed to get changed and get in touch with an attorney fast, before Douglas tore himself away from the mirror. "I have to go. Really."

"Anything I can help with?"

"Just call the police. And do you know a lawyer?"

"Me?!" Zinnia followed Jessamyn down the staircase. "What do I need to go calling Andrew Kingston for? I didn't commit the crime. I was the victim! No, you were. Anyhow—"

Andrew Kingston! "That's right!" Jessamyn hugged her at the base of the stairs. "I'll text him." She had his number thanks to their being in the Chamber of Commerce together.

"Zinnia. Lock the doors and turn on the No Vacancy sign. Wait for the police. I'll be back."

It was faster to run to Sweetwater Hotel from Gingerbread Inn than to start her car, drive, and park. The cold air invigorated as much as it solidified her resolve.

On the way, she sent a text to Andrew Kingston. *I need help. Stat!*

A reply came immediately. *I saw a news story that you'd been found. I thought I might hear from you.*

Man, had everyone actually known about her identity? And protected her? Sugarplum Falls was the best place to be.

She finished texting her request as she reached Sweetwater Hotel, gathered her wits, and squared her shoulders.

At the big, glass entrance of Cliff's hotel, she pushed the door open and stepped inside. The clock chimed nine thirty.

Running away isn't the answer. If I can reason with Douglas, I'll finally be free.

Could Douglas understand reason? He just had to—and she had to take that risk.

Over at the desk, however, a horrific sight greeted her: Cliff, his employee with the slicked-back hair, and Bluebeard all stood looking more than chummy. Cliff even grasped hold of her money bag. Slicked-Back Hair thumped Bluebeard on the back—giving him a jesting look.

Jessamyn stumbled backward, sinking into the shadows just outside the door, praying none of them had noticed her.

Cliff? Cliff had not only accepted the reward money from Douglas, but he was also in cahoots with Bluebeard?

Chapter 37

Cliff

Fifteen frustrating minutes passed, with no more word from Andrew. He couldn't stand the tension anymore. He had to confront Tarquin about this face to face, like a man.

Cliff strode out into the main room of Sweetwater Hotel.

Tarquin smiled down at the front desk computer screen. Like, with a gleeful, greedy grin. And he was singing that same weird, overtly materialistic Christmas song from earlier. "Hello, Cliff, my friend. Isn't this a fantastic night?"

"Sure." Cliff's spine tingled. A strong feeling to go back to his office filled his whole frame. "Just saying hi. Back in a few."

He ducked behind the wall that separated the front desk from the workroom just as a man came charging into the foyer through the main entrance of the hotel. His eyes were crazy, and he looked like he might be dangerous. He sported a soul patch in an unnatural color.

Quickly, Cliff inventoried the man's appearance, in case he had to make a police report later. *Five feet nine inches, medium build, yellowish-green eyes, and a flat-top haircut like ex-military who never left it behind. Oh, and that weird dyed-blue soul patch on his chin.*

"Take it, Shark. It's not all there, but I'm done with this shakedown. She and her clerk are going to call the cops, so you better believe I'm out of here. Don't tell me to come back. That's all the cash the lady had, and I checked everywhere, even hacked into her accounts. They're empty as my karate fist." He held out his palm, and brass knuckles glinted. "Not that I can't do some damage with it when I want."

"Shut up, Nardo," Tarquin growled.

Nardo threw a cloth tote bag on the counter. It had the logo for

Gingerbread Inn emblazoned on the side. "Take it, and then leave me out of anything else."

Cliff shrank back—but only for a split second. No *way* was the financial exchange for an extortion scam happening in *his* hotel.

Because that's exactly what it had to be, right? Cliff might live in Sugarplum Falls, but when he'd been a homeless pre-teen, he'd seen things while on the fringes.

Nobody used the Sweetwater Hotel as a meeting place for crime.

Cliff strode out into the open and placed his hand on the tote bag with the Gingerbread Inn label. "What've you got here? This isn't a Sweetwater Hotel item. You have the wrong hotel, sir." Cliff leveled a look at the thug, who stood his ground.

Bold.

The brass knuckles glinted in the overhead lighting.

Could I take a guy with brass knuckles? He gulped—not in fear but to swallow it.

"Who's your friend, Tarquin? What's going on?"

Tarquin broke into a laugh, as if this situation could be shoved under the rug or brushed aside as a pure misunderstanding. "Cliff, hey. This is a misunderstanding. It's not what it looks like."

"I hope not, because it looks illegal, Tarquin."

"Tark, I wasn't kidding," said the thug. "I'm done being your henchman. She called the cops, and they'll finger me, and I'll get ten years. I'm not going back to the big house. Not for you. Not for nobody."

The front doors of the hotel clunked, as if someone had passed through them, but no one was there.

Cliff redirected his gaze to Tarquin. "Not looking great, *Tark*." For a thousand reasons, and most of them led back to his lying, cheating, embezzling, extortionist business partner.

Tark the Shark! Douglas had used that name—had chortled that Cliff would obviously know the guy.

Jessamyn had called her intimidating creditor a shark.

How could this all have been happening right under Cliff's nose? Under his *roof!*

"Not great at all." Venom laced his words, but he smiled through clenched teeth.

"Nardo, I've always been fair with you. More than fair."

The guy with the blue beard shook off Tarquin's placating slaps on the back. "Not looking great to me, neither. Tark the Shark," Nardo said. "I'm done working for you. Shake down your own defenseless women."

Defenseless women, as in Jessamyn, owner of this tote bag of cash.

"What all has Tark made you do, Nardo?" Cliff asked while staring a molten-lead hole through Tarquin.

But the guy strode out the door—where Jessamyn stood outside, watching the whole exchange. Sheer horror marred her face. She turned and broke into a run.

Tarquin would have to explain later. Cliff raced after her, all the way down the street to Gingerbread Inn.

"No!" she yelled. "You stay away from me! You liar! You snitch!"

Snitch! Liar? "Jessamyn!" Cliff chased her to the porch of her hotel, where she went inside and locked the front door. Cliff pressed his head against the glass, his heart chugging like a steam train's engine. "Please! Listen to me?"

"Are you kidding me?" she said through the glass, her voice muffled. "You were just holding a bag of money and chumming it up with a man who has made my life a living terror for over a year. You were *smiling* with him, Cliff. I knew it! I can't trust you, and I can't trust anyone. Now, go away!"

Thank goodness he hadn't texted an admission of his being Santa Cliff. That would've muddied the waters even further right now.

"I can't go away, Jessamyn. I need to know if you're leaving with Douglas."

Just then, who should zoom up to the steps of Gingerbread Inn but Valerie Vanderhoff sitting in *The Warrior.*

"Mr. Rockingham!" She used her most warrior-like voice. "Are you aware that the trash can in front of your hotel is overflowing with recyclable plastic bottles that will harm the environment? I was standing outside your hotel, attempting to clean it up when you charged past, ignoring me, and came to bother this poor woman, who—for the record—takes care of her hotel's front trash can." She gave him the world's stinkiest stink eye.

"It's the middle of the night, Valerie, and now's not a good time." Cliff backed up against the glass of the front door to Gingerbread Inn.

Jessamyn still stood in her lobby, as if waiting for him to provide a real explanation. If only she could understand everything at a glance—that this was all Tarquin!

"Please, Jessamyn," he pleaded. "It's important that I tell you something right now."

"You can't come in."

"Then, can you come out here? Please?"

Jessamyn shut her eyes, tilted her head back, and then shook herself and came out to join him in the cold. Clearly, he wasn't welcome inside.

"Did you take Douglas's reward money?"

"What?" Cliff's heart clutched. "I can't believe you're even asking me that."

"I can't believe you're deflecting and not answering the question. Why were you holding a bag of money that thug took from me? Why were you hanging out with Bluebeard and the Shark? I can't trust you."

"Why can't she trust you, Cliff Rockingham?" Valerie Vanderhoff climbed the stairs and again inserted herself where she didn't belong. "The fact that you're a known litterer? She does need to understand that before she gets serious with you. It should drive the opinion of any sane woman."

"Excuse me, Mrs. Vanderhoff." Cliff's fists clenched and he drew a calming breath. "Can I discuss recycling with you another time?"

Mrs. Vanderhoff pushed out her chin, but then she huffed in defeat. "Fine."

Whew. Cliff turned around to face Jessamyn. "I'd never take that reward!"

"But you did tell him. You told Douglas I was in Sugarplum Falls."

"Not me." But had Lark? She knew—she'd been the one to inform Cliff. "I'm so sorry, Jessamyn. I wouldn't hurt you for all the money in the world."

180

"But you know who did tell, right?"

"I—" Would Lark really? As in, to protect Cliff from Jessamyn? Lark thought the worst of Jess—without reason. "Jessamyn, are you going back to Douglas?"

"I don't know if I am."

Those words gave him a glimmer of hope. "Can I convince you otherwise?"

"There's a lot to work out, legally."

"But you didn't marry him, did you?"

"I don't know. I left him at the altar."

Cliff's brain turned into the Norwegian painting where the man screams and melts simultaneously. "You left him at the altar?" That changed everything. "No apologies? No explanations?" Sure, he'd forgiven Kiva when she'd begged him to, but that wedding disaster had been ages ago, when they were too young.

"I don't feel sorry about it one bit."

Unfortunately, Mrs. V hadn't left. In fact, she still rode her freight-train of warrioressness at full speed. "I'm only giving you leeway, Mr. Rockingham, because you waded into the lake for me four weeks ago and retrieved that blue bottle, the one with the scroll inside. Did you read the message? I bet you did. You probably tried to save the person who wrote it, knowing you. You always demand so much of yourself. What did you do to help the poor forlorn litterer? I hope it involved a short lecture on the sanctity of our lakes and rivers."

As Mrs. Vanderhoff's rant wound to a dull roar, the tightness on Jessamyn's expression melted. It went from disappointment in Cliff, to shock, to horror, to dismay, to fear, to betrayal—all in the course of that brief diatribe.

"*You're* Santa Claus from San Nouveau?" Her voice was a thread, quivering and taut with disbelief.

Cliff couldn't deny it. Not even physically. Paralysis struck. "I—I've wanted to tell you."

Jessamyn backed away. "Get. Away. From me." Stomping inside, she shut off the light in the foyer of her hotel, pointed fiercely at the glowing *No Vacancy* sign, and disappeared beyond his view.

No vacancy.

No room for Cliff's explanations, his empty excuses, or his stark admissions.

No room for Cliff.

Chapter 38

Jessamyn

Pure, unmitigated betrayal.

At her laptop in her sad little bedroom, she stabbed her fingers at the keyboard, sending one final message to Santa Claus in San Nouveau.

Yes, I left Douglas at the altar. No, I'm not sorry. Not one iota. And I never will be.

Look, I'm through being someone's project. Don't contact me again, in any way, shape, or form. Goodbye, Cliff.

Jessamyn slammed her computer shut with so much force she could've broken the screen.

Douglas was probably still on camera at Sweetwater Hotel, expecting her return.

No way could she go there to give him her ultimatum or her breakup speech. That place was infested with liars—including Blue Soul Patch. Why had he ended up there with Cliff?

Was Cliff in on the extortion? Had he ratted out her whereabouts to Douglas at the same time as being in cahoots with Not-Bernard? And why? For the money? Because he was operating in the red?

None of it computed, and yet it all computed at the same time. Every arrow pointed right back to Cliff Rockingham. Worst of all, he'd been duping her by pretending to be someone he wasn't—or at least by pretending not to be someone he was.

Oh, her head spun!

It all came down to one *glaring* fact: Cliff lied.

Even Douglas Queen never *tricked* Jessamyn.

Cliff had out-and-out deceived her. And worse, betrayed her.

Meanwhile, Douglas, for all his faults, had at a minimum been up-front about his identity as a user of people, about his intention to use Jessamyn as a project, about his growing feelings for her, and, ultimately, he'd proposed. Whether it had been to feed his enormous ego or not, Douglas had not lied.

Cliff. Lied. As a rule.

There was no going back to Cliff.

Never.

Not ever.

Even if her heart begged for it.

I have to stop right now. I have to stop depending on others and work to solve my own problems.

Bluebeard wouldn't be returning. However, that didn't suggest that her finances were safe. Not as long as Tark the Shark was still out there. He'd hire someone else to persecute her in Bluebeard's place. Maybe someone worse.

If only there were a way to get out from under the thumb of the man she'd foolishly borrowed so much money from, the man Bernard referred to as Tark the Shark.

Her phone rang. "Hi, Jessamyn. This is Andrew Kingston, your attorney. I have some information for you."

Chapter 39

Cliff

Cliff stared at the stack of emails he'd shared with Jessamyn—the correspondence he should've cut off weeks ago. Or should never have begun in the first place.

I left Douglas at the altar, and I'm not sorry.

Fifteen minutes ago, if Jessamyn had opened the door of Gingerbread Inn and allowed Cliff to give his explanation about the events of the evening, he would have given anything in the world to do so.

Then, this email's notification had sounded, and he'd opened it assuming she would have a few quiet words of goodbye.

Fat chance. Instead, the content was covered with barbs that gouged him deeper than anything she could've imagined.

Left him at the altar. And she wasn't sorry about it. Married him, and was sorry. But pretended she hadn't married the guy. It was such a tangled web of nonsense and fiction and deceit!

Every old wound Cliff had received from Kiva ripped open again in a single moment, laying him bare and raw and bleeding.

Left someone at the altar and didn't care. Jessamyn was as heartless and cold as the younger version of Kiva. If he were to let Jessamyn into his heart, she'd very likely do the same thing to Cliff as she'd done to Douglas Queen.

Forget it. Cliff was not treading into that territory again. Not a chance.

As deep as the betrayal by Tarquin stabbed, Jessamyn's true character coming to light pierced him even more.

Cliff closed his eyes, as if it could shut everything out. As if it could make the truth go away.

Chapter 40

Jessamyn

Morning dawned. Jessamyn had barred herself in Gingerbread Inn. No matter how many times Douglas pounded on the front door, she'd kept it locked.

"I know you're in there, Sammie," he'd hollered. "Tarquin told me you're the owner of Gingerbread Inn. He said he'll buy it from you. You won't be out anything."

Wrong. She'd be out everything.

Douglas had camped out on the front steps for several hours, dialed the desk phone nonstop, and demanded she come out until a local police officer came and asked him to quiet down. This was Sugarplum Falls, and he might be famous, but he was disturbing the peace.

After that, Douglas had holed up in his car, watching the place.

Great. Under siege in her own hotel.

Bleary-eyed and sick to her soul, Jessamyn made her way to the breakfast nook and poured herself a bowl of cereal. No guests needed breakfast, since they'd all been rerouted to Sweetwater Hotel for the past night, while the carpets finished drying and the flood-smell went away.

Exhausted, she wrote a few words on a napkin. Then, she asked Zinnia to tape them to the glass front door.

Douglas, I need a breather.

"He saw me," Zinnia reported. "He raced up the steps and read the note. Then, he pointed at his watch and shouted, 'Tell her to meet me at Sweetwater Hotel at six tonight.'"

Six? It still stunk, but at least Jessamyn could breathe for the day.

Running away was a bad option, as she knew from experience. A useless option.

Talking to him face-to-face, while terrible, could be worse.

I miss Cliff. I hate him, but I miss him.

Zinnia limped back into the room, after getting herself a sweet roll and a mug of cocoa.

"You all right?" Jessamyn jumped to get her a chair.

"As soon as the ibuprofen kicks in I will be." Zinnia plopped down and took a bite of her pastry. "Weird not to have any guests here. Makes the place feel like a ghost town in the Old West."

Yeah. "I'm really sorry for what I did to you, Zinnia." Jessamyn had never intended to put her coworker in danger. "I'll make it up to you somehow, someday."

"You make it sound like … like you're leaving."

"I had a good, long talk with myself last night."

"And?" Zinnia set down the sweet roll and wiped her fingers on a napkin. "I don't like the look on your face, Jessamyn. It's a *giving up* face."

Why not give up? Gingerbread Inn was a dream, but dreams ended. People woke up. *Like I woke up to the fact Cliff is a liar and probably took my loan payments* and *Douglas's reward money.*

"I'm not giving up, I'm making a new choice." The words had an empowering lilt, but they were still code for surrender. "It's hard to say goodbye, especially to something I knew would've made my grandma happy, but it's over. The world knows where I am now, and Douglas insists."

"Insists what?"

What, exactly? Well, Jessamyn knew without even having the direct conversation with him. "He insists that I come back to Darlington with him. Start a life together. I am so tired, Zinnia. Tired of running, tired of fighting. Douglas isn't that bad. He makes me feel beautiful and wanted. Why not just go? It'd be so easy."

"You'll do no such thing!" Zinnia slammed her cocoa mug down hard. "I refuse to believe what I'm hearing, Jessamyn. You're not that girl. You are someone who fights!"

How could Zinnia believe that? "No, I'm someone who runs away." Case in point, her current life, and the shambles she'd made of it. "I endangered you by being such a coward. I'm sorry."

"Stop apologizing to me and do the right thing!"

"I'm *married* to him. He has the paperwork to prove it."

"You didn't say *I do*, did you?"

No, she hadn't. But the marriage license proved otherwise. "I signed on the dotted line." She stared at the untouched cereal that grew soggy. "The eyes of the law insist." Probably, but Andrew hadn't said he had *good news* in the text to her. He'd just said news, which implied *bad news*.

He'd be over later that morning to deliver it in person.

"You need an annulment." Zinnia frowned. "Like Esther Lang got."

"On what grounds?" Though, it was true—the mayor's daughter had obtained one. It just seemed so impossible for Jessamyn, considering Douglas's fame and his infinitely deep pockets.

Jessamyn needed to tell someone. Someone who'd truly get her feelings.

"Esther had a rough go with a broken marriage. Maybe you should talk with her. Me, I only married my husband and we stayed together until he went to heaven. Then, I found you." Zinnia's face softened. "Honestly, Jessamyn. I don't get why Douglas Queen wants you to come back so much. Other than you *must* be the best thing that ever happened to him."

That was an easy one. "He has this insatiable need to show the world he wasn't rejected. He has to be *wanted*. By literally *everyone*. He wins over every holdout."

"Ah."

"He's already announced that I've been located with a head injury after a car accident landed me in a new town with a new identity."

"Amnesia?" Zinnia snorted and rolled her eyes. "No one's buying that, I hope."

"Amnesia." Far-fetched, true. "It's completely appropriate to the soap opera life I lived while I dated him."

"You have to get away, girl! Jessamyn!"

"I don't know." Jessamyn exhaled, just so tired. Just so done. "Look, might as well start calling me Sammie."

"But, you're not Sammie. You're Jessamyn, and you own Gingerbread

Inn, and you're your grandma's granddaughter, and you make the world a better place with hope and healing for all your guests." Zinnia popped the last bite of her sweet roll. "There. We solved it."

"Solved what?"

"The fact that you're going to lawyer up. And you're going to live the life you want to live—with the man you're destined to live it with. Or without one. But it's your choice! Full stop."

Lawyer up? Jessamyn's chest buzzed in the aftermath of the energy of Zinnia's pep talk. "Lawyer up? For an annulment?" she asked.

"Exactly." Zinnia rolled her eyes. "You already contacted Andrew Kingston. He's the best lawyer in town."

"He's the only lawyer in town."

A voice inside Jessamyn said, *do this.* For once, Jessamyn saw a way through!

"Good." Zinnia picked up her plate. "You'll explain everything to that man when he comes. I have an errand to run."

Jessamyn steeled herself for her meeting with the attorney in a couple of hours.

Her nerves failed, though, as she got dressed after showering. Would an attorney even understand?

Tell Esther, Zinnia's voice re-echoed in her mind. Jessamyn put her hair up, and called her friend. "Esther? Do you have time for a story?"

"Is it the story I've been waiting all these months for you to tell me?" So, Esther knew too? "I'll be right over with cranberry turnovers from Sugarbabies."

Telling it all to someone who could understand the depths of the agony—from the side of the person who ended things—liberated her, a bird freed from a cage at last. "Thank you for coming—and for listening," she said as Esther came through the door.

"You deserve to be happy, Jessamyn." Esther hugged her, wiped a stray bit of white glaze from Jess's chin, and then smiled. "You will love Andrew. He's not only empathetic, he's able to see solutions in a flash."

"You could tell I'm balking?" Was it that obvious? *What will Douglas do when he gets hit with a lawyer?* "Douglas has only the highest-priced legal help on his side."

"Andrew can handle it."

Jessamyn hoped so.

"Well, I'm only going to ask his advice. Informational meeting. I can't make any snap decisions." Snap decisions had ruined her in the past. "But I'll be honest, it'd be so much easier just to give in, play married to Douglas, and then wait for him to divorce me after he tires of me."

But then she'd have to do things with him she never wanted to do—married things. And now that she'd fallen in love with someone else, she'd be disloyal in her heart.

The dilemma impaled her, like the horns of a raging bull.

"No way are you going to do that, Jessamyn." Esther hugged her. "Let Andrew help you."

"I—I'm going to at least get some information."

An hour later, Jessamyn was seated across her desk from Andrew Kingston, attorney at law. "Lawyer-client privilege is in force. Tell me everything—and what you want to have happen."

As the details spilled forth, she kept her composure. Christmas miracles did exist!

Telling him was not only like flying from the cage, it was soaring so high the cage was nothing but a tiny dot in the distance.

Best of all, she was taking control of her own life. Hiring legal help wasn't running away from her problems, and it sat squarely outside the definition of letting others solve her problems.

Chapter 41

Cliff

Cliff paced the lobby of Sweetwater Hotel.

Instead of confronting him with preliminary accusations about the extortion that Tarquin might be able to explain away—and that might make Tarquin skip town—Cliff had given the guy a big list of tasks to handle for the morning. Keeping the man hard at work and in the semi-dark about Cliff's suspicions seemed like the smartest option—for now. Sure, there'd been the brief incident with Nardo, but Tarquin was the type to hope that others swept suspicious moments aside, based on past character experience.

Cliff wasn't sweeping anything until he had proof from Andrew one way or another.

Meanwhile, the world had nothing to offer Cliff in the way of hope. No girlfriend, no best friend, and a business partner who was stealing him blind, and possibly harassing innocent people—with a home base at his own Sweetwater Hotel.

What killed Cliff most was the fact he'd fallen for Jess—truly felt deep love for the woman. Why? Why lie to him? Why keep the fact of her flight from her ex at the altar from Cliff? If she'd told him herself, been up front about it, things might have been different.

A tall woman with a crazy hairstyle strode into the hotel. She peeled off her scarf, revealing her face.

"Zinnia?" he asked. Unmistakably, she was the clerk from Gingerbread Inn. "What is going on? Do you have more plumbing problems? I can't take any more guests today. We only had the top floor remaining, and someone bought out the rest of those rooms." A blessing and a curse.

"It's not that. I'm here with a message."

From Jessamyn? His eyes must have narrowed, because Zinnia frowned at him.

"It's not from Jessamyn, but it's about her." She lifted her scarf and wound it around her face again, but just before covering her mouth, she said, "Call Esther Lang. Tell her I sent you. Ask her Jessamyn's story, and tell her it's life or death."

"Esther Lang? The mayor's daughter?"

"How many Esther Langs do you know, fool?" Zinnia strode back out of Sweetwater Hotel, leaving Cliff with a choice to make. But it wasn't a hard choice. More information was what his soul craved, even if it feared that information more.

***

An hour later, Cliff sat across the table at The Cider Press from Esther Lang.

"I take it this is not your Mr. Darcy moment." Esther pulled a frown at him. "Or, your Mr. Bingley moment, as the case may be. Whatever, you shouldn't be doubting our girl Jessamyn, you know. She's as pure as the driven snow."

"You do know she left Douglas Queen *at the altar,* right?" That phrase should be a rusty barb to Esther the same as it was to Cliff.

"Because he had a god complex." She rolled her eyes.

"Because he's famous? A lot of famous people have egos. She knew that going in, I'm sure."

"Cliff, you're not listening. He thought he'd *created* her. He fell in love with his so-imagined creation, not with the woman herself, the goodness of her heart. He knew nothing of her inner self. All he cared about was the appearance of her, the dark-haired automaton he'd fashioned."

Jessamyn *had* mentioned a Pygmalion thing. But wasn't that just her fiancé being an egoist about wedding plans and making them too overblown? "Go on. I'm listening."

"Keep that up, please. You'll be glad you did."

Esther launched into a recap of Jessamyn's wedding day. She'd tried to leave her hair down, and Douglas had disagreed—as he had done with a hundred other details about their wedding—and her parents had backed Douglas's opinion. When Jessamyn saw the writing on the wall, that Douglas would forever be micromanaging her life, and that her parents didn't support her, she bolted.

However, with her grandma Ginger's recent death, she'd had nowhere to run. Three months, she'd gone into hiding, unsure what to do, other than knowing she wanted to live better than she'd been living. In a moment of weakness, she'd borrowed money from an unscrupulous source, one she'd overheard Douglas mentioning with a business partner sometime or other, not realizing that the lender was nothing but a low-profile loan shark. She'd assumed his *Shark* moniker had something to do with investments, like on a famous reality television program.

Though that choice would turn out disastrously, in the meantime, it had allowed her to open a hotel in Sugarplum Falls, after she met Esther in Los Angeles, and Esther had gushed about the virtues of small-town life.

"So you can see, she was alone and in deep water."

"Douglas didn't lend her the money?" He knew this, but he felt compelled to double check.

"No, of course not. She was hiding from him."

Good point. That settled any vestigial doubts for Cliff, and redirected all suspicions back at Tarquin. Tark the Shark? How could Cliff not have been aware of an extortion ring centered in his own hotel?

"So, he gave her a makeover? That was her complaint?"

Esther huffed. "Didn't you ever watch the show?"

"What show?"

Esther leveled a look at him. "*Douglas Creates a Goddess*. Hello? Well, I guess the official title is *Queen of the Queendom*, but everyone just refers to it by the fan name."

"I'm running a hotel. I don't watch much TV." Particularly not reality shows.

"It's been on the air for years." Esther huffed. "Anyway, Douglas falls for his creations every time. He's married several of those women—and then left them within six months."

Bile rose in Cliff's throat. "And Jessamyn fell for that anyway?" She seemed far too bright for that! Too self-assured, as well!

Maybe he didn't know her as well as he should. She'd hinted at shame about her past weakness, at being too willing to be molded, about her parents' pressure, about her unsure self-image, about being afraid of everyone's opinion.

But he'd never dreamed something as huge as this was why.

Lark told me like it should be a category 5 storm warning. But I downgraded that hurricane.

He should've taken heed—and been more compassionate.

Leaving a guy like that at the altar actually sounded like the only possible escape route.

"But if she knew the format, she still was too smart to be manipulated." He had to think the best of her.

"It'd been a few years since he'd allowed himself to propose, and the whole viewing audience was pulling for them. Douglas and Sammie were practically one of those combined-names couples, though theirs didn't sound right together. No one could make one work. Dou-mmie went around social media for a while."

Dummy. That sounded about right. But applied to himself for not listening better, for not supporting her.

Geez. Cliff dragged his hand down his cheek. A lot of things now made more sense, but not everything.

"He put out a reward, trying to find her. Didn't that mean he was sincere?"

"You should read a *little* more celebrity news, my friend." Esther pulled up an article on her phone. "Look. He claimed terrorists kidnapped her."

So Douglas hadn't been lying about the kidnapping thing? Or about pinning it on the people of Sugarplum Falls? Cliff recoiled. If that news went out, if Sugarplum Falls were implicated in an albeit absurd kidnapping plot, that could turn public opinion against the place instantly. It would ruin the whole town's economy far worse than any lack of snow on the ski slopes!

"Why? Why would he say something so unbelievable?"

"To deflect rumors that she left him based on *his* qualities. And his audience gobbles up the unbelievable." Eye roll.

"What an ego-motivated move!"

"Jessamyn's choice to leave him at the altar and then to evaporate from the public eye was not only rational but also courageous."

"Yeah." He'd seen that, too.

"Some would argue that she shouldn't have let it get that far, but under the pressure of the public eye a show like that might produce, and how young she was, and the power imbalance—it all looks a lot more understandable."

"Reasonable, even." Cliff shut his eyes.

Forgivable.

Early in their emails when he'd been masquerading as Santa Cliff, JW had mentioned never wanting to be someone's project ever again.

Well, no wonder!

Meanwhile, Cliff had been chucking salt in that wound unwittingly. What an insensitive lout thing to do.

"Answer me this, Esther. Is she married to him?"

"He says so, and she says not." She grimaced. "It's murky. I know she's trying to sort that out."

"She is?"

"A few hours ago, she asked me to come by. I recommended she hire Andrew Kingston to sort it out. He helped me get an annulment. I don't know if that's what Jessamyn wants. She doesn't know what she wants. Other than the fact that until a few hours ago, I'm sure she wanted you."

"But she doesn't anymore? Did she say that?" The way he'd treated her, and the lies he'd told—he didn't deserve her love. "I've got to make things right with her, Esther."

"It's your Sherlock Holmes light-bulb moment, I see." Esther reached across and punched him in the arm. "Good luck. How are you going to do it?"

He had no idea. "I'll let you know. Thanks, Esther."

"Don't thank me yet. I haven't told you the worst part of it."

"Worst?" Cliff asked.

"She's closing Gingerbread Inn."

"What!"

"She says now that the world knows where she is, thanks to whomever tipped off Douglas about her location, she'll never have any peace, for one, and for another, the person who has been pressing her for loan repayment will never relent. She is letting Gingerbread Inn go and …"

"And?" Cliff couldn't breathe. He couldn't lose her! Not when his heart finally understood her reasons, not when he could allow himself to love her fully, not when it was time to beg on his knees for forgiveness! "And what will she do if she leaves?"

"And she doesn't know yet. Maybe go back to Darlington with Douglas Queen. Path of least resistance."

"Esther! No!" That couldn't happen. "I thought you said annulment was in the air."

"Going back with Douglas Queen might have perks. Being the man's wife for a while could be an indirect path to what she wants. Jessamyn is resourceful. She's not going to stick to Plan A if it isn't working and there's Plan B, C, or D."

Cliff panicked. "Perks? Like, money? And fame?" And honeymoon activities?

"No! Do you know her at all? Geez. Like getting the spotlight off herself. Former wives of TV celebrities fade quickly. It might be a path to the non-fame she is seeking."

Former wives. "So she'd play married and then divorce him?"

"She figures he would divorce *her* once he tires of her. Look, the girl has been put in an awful spot. And the people she actually loves and cares about haven't been there for her, *Cliff.*" Esther leveled a mean look at him. "She doesn't need a rescuer, but she does deserve loyalty. And people not jumping to conclusions about her motives."

Esther's words skewered him. Cliff jumped up, nearly spilling his cup of hot cider. "Thanks, Esther." He shook her hand. "I appreciate it more than I can say."

He rushed out of The Cider Press and into the cold, nearly slamming into a Goodwill Santa with a bucket and a bell.

There was no more time to waste. Cliff had to do something to fix all the idiotic things he'd done to hurt her. Jess was the last person on earth who deserved to be hurt.

Cliff had to make this huge.

Chapter 42

Jessamyn

At midmorning of the longest day of Jessamyn's life, the now-closed Gingerbread Inn had been devoid of guests for the past several days, since the water-main break, so it shouldn't have felt twice as empty when Jessamyn packed up her few personal items into three suitcases and a box and placed them in her jeep.

Then, she went back inside Gingerbread Inn for one last look around. Now, all she had to do was wait for Andrew Kingston to show up.

Part of her ponytail came loose and fell into her eyes. She shoved it back as Zinnia came through the lobby with her own box of belongings—probably chock full of caftans.

"I'm gonna miss this." Zinnia gave Jessamyn a hug. "You sure you can't stay? When he was zip-tying me, Bluebeard muttered stuff about never coming back to Sugarplum Falls, that this wasn't what he'd signed up for. I think you're safe."

"Maybe from that guy, but guys like Tark the Shark always have another thug lined up to do their bidding. I guess I'm just tired."

"You do know Cliff Rockingham had a girl leave him at the altar. That's why he freaked out so bad when you said you stood up Douglas for your wedding. Sorry, I was eavesdropping. I couldn't help it."

"Don't worry about eavesdropping. We were in public." Jessamyn sighed. "And yeah, he told me about his ex." But not about the leaving at the altar thing, just that she'd been a gold-digger. "Besides, Esther did talk to him, and I don't see him standing here asking me to stay."

I look like a gold-digger to Cliff. He thinks I only cared about Douglas's money. He probably thinks I stole money from Douglas and skipped town on our wedding day.

Well, no wonder he hated her, was happily letting her go.

"You're slumping, girl. What are you going to do? Don't say you're going back to Douglas Queen."

"I'm his wife." Jessamyn's throat constricted as she spoke the words, and her voice cracked. "I think. Andrew Kingston said he has news."

The front door thumped closed.

"His wife? Are you sure about that?" a man's voice boomed through the air. "Hi, Jessamyn. Nice to see you again." Andrew Kingston looked officially like an attorney in his three-piece suit. "Do you want me to share the results of my research with you in private?"

Zinnia saluted. "I'm out of here!" She dashed to the coat tree and picked up her spacious wool cloak. "But can I beg for an update later?" She rubbed her hands together in begging. "Please?"

"If there's good news," Jessamyn said, and Zinnia left. "Well?" she asked Andrew.

"I have bad news and good news. Which do you want first?"

Jessamyn sucked in a sharp breath. Any more bad news and she'd burst.

"She wants the good news first!" Through the door strode Lisa Lang, mayor of Sugarplum Falls. "That's why I'm here." The woman's presence filled the whole lobby.

"Hello, Mayor Lang." Jessamyn shook the woman's alarmingly firm handshake. "Merry Christmas."

"Indeed! For you, especially." The mayor looked around. "Why does Gingerbread Inn look like a Halloween movie set instead of the bustling poster child of the state's top Christmas town? Where is everyone? And I thought it was supposed to smell like spices in here. It's too faint. Should I buy you a pumpkin spice candle? Easy fix!"

"What's going on, Lisa?" Andrew might be the only person assertive enough to put the mayor back on the rails. "Is everything all right?"

"More than all right!" She quit inspecting the hotel and turned back to Jessamyn. "You're officially the face of the state's tourism website. Well, Gingerbread Inn is. And if you want to be, you can have your face on there, too."

Uh, that was the last thing Jessamyn needed—more public face-time. "No pictures of me, please."

"But do you want the placement?"

"Of course! Thank you!" For a second, it felt so real, reaching the goal she'd been striving for all month. "Except, I mean, are you sure? Gingerbread Inn is so small, and—"

And it's going out of business. She couldn't bring herself to utter the words yet. That would make it too real, and Jessamyn dreaded a public breakdown.

"Totally sure. You earned it! Solo placement, sweetie."

"Solo? But I thought they wanted to feature two lodgings, one large hotel and one small. What about Cliff?" The words came out small, the mouse having returned.

"Cliff? He's the one who requested it. He asked to be removed from consideration."

"But he needed placement, too! His hotel—" Jessamyn stopped herself. Cliff would likely have all the money he needed now, thanks to getting the reward money from Douglas.

"What about his hotel?" Mayor Lang said.

"His hotel is iconic," she backtracked, shoving her hands in her pockets. "It's the true face of Sugarplum Falls for tourists."

"Not anymore. That's this place. If you erase the Halloween abandoned-house vibe, I mean. Where is everyone?"

"There was a flood." Jessamyn pulled her hands from her pockets. "Mayor Lang, I think I have something I'd better tell you."

Andrew Kingston stepped between Jessamyn and the mayor, staring down Jessamyn. "It's *thank you, Mayor Lang,* isn't it?" He urged her with his eyes, and then turned back toward the elected official. "Lisa, I hate to interrupt this celebration of great news, but would it be okay if I finish up this official lawyer-client meeting with Miss Fleet? I'm due at the courthouse soon."

"Of course!" Mayor Lang pushed him aside and hugged Jessamyn. "We're so happy you're in town, Jessamyn. I can't gush enough about how your lodgings have created a domino effect of getting everyone else to level up their establishments' authentic and personal flairs. You started it, and I only wish I'd been an investor in Gingerbread Inn. It's big—and it's only going to get bigger."

She turned to leave, but Jessamyn stopped her. "Just one last thing, Mayor. When did Cliff Rockingham say he didn't want to be featured on the website?"

"Twenty minutes ago."

"Why would he do that?" Jessamyn asked, her voice cracking.

Mayor Lang's eyes twinkled. "I think that should be self-evident." She patted her heart rhythmically—bad-dum, bad-dum, bad-dum. Then, she winked like she'd orchestrated everything around her personally, and left.

Twenty minutes ago? He'd been thinking of her, helping her, not out joyriding in his new luxury truck or hiring every contractor in the city to rework Sweetwater Hotel? Not having a celebration meal with Bluebeard and Shark about her demise?

Maybe he really didn't turn me in. But I'll bet he knows the person who did.

She soured again.

When the door shut, Andrew turned the lock. "Enough interruptions." From inside his briefcase, he pulled a large envelope, which he dumped out. "This is the marriage certificate you signed."

"How did you get that?" Jessamyn's hands flew to her mouth. She'd stealthily replaced it last night, after taking a photo and sending it to Andrew. "Did Douglas Queen give that to you? I can't see him handing it over to anyone. Even a lawyer with a subpoena."

"Unless it was worthless to him."

"How could it be worthless? Contracts are contracts, and I signed, Mr. Kingston. That is my signature, and I can't deny that in or out of court."

"Call me Andrew, since we'll be Sugarplum Falls neighbors."

Uh, about that. "Probably not, to be honest. I'm closing Gingerbread Inn." Shuttering her dream. "I should've told Lisa Lang, but I chickened out. As you can see, I've got more going wrong in my world than just my marriage, Andrew."

"Well, let's talk about the marriage first." He unfolded the piece of paper. "When you contacted me, I could have gone to Mr. Queen's lawyer, but I decided to jump the line and go see him instead."

"Unorthodox."

"Yeah, but he was in town, and he seemed anxious to speak to me directly, to show me his evidence, and to convince me to convince *you* to see things his way."

It was just like Douglas to use backdoor methods to get to people, including to Jessamyn. He'd won over Mom and Dad, used them to manipulate her into getting as close to the marriage day as she had. Without that, she never would've put on a wedding dress that morning. "And?" she asked.

"And, when I saw him, he was very matter-of-fact about the documentation of your marriage."

"I know." Jessamyn's heart fell. "Did he send it with you as a means to convince me?" She'd never specified whether she wanted the bad news first, but it sure seemed like Andrew was spooning it up for her.

"You asked about the possibility of an annulment," said Andrew.

"Honestly, I doubt he will consent to an annulment. I know Douglas Queen. He's not the type to give in or give up. Ever." Case in point, the eighteen-month manhunt he'd conducted to find Jessamyn. "I just wish I knew who tipped him off to my location." If it were Cliff, or someone he'd told …

"I'll get to that."

Jessamyn's eyes flew wide. "You will? How would you know any of that?"

"First things first, please." He pointed to Jessamyn's signature on the line. "Now, I noticed that you signed the certificate Sammie Westwood."

"Yes."

"That's not your legal name."

A knocking went through her knees. "No, but it's what everyone knew me as." Recognition dawned. "Does this make the certificate invalid?" She had to swallow hard, but her mouth was dry.

"It's something we could argue in court."

"Oh, we do not want to go to court against Douglas. He has big money and a vicious legal team." Jessamyn had seen them in action over a petty copyright suit. "I'd rather even spend a year married to him than endure that."

"That's what we'd have to do if …"

"If?"

"*If* your non-marriage had occurred in a state where all that's necessary is a signed license. However, in this state? The law requires not only the license—which is permission to marry—but also a marriage certificate *and* signatures of witnesses to the subsequent ceremony."

"But I signed. And so did the officiator." The man had been someone Douglas had chosen, not Jessamyn's lifelong pastor. It'd been someone famous, for the TV show's sake—another huge sticking point for Jessamyn. "He witnessed our signing."

"Correct, but do you see this line?" Andrew pulled out a similar piece of documentation, but a template. He pointed to two additional lines on the bottom of the large paper, two lines that were conspicuously missing from the copy Douglas had brandished at Jessamyn and to all his fans time and time again.

"What is that line?"

"That's where two *additional* witnesses must sign *after* the ceremony, certifying that both parties actually uttered their solemn vows. No signatures? No valid marriage according to the state."

"Does that mean—?" A thousand bells rang at once, Christmas morning, New Year's morning, last day of school! "I'm free?" Jessamyn squeaked. "From Douglas's grasp?"

A grin spread over his face. "Yep, in black and white."

The cuckoo clock and the town clock sounded at the same time, as if on cue.

Freedom did ring!

"How did Douglas take the news?" she asked.

"Based on his social media feeds—of which there are a supernaturally large number—he left town, saying he'd found you but he'd only been looking for you to make sure you were safe. Now that he'd satisfied all his concerns for your *safety* from the so-called *kidnappers*, he was going to head back to the city, and the two of you would have to take things slow and work things out if it was in the cards for the two of you."

"It's not. In case you're wondering."

"I should hope not, after what Cliff gave up for you."

"Cliff! He's the guy who took Douglas's zillion-dollar reward for telling where I was."

"Not Cliff." Andrew shook his head.

"If not, then someone working with him to ruin me and shut down the hotel."

"What are you talking about? Cliff is in love with you. The guy who took the reward was— you know what? I've actually got a few people waiting. You'll get the whole story soon." He sounded disappointed, like Jessamyn had let him and Cliff and the whole town of Sugarplum Falls down by casting aspersions on Cliff's integrity.

But all signs pointed directly to Cliff or someone Cliff had conspired with—and they flashed in neon. Jessamyn might have fallen for him at first, but she wasn't stupid.

"Can I ask one more question, Andrew? I have a much bigger problem than Douglas, to be honest." One she couldn't solve, and one of her own making.

"You're kidding."

"No. Have you ever heard of Tark the Shark?"

"As a matter of fact." Andrew looked over his shoulder. "It just so happens that I have a side business as a private investigator. My first client has something to tell you about Tark the Shark."

"Who's your first client?" Jessamyn's foundations rumbled.

"Cliff Rockingham."

"Was that the bad news you referred to? Because I'm not sure I can see him."

"He said you'd say that." Andrew chuckled.

Seriously, Cliff wasn't among the top seven billion people she'd be happy to see today. He'd better come clean about his involvement with Bluebeard. She needed to know whether he'd betrayed her in *that* way, at the very least.

The fact he'd been Santa Claus of San Nouveau paled in significance to such a huge betrayal.

"If you say he has information about Tark the Shark I guess I'll see him."

For the last time.

That thought should not break her heart.

"One second." Andrew lifted his phone, dialed, and said into it, "Okay, you can bring them in." Then, he unlocked the front door to leave for court—inviting in several unwelcome or unexpected faces. Including a pair of police officers.

Chapter 43

Jessamyn

The door of Gingerbread Inn rattled as it closed behind Andrew, and two uniformed officers marched up to her, one with a mustache and one tall and thin. Mustache kept a heavy hand on the shoulder of a handcuffed Bluebeard.

"Bernard?" Jessamyn winced and thanked heaven above that Zinnia wasn't here to be accosted by the sight of the man who'd tied her up and threatened her life.

"It's not Bernard." The officer held Bluebeard in a tight grip.

Another pair of officers entered. They flanked a familiar-looking man wearing a very nice suit and a matching pair of handcuffs.

He looked familiar. Was that—? She peered closer.

That was the guy from Sweetwater Hotel's front desk. The one she'd seen holding the tote bag of money with Bluebeard and Cliff. Why did they have that guy from Sweetwater Hotel along for the interrogation? He looked annoyed and like he might blow his stack. Was he in on it? A stooge for Bernard?

She shrank back until her spine hit the countertop of the check-in desk.

When she'd seen him before, he'd looked slick, professional, and on top of things. Now, he looked sinister.

"Miss Fleet, is this the man who was extorting you?"

Jessamyn's glance darted between the two men. "You mean Bernard?"

"It's not Bernard. It's Nardo," Bluebeard said.

"He's not Tark the Shark. He's nothing but his henchman."

"There was a statewide BOLO for Tark the Shark, so we appreciated the tip. We didn't act right away, wanted to catch them both redhanded. Good thinking, putting the name of your hotel on the cash bag."

Jessamyn hadn't planned any of that.

"Federal Marshals want Tark for his fraudulent loan business, and we've got him on some new embezzling charges for falsifying plumbing bills from our own Draven Porter." The officer leaned on Tarquin, hard. "Not cool." At which, the man sniveled.

"What do you need from me?" asked Jessamyn, starting to feel relieved.

"We just needed you, Miss Fleet, to confirm that Bernard was in your place of business." He looked giddy at poking the bear, and Bluebeard's shoulders sank.

"Many times, but he only brandished a weapon once. That was when he tied up Zinnia."

"Armed robbery." Mustache Officer frowned and took Zinnia's contact information.

"I don't have specifics on the amount he took from me, I'm sorry." Again, if only she'd been Jane Bennet and not Kitty, a crime ring could be taken down.

"Don't worry, Tark kept those records to the penny." The officer grinned. "He was meticulous."

He did not look meticulous.

Jessamyn's disbelief must have shown on her face because Mustache Officer chortled.

"Not Bernard. *This* guy." He aimed a thumb at the man from Sweetwater Hotel. "Meet Tark the Shark."

After a bomb detonates, they say that ringing in the ears causes temporary deafness. Jessamyn could attest to emotional bombs creating a similar effect. Officer Mustache moved his lips, but Jessamyn heard nothing.

She gripped the edge of the countertop behind her. All this time, she'd pictured the loan shark holed up in some back-alley hovel filled with smoke and counting his stacks of gold. But no, he'd been in Sugarplum Falls, a stone's throw from Gingerbread Inn. Boy, she'd really love to throw a stone this time. Right at his smug nose.

Tark the Shark? Inside my Gingerbread Inn? It felt so defiled and polluted! *Get him out!* she yearned to yell, but she bit it back.

"With your testimony, this shyster will be locked up for a long time." Officer Mustache smiled. "There will be a huge team of government prosecutors involved."

"True," said the tall-skinny officer. "But thanks to you and your boyfriend's help getting us access to all Tark the Shark's business files—which are detailed to the point of obsession, we thank you, Mr. Tarquin—the case is open and shut. You never have to worry about being bothered by him or Bernard again."

"It's Nardo!" Bluebeard cried in agony, and the officers shuffled the men toward the door.

Sandbags of worry fell from Jessamyn's shoulders. For the first time in almost a year, her neck muscles relaxed, and her head dropped to her chest. Deep exhale. She peeked an eye upward.

"I knew I hated you!" Tark yanked himself away and came back at Jessamyn.

Officer Mustache yanked at the guy's shoulder, pulling tight. "Use manners around a lady, Tark. Let's go."

Mr. Tarquin's eyes narrowed to shark-like slits. "Lady? She's nothing but a two-bit television actress."

"You persecuted me, sending Nardo over to threaten me time after time?" Jessamyn asked. "Meanwhile, you lied to Cliff about everything—right down to the plumber."

"I kept both Cliff *and* you worrying about solvency. I figured after a while you would both give up and sell your hotels cheap." He shot a sneer in Bluebeard's direction. "I was patient, kept working my plan—but then I saw your face in person when you came through touring Sweetwater Hotel with hotshot here. Douglas's reward was enormous, but I figured it would climb again. When it hit the dollar amount I needed, I played my ace and cashed in. A big sum up front from Douglas Queen was better than a pittance trickling in from you."

"Pittance! It was my entire profit margin!" Then it hit her—"You turned me in to Douglas?" A gasp exploded from her lungs. *Tark did it? Not Cliff?*

"Sweetheart, somebody was going to do it sooner or later."

Her head spun. What else was Cliff innocent of doing?

"And Cliff wasn't part of Nardo's and your business?" He hadn't been holding the tote bag in glee, like it was a Christmas gift of stolen money?

The doors flew open. In strode Cliff. "Here." He threw a bag of money onto the floor at Tarquin's feet. "That's the interest you charged her."

"Where did you find that?" he growled.

"Laundry room, Sweetwater Inn." Cliff kicked Tarquin's ankle, making him curse. "Where you had several other bags of cash that I've handed over to the authorities." He looked at Jessamyn. "That's the amount you overpaid, Jess. Every penny accounted for."

But—

"But I legitimately owed him money, Cliff. I took out the loan."

"But you'd already repaid him triple that amount, according to his records. He apparently counted on you not being able to keep track, due to the pressures he placed on you and the lies he probably had Nardo telling you." He faced Tarquin again. "Apologize."

Showers of sparks fell all around her. Cliff not only hadn't turned her in to Douglas, he also wasn't working with Tarquin to ruin Jessamyn's life! She could trust him again! He wasn't her enemy—he was the man she'd been wishing he was all along! Even when she'd been talking to him as Santa Claus of San Nouveau.

Cliff leaned toward Tarquin, menacing him. "Now."

"I'm sorry." Tarquin spat it.

"That's the confession we need," the tall-skinny officer said. "Starting with *Nardo was getting nowhere with your payments.*" He tapped his chest next to what looked like a vest camera. "Thanks, Cliff. Thanks, Miss Fleet. Or, should I say, Westwood?" His eye twinkled like he had a crush on her old persona. "I really liked you on that show, and I am glad you didn't end up marrying that guy but came to Sugarplum Falls instead. We have all been pulling for you these past few months."

"You knew?" Jessamyn winced.

"Oh, sugar, everyone knew." Tarquin rolled his eyes. "Get me out of here. It's too syrupy."

Cliff tapped Officer Mustache's shoulder. "May I punch him?"

"It'd be assault, but I bet you wouldn't have any witnesses who testified against you." He chin-jutted at Officer Tall. "Shut that body-cam off?"

Cliff made a fist and wound up. He hauled off and swung—stopping a fraction of an inch from Tarquin's wincing nose. "I won't give you the satisfaction. Merry Christmas."

"You're too much of a wimp."

"No, actually, Tarquin, I'd prefer if you're the prettiest guy in prison."

The police marched the alleged culprits out of her hotel, leaving Jessamyn eye to eye with only Cliff Rockingham.

Jessamyn's heart lodged in her throat. The air buzzed, hummed, vibrated.

"I guess I'll go." Cliff reached out to touch her arm. But he dropped it—just like he'd nearly hurt Tarquin with a touch. "I'm going for a jog where you first started saving my life. If you want to talk, I think you know where to find me."

Saved his life! But he'd been the one doing the pseudo-saving.

"Cliff?" But he was gone. However, she did know exactly where she'd find him.

***

In multiple senses, Jessamyn was free. Free of Sammie. Free to be herself. Free at last to be Jess Westwood, the girl she'd grown up as. Free of Douglas Queen's insistence that they were married. Free of the frightening visits from the loan shark and his thug.

Most of all, she was now free to pursue her dream of running a hotel, the beautiful and charming Gingerbread Inn, in Grandma Ginger's honor right there in Sugarplum Falls. And doing it well—thanks to the patronage of Mayor Lang and the state's tourism website.

Everything on Jessamyn's horizon looked clear and without obstacle.

And yet—cords bound her. Cords she couldn't ignore, and didn't want to.

After getting something to eat to settle her stomach, calling Zinnia and giving her the good news, and fixing her hair, Jessamyn climbed in her jeep and drove to the Falls Overlook.

I have to talk to him, work this out, tell him I'm sorry.

When she arrived, the parking lot was empty. True to his word, he must've jogged, not driven to the place he suggested they meet. If she was even right about where he meant.

Jessamyn's mouth dried. A mostly empty water bottle sat in the console cup-holder. She tipped the remains to her lips, but it was frozen solid, and a little circular ice cube bumped her lip from inside the blue plastic container.

But—that bump gave her an idea. Jessamyn opened the glove compartment, from which she took a Burger Shack napkin and a pen.

Dear Cliff, she began.

When it was through, she scrolled it as well as she could, tucked it into the water bottle, and replaced the lid. Then, with shaking knees, she walked to the railing, climbed on the lower rung, and held the bottle aloft.

Would he come?

Chapter 44

Cliff

Cliff covered the distance between the frozen pool beneath the falls and the upper overlook twice, three times.

Jessamyn hadn't come to the Falls Overlook.

His thighs and shins ached with the effort. In his usual runs, he only took the hill once. After three passes, he felt the burn—and not just in his body.

She hadn't come back to me.

Not that he could blame her. Cliff had been a total jerk to her: lying about who he was, calling her his project—a label unwittingly designed to cut into her deepest tender spots—overreacting to her perfectly reasonable choice to leave a controlling jerk and not marry him. Just because Cliff had been victim of a superficial, ghosting fake, that didn't directly translate to Jessamyn being one too.

I'm sorry. The chant accompanied the rhythm of his footfalls on the frozen-mud of the jogging trail.

I was wrong.

Can you forgive me?

Had his withdrawal from the state tourism website been enough to prove to her he'd do anything to keep her in Sugarplum Falls? To prove how desperately he wanted another chance despite how little he deserved it?

As he crested the hill for the third time, there was a movement in the distance. Someone was at the railing—and leaning dangerously forward!

Cliff shifted into high gear, speeding up the remainder of the hill, despite his spent muscles. "Wait!" he cried to the unhappy person, who seemed bent on self-harm. "Stop! It's going to be all right."

A woman turned to face him, her face sporting a smile—and a blue plastic bottle in her hand. "Cliff! I thought you were never coming."

"Jess?" he said, completely out of breath as he grew closer.

But it was Jessamyn who closed the distance between them. She ran to him, throwing her arms around his neck. "I was worried you thought I wasn't coming. I'm so sorry I was late."

She bathed his neck with kisses, throwing him into a happy confusion. "Jess, I'm the one who was late." Cliff hugged her supple body to his tired one. "I didn't know about your nightmare of a relationship. I'm so sorry for getting upset that you left him at the altar. I'm so happy you did."

Jess pulled him tighter. "Did you know that I'm in love with you? That now I'm finally free to love you?"

Cliff took her hand, but then, he withdrew it, yanked off his glove, and then hers. Pressing the skin of his palm to hers, he led her to the bench overlooking the late-afternoon view of Lake Sugar's frozen surface, which stretched to the western horizon.

"I'm not sure I understand," said Cliff.

"Let me tell you what happened this morning."

"Besides the arrest of my so-called best friend and business partner with the help of the local private investigator?" Tarquin's betrayal still stung deeply, but he'd deal with that later. "What a day! Go on." Cliff might as well get the whole enchilada at once.

"It started yesterday when I decided to stop asking others to solve my problems—and when I decided hiring a lawyer wasn't the same as asking someone else to rescue me."

Jessamyn explained the revelation from Andrew Kingston about the marriage certificate.

"So, you see, I never said I do. So ... I didn't! And we aren't, and we never were." Tears welled in her eyes, making them glossy, and making their honey-brown depths look fathomless.

"Jess, I'm so happy for you."

"Me, too." She swatted a tear as it fell. "To be honest, I felt so guilty falling in love with you. Kissing you felt like a betrayal of your feelings, like a lie, though it was the truest thing I'd ever done. To keep you safe, I built up every wall in the world. I'm so sorry, Cliff. Can you ever forgive me for being so deceptive?"

On that scant invitation, Cliff took her close in his arms, placed a soft kiss on her temple, and then used his thumb to wipe away another escaped tear. "I need to beg the same thing of you."

"You did nothing wrong, Cliff. Yes, you claimed to be Santa, but you tried to help me, to answer my cry for help."

"I went about it in the worst way possible. You ended up hearing the truth about your message in the bottle from Valerie Vanderhoff. I lied to you."

"Maybe." She closed her eyes and chuckled, then opened them and smiled. "But your heart was good. I wouldn't have accepted help from anyone but a stranger, and you were … the stranger's agent. An incredibly handsome one, with crystal-blue eyes that weaken all my defenses."

He weakened her defenses? "Is that so?" Cliff slid closer to her on the wooden bench, placing an arm around her waist. "I called you my project. Can you forgive me?" He bit his lip. "I—" He cleared his throat. Twice. "I was living under some kind of misconception that I had to *pay it forward* in order to make up for a deficit I'd accrued when the Houstons helped me and my siblings back when I was a kid. That until I'd contributed to significant change in an individual's life, I shouldn't let myself fall in love."

"But," Jessamyn pressed her brows together, "I thought you loved the girl who …"

"Kiva?" He explained the reason for Kiva's appearance and how his feelings for her had changed years ago.

"So, you were *her* Christmas project?"

Now that was rich. "Jessamyn, can we start fresh?"

"Fresher than a batch of newly baked gingerbread?"

"What about gingerbread-man-topped oatmeal? That takes less time, and I'm anxious to get started."

"Me, too," Jessamyn said, lifting her eyebrow in a different kind of invitation. She took his cheeks in her hands and pressed a soft but intentional kiss to his mouth. "Very anxious."

The kiss lasted until a lonely, displaced seagull landed on the bench, knocking something onto the ground with a clatter.

"Don't litter!" Valerie Vanderhoff appeared immediately, as if an apparition of a warning ghost. "Will you young people never learn?" She bent and snagged it, stuffing it into the trash bag attached to her cross-body bag, hanging from her hip.

"Oh!" Jessamyn said, lunging for the lost bottle. "That was a message for—"

"Mrs. Vanderhoff!" Cliff stood up and tried to retrieve it, but Mrs. V scooted away.

"I expect the two of you to join this millennium and use electronic communication just like every other sane person." And with that, she disappeared down the crest of the hill.

Cliff sat back down. "I'm sorry. I couldn't grab it."

Jessamyn sighed, rested her head on his shoulder, and they looked out at the western horizon at the edge of Lake Sugar.

"Look! It's snowing!" Cliff pointed to the first heavy flakes. "I think it was just waiting for us to get our hearts straightened out."

"Let's keep them straight so the snow can keep falling."

"Deal." Cliff gave her another long, luxurious kiss.

The first of as many as there were snowflakes falling in Sugarplum Falls.

Chapter 45

Cliff

One year later

"**H**appy holidays!" Jessamyn came into the lobby of Gingerbread Inn and greeted Cliff. "You're dashing, I must say."

"You look even prettier this morning than you did last night at the rehearsal dinner." He kissed her cheek. The Gingerbread Inn still had up the wedding dinner decorations, in addition to the holiday décor. Some might call it cluttered, but it worked.

"And I expect you'll look even more beautiful by moonlight tonight on the roof of the Sweetwater Hotel, with your pastor from home asking if you'll be my wife."

"I'll be saying yes." She pulled out a package. "I have an early gift for you."

"But Christmas isn't for three weeks. Oh—you mean wedding gift."

"Open it."

"I didn't get you anything yet." He winced. "There's so much else to do, what with opening the roof of Sweetwater Hotel to guests as soon as the wedding is over."

"They'll love it there. The view will make their stay magical. Grandma Ginger would definitely approve."

"I expect Heaven will let Grandma Ginger be there with us in spirit tonight."

"That would be sweet. And she'd probably be wearing a matching Christmas-print caftan as her angel robes to match Zinnia—and the rest of my hotel guests' favorite perk."

"My hotel guests' favorite perk is the view from the roof. Unless it's breakfast. I get good reviews for both on the state tourism website. Almost as good as the reviews for your gingerbread man oatmeal."

"You deserve them." Jessamyn encircled his waist with her arms and looked up into his eyes. "Now, open your gift." She slapped his chest with both hands and then scooted off. "I'll be back, but take your time savoring the gift."

Cliff sat down on the staircase. He'd better check it out quickly, before either of Jessamyn's parents appeared. They were in town for the wedding and anxious to win his affection. It would be a hard race for that win, but he'd get there. Jessamyn had already begun to work through her feelings about their mistake.

It hadn't hurt that Douglas had married his next protégé. Jess's parents had finally let go of the dream of their daughter marrying him and getting his fame and money.

Shudder.

He tore off the paper, and inside was a clear plastic water bottle—with a note inside!

Ah, that bottle! It was from that day a year ago—the first day of their real life together. Jessamyn must have retrieved it from Valerie Vanderhoffen. Cliff unscrewed the cap and tipped out the scrolled paper that Jessamyn had inserted just for him.

Dearest Cliff—

For the past while, you've been my Mr. Darcy, my Santa Claus, my competitor (briefly), my billionaire on San Nouveau, my Mr. Bingley, my coworker, my favorite-ever kissing partner, and most of all my best friend and confidant.

You came to my rescue, you sacrificed for me, and you gave me all I knew I wanted and didn't know I needed. Can loving you be my Christmas project?

Your Jess

She peeked around the corner of the breakfast nook. "Did you read it?"

"I'm going to read it every day of my life with you." He accepted her into his arms.

"That's going to be a lot of days." She pressed her lips to his cheek.

"It's going to be all the days." The cuckoo clock chimed that it was time to leave to begin the first day of their forever love.

Epilogue

Chelsea

Chelsea Sutherland tidied the Christmas sheet music. She pressed three chords on her piano in succession, and sang the holiday lyrics—alone.

Wyatt was late. Again. After ten years in the trio with him she should have been used to it. If he weren't so charming and easy-going, she probably wouldn't put up with it.

Heath, however, would snarl. In fact, her brother might be snarling at both Chelsea and his lifelong best friend Wyatt right now, two hours away from Sugarplum Falls at his apartment in Caldwell City. He'd texted to say he was waiting for Chelsea to patch him in on a call so they could practice for the umpteen community Christmas events Dad had booked for them to perform.

Sutherlands did love their community events—from the Waterfall Lights, to the Hot Cocoa Festival, to the town Christmas play, to summer nursing home performances, Christmas Tree-O was slated for them all, thanks to Dad's enthusiasm for supporting the community.

She spelled the word *L-A-T-E* on the Scrabble game at the table, then took one of the mugs of hot water with lemon juice and honey from the top of the piano and sipped it. Singer's Tea. It prepped the throat for singing, which she may or may not be doing tonight, if Wyatt didn't show up soon. She had work responsibilities to catch up on, and another family event later. Their practice time window was closing.

"I'm here." The front door of her cottage creaked open, and through it poked Wyatt's head. "You're already at the piano?" The rest of him came in, all six feet of his tall, dark and handsome relentless charm. Unpunctual relentless charm. "Is Heath steaming as much as that cup of whatever you're holding?"

"Here. I made you one, too."

He strode over and took the cup, his fingers brushing hers before sipping it. "Mmm. You left out the ginger."

"You do hate ginger." Especially in Singer's Tea. "I'll see if I can get Heath patched in." The wireless connection wasn't always the greatest there at her cottage outside of Holly Berry House near the edge of the woods. It'd be so much less of a pain if Heath would just drive over to Sugarplum Falls for at least one practice before they had to run the gauntlet of holiday events they were booked for entertaining at.

Wyatt unbuttoned his jacket and tossed it over the back of a dining room chair, like always. "I brought your mail. I was up at the house, and your mom asked me to drop it off." The envelopes and magazines slapped against the antique wooden tabletop. "It's not all bills. You're lucky."

"Any Christmas cards?" she asked, but a crackly voice interrupted.

"Hey, guys." Heath's face appeared on the computer screen. "You're late, Wyatt."

"Yes, but I brought your sister's mail, so I'm forgiven. She always forgives me when I do a little nicety for her."

"Keep your niceties to a minimum." Heath and his big-brother sternness. "Now, because you're late, I only have seven minutes before I have to leave with Odessa for her Lamaze class, so let's get cranking."

Good. Finally.

Chelsea parked herself at the piano bench and flipped through one of the binders containing their repertoire of bubble-gum Christmas pop.

"Since I'm out of town, let's keep everything as easy as possible this year." Heath took charge, as always. "As usual, I'm on lead. Wyatt and Chelsea, you're on harmonies. Start with 'Holly Jolly Christmas,' and then move through 'Rockin' Around the Christmas Tree,' and 'Santa Claus is Comin' to Town.'" As lead, Heath also made the decisions. It was easier that way, since Chelsea was the younger sister, and Wyatt was too chill to bother challenging Heath's dominance. Sometimes it seemed like Wyatt only sang in Christmas Tree-O to keep Heath happy.

And probably for all the girls who mobbed him after every performance, batting their eyelashes and asking if he'd autograph something for them.

Minor celebrity status in Sugarplum Falls had its perks, at least for the guys of the group, if not for Chelsea. In fact, Heath had met Odessa after their performance at the Waterfall Lights event two years ago. Now they were married, and any day now Chelsea would become an aunt for the first time at age twenty-six.

"Let's run through 'Holly Jolly 'to start." Heath's voice cut out as the image of his face fizzed. "Hav- holl- Chri-" came through in crackling zaps. "Hey, why aren't you guys coming in? Chelsea, you're supposed to harmonize, remember?"

"You're cutting out, man." Wyatt took a gulp from his mug. "You gotta sing louder."

"If I sing any louder, I'll wake the baby inside my wife's abdomen. Now, let's go."

But it wasn't any use, as the connection worsened, no matter what Chelsea did to rejigger it. Her tech skills failed for once, and their practice ended without a single full run-through.

"Bye, guys. I'll"—crack, snap, pop—"Cocoa Festival, if I can." Heath disappeared from the screen.

Wyatt's head snapped and his gaze met Chelsea's. "Did he just say *if I can?* What's that supposed to mean?"

"It means that as long as Odessa doesn't have the baby, he'll trek over to Sugarplum Falls for the Hot Cocoa Festival on Saturday night."

"No whammies." Wyatt set his mug down.

"He'll be there. He's just nervous," she said. "New dad stuff."

Though, Odessa wasn't due until Christmas day. Heath was being flaky.

"Maybe we should run through our parts." She played the full chord, but Wyatt patted her shoulder and went to the table.

"Nah, we know it well enough." He picked up her mail and sank down on her vintage sofa with its nubby red and green plaid fabric. "Junk mail, junk mail, catalog." He tossed the successive pieces into a new pile on her coffee table. "You actually buy anything from this?"

"It's addressed to the cottage resident." She yanked the non-essentials away, creating order from the chaos he was creating in her room. "It probably comes because of Grandma."

"Your grandma died a long time ago." Ten years ago, or more. "And she's still getting catalogs?"

"Catalog databases don't know that." And Wyatt didn't need to know that Chelsea had ordered a pair of cute puppy-face socks from that catalog to keep her feet warm. The Holly Berry Cottage could get drafty. "They're ones and zeros."

"Like the statistics you work with all day?" Wyatt kept snooping through the stack, tossing sweepstakes offers and gardening supply catalogs hither and yon. "You have rescued those big pharma beggars so many times. Are they ever going to promote you?"

"Someday, maybe." She'd only been there about a year and a half. "I don't want a promotion now." Didn't deserve one yet. Nice that he kept track of her life's goings-on, though. Sweet. Better than any other guy she'd ever spent time with. She gathered up another sorted stack and whisked it into the trash can. "I like working remotely where I can control my environment." And help local family members as their *I can't get my document to open* go-to person.

"And wear pajamas all day." Wyatt smirked at her gray sweatpants.

"These are not pajamas." Even though they did closely resemble her gray pajama pants. Those were fuzzier. "You're just jealous because you're forced to wear a suit and tie to North Star Capital every day, and I get to be comfortable."

Okay, slovenly was probably a better word for it. But she had her reasons for looking this way to solve everyone else's math problems. Good ones.

"Yeah, whatever." Wyatt tugged a cream-colored envelope from what remained of the mail stack and began tearing it open. "Hey, what's this? Somebody is splashing out on very nice envelopes for the Christmas cards this year."

Chelsea reached for it. "You do know that opening other people's mail is a federal offense."

"No, stealing other people's mail is." He passed it to her.

She pulled the card and photo out of the linen envelope with a *nyah, nyah* in his general direction.

However, the second she saw the contents, she dropped them like hot coals.

Mr. Sheldon and Mrs. Lisa Lang announce the marriage of their daughter ...

Oh, no. It couldn't be. Not Esther. Not with Fargo. This was too cruel to be real.

"Are you okay?" Wyatt picked up the piece of embossed card stock from atop her puppy-face sock where it was burning her toe. "You look like you've seen a ghost."

More or less. "I wish they'd both expire and *become* ghosts this very moment." Before they could invade Chelsea's world and haunt her entire Christmas season.

"Is that any way to speak about a Sutherland cousin?" Wyatt glanced down at the photo in his hand. "Oh, never mind. It's Esther. I get it."

No, he most certainly did not get it. "Esther is only half the horror."

Wyatt looked closer. "Let's see." He mumbled the details on the invitation under his breath. "Mr. and Mrs. Frye cordially ... the last Saturday before Christmas, nuptials, twenty-two hundred Poinsettia Drive, RSVP ... So?" Wyatt looked at her. But then his arm dropped at his side. "Just a second. This isn't *Fargo* Frye, is it?"

Chelsea nodded.

"Your useless college boyfriend? Heath told me all about him."

Um, not all about him. Nobody but Chelsea knew *all* about Fargo Frye and the decimation he'd inflicted on her life that last semester before Fargo graduated and Chelsea earned her degree in mathematics and statistics. "One and the same."

Wyatt's upper lip curled. "Well, he's getting what's coming to him if he's marrying your cousin Esther."

"That's one way to look at it." But still, it burned like a cinder in her eye. Her horrid ex-boyfriend was marrying into her family, marrying her meanest cousin, even if they had been best friends when they were small, and Chelsea would have no excuse to avoid it.

Esther Lang, hairdresser to the starriest stars in all of Caldwell City. To hear her tell it, she was practically an A-lister herself. "Honestly, Wyatt. I just can't take it."

"Allow me to do the honors, then." He chucked the card in the trash can. "Skip it. Then you don't have to watch the staging scene for the mutually assured destruction live and in person."

"Hey." Chelsea reached into the can and sifted through the Christmas sale coupons and glossy offers for porcelain cat figurines to grab out the invitation.

"Why are you getting that out?" Wyatt went back over to the piano and set his mug on top—not on the coaster. "Forget it."

Forget? As if. As if she'd forgotten about Fargo Frye and what he'd done to her for even one single day since their breakup a year and a half ago. Oh, what a fool she'd been.

Couldn't Chelsea just sink to the bottom of Lake Sugar instead?

"Stop looking for it." Wyatt tugged it away from her again and sent it Frisbee-sailing to the trash can. "You're being a glutton for punishment."

"It's not like I can skip attending it." She plucked it from the trash and set it on the table.

"Of course you can. It's a last-minute holiday wedding, and everyone is really booked up at the holidays. They can't expect you to change plans around them. You're busy. You have a life. Lots of musical commitments to boot. You're not indebted to them, and certainly not to Fargo Frye, of all people."

Yes, she was. Indebted for her complete lack of self-confidence, for her lack of desire to date, for her year of hibernation, thank you very much. "It's a Sutherland wedding. I'm a Sutherland."

Wyatt looked unmoved. "Sutherlands always have plans. You have plans. Just attend whatever plans you already have in place. Give your regrets. Send a chintzy gift. In fact, re-gift something tacky. Or buy them an impersonal gift card in a low dollar amount to a restaurant you know they'd both hate. Just get it over with and then skip the personal appearance. That's what I'd do."

That probably was what Wyatt would do, but with more flair than

Chelsea would be able to muster under the circumstances. "It's at twenty-two hundred Poinsettia Drive. Does that address ring a bell? My parents' house?"

Fifty yards away from where Chelsea lived in the property's original cottage was Holly Berry House, where Chelsea grew up.

"In fact, I'll likely get roped into helping decorate for the thing, as part of Sutherland solidarity. Which is usually a beautiful thing. Just not in this instance."

"Tell me something, then. Why are you just finding out about it?" At this, Wyatt blinked madly. He had thick, dark eyelashes for a guy. So unfair. "Don't you think your mom would give you a heads up if you were expected to be there? Surely they know you're not going to want to subject yourself to it. They only sent you the invitation to be polite."

Good point. He made such a good point. Chelsea pulled out her phone and dialed. "Mom, there's a wedding planned at your house? How long has this been on the books?"

"Esther's scheduled church ended up with bats in the belfry. There was a remediation closure at the last minute, so I volunteered the house, which she said she'd wanted to use for her reception in the first place. Lisa is thrilled."

Of course Mayor Lisa Lang was thrilled. Holly Berry House was the best place on the planet to have a daughter get married, if you were a Sutherland. In fact, Chelsea had always dreamed of her own reception being held there, with the grand staircase bedecked with garland, blazing hearths, steaming hot cocoa scents from the kitchen—and music. Lots of music wafting through the rooms.

"You're volunteering the house for a wedding. Right before Christmas. With zero notice."

"I'd do anything for Aunt Lisa and Uncle Sheldon, they've been so good to us." Mom did love her sister-in-law. So did Chelsea, for that matter. Aunt Lisa was pushy but loving, and one of Chelsea's biggest cheerleaders. *Unlike her sour daughter.* "Uncle Zeke just finished divinity school and will perform the ceremony."

"Zeke, Zeke, the Black Sheep? And he finished divinity school?"

"Finally something complete. We couldn't *not* reward that by including him. In fact, it'll be all in the family, and such a joy to have every single person in Grandma and Grandpa's posterity there. No empty chairs. They'll be smiling down from heaven."

No empty chairs? Not even Chelsea's? That sealed that. She looked up at Wyatt after hanging up.

"I heard." His chin wrinkled in a frown.

Seeing Fargo again, for the first time since he so ruthlessly tore her self-worth apart, and him all starry-eyed over none other than Esther? Chelsea squeezed her eyes shut and pulled her head down, turtle style, into her bulky, misshapen sweater.

What am I going to do?

To read the rest of Chelsea and Wyatt's song-filled, brother's-best-friend romance, check out *Christmas at Holly Berry Cottage* next!

Author's Note

All stories in the Sugarplum Falls Romance series are clean, standalone holiday romances. They're arranged in a loop. Book 1 introduces characters from book 2, and so forth, and then The *Christmas at Gingerbread Inn* loops back to *Christmas at Holly Berry Cottage*. This means readers can begin at any point in the series and then complete the loop and meet the many recurring characters from the charming small town. The books can be read in any order, but they are best enjoyed as listed on the following page.

The Sugarplum Falls Romance Series

Christmas at Holly Berry Cottage
Christmas at Turtledove Place
Christmas at Angels Landing
Christmas at Sugarplum Falls
Christmas at Gingerbread Inn

For a bonus sampling of Christmastime in Sugarplum Falls, grab the wonderful, sweet falling-in-love story between attorney Andrew Kingston and the feisty, cider-shop-owning Poppy. Sign up for Jennifer's fun, effervescent newsletter full of freebies and stories and receive Christmas at The Cider Press [here](#) *for free.*

Jennifer's Other Holiday Romance Series

Christmas House Romances
Snowfall Wishes Romances

About the Author

Jennifer Griffith is a *USA Today* bestselling author. She lives in Arizona with her husband, where they are raising their five children to love Christmas. She tries to put more lights on her tree each year, and she wholeheartedly believes the best way to kick off the holiday season is to sing Christmas songs with her husband's extended family for two to three hours on Thanksgiving night.

Manufactured by Amazon.ca
Acheson, AB